Celeste slapped Jean-Jacques's face, and it must have stung quite a bit because he held his hand to his cheek for some time without saying a word. It wiped away the smile. He noticed Phillipe's portrait. "But then you are in love with him, n'est ce pas? It isn't security; it's passion, eh, Mademoiselle?"

"I'd say it's none of your *damn* business!"

He was angry with her but doing a fine job of hiding it. "All right. Get your shawl, it's very cold where you're sleeping tonight. Disturbing the peace, fighting in the streets, rioting, wearing the cockade and the skirt, striking a man of the force; I think that should be enough to drag you to prison for a long day and night of interrogation. I want to know all their plans, and how they affect the citizens of Paris."

"I'm not going anywhere with you!" She stood her ground with her arms crossed, and her legs firmly planted on the wooden floor of the apartment.

He picked her up in his arms and hurled her body over his strong shoulders as if she were a sack of flour. "Oh, yes you are."

"Put me down!" she said.

"No," he said as he slammed the door shut behind him with his foot, turned into a lane, and headed into the busy streets filled with citizens walking to work.

Celeste saw a crowd of neighbors, mostly women, gawking at the two of them and was suddenly inspired.

"What about my rights! I'm a good citizen of France!" screamed the humiliated artist at the top of her voice.

"Citizen, indeed. Pretend all you want, you're nothing but a woman of France, and you have no rights," Jean-Jacques said.

The Diary of Jean-Jacques Coupier
by
Hollie Van Horne

An original publication of Time Travelers

Time Travelers
P.O. Box 361
Columbiana, Ohio
44408

ISBN: 0-9674552-1-9
Library of Congress Control number: 2002091675
First printing June 2002
Series book 5

Printed in the U.S.A.

Cover art: Lange Design
www.langedesign.org

Other books by Hollie Van Horne:

Reflections of Toddsville (Book one)
Wild Roses for Miss Jane(Book two)
McKnight's Revenge (Book three)
When We Do Meet Again (Book four)
Speak of the Dead (Mystery)
The Diary of Jean-Jacques Coupier (Book five)

Coming soon:

Portrait of Lydia (Book six)

Beneath the Wings of Isis (Book seven)

This book is dedicated to
Madame de La Tour du Pin,
Claire Lacombe,
and the women of France 1793

The Diary

of

Jean-Jacques Coupier

by

Hollie Van Horne

Time Travelers   Book Five

Prologue

Phillipe de Brouquens kissed the sleepy young woman and then moved from her side on the bed and began to dress. He looked once or twice at his lover as he pulled on his pants and reached for his shirt, then darted a quick glance out of the street side window. His unmarked carriage and its driver waited for him. He'd given his servant strict rules as to when and where to wait, at what hour he would leave for home, and how much he would pay him to keep silent about the matter. He had been with his lover for two weeks now. Living, sleeping, dining, and loving in their small townhouse apartment. It was enough to satisfy his desire for her for another month.

He felt her stare on his neck. Her naked body, covered lightly with the bed sheets, was inviting him to return to her embrace. Her breasts, hidden only by her long blondish-brown hair, begged to be teased with his usual tantalizing caress. Her lips parted waiting for his farewell kiss. Her warm fragrance that still clung to his own skin, seduced him to take her again before he left. Her somnolent, satisfied smile was an invitation a stronger man would not have ignored. Her eyes glowed with the inner light of a woman in love.

Then they narrowed suspiciously, and she said, "Are you ashamed of your love for me? Is that why you look to the streets all the time? To see whether anyone noticed your carriage? I do not understand, Phillipe," cried Celeste Lacombe. "Why must I stay in this hell hole when I could live with you in your fine estate as your wife? You said that your father was a reasonable man. Well, tell him that I am the woman you love, and you won't have to make such a long trip here to visit me anymore."

Phillipe de Brouquens thought of his massive country estate in Bordeaux, a good 350 kilometers from Paris, and wondered how long he could keep his affair with the common yet gifted and beautiful Celeste a secret. "You know my father will have none of it," said Phillipe.

"I think you are lying to me. I don't believe you even mentioned me to him. I think you have another woman."

"Another woman? How? *Why?* You alone consume my every thought, my every minute."

"Then why can't I meet your father and mother?"

Hopefully, no one in Rue Neuve-des-Petits-Champs in the Lepeletier section of Paris had noticed his interference in Celeste's life. Who was she to question a bag of gold or her new position at the print shop? Many women's names were still sitting on a lengthy list for the job she held; but Celeste, whose name was almost the last one on the page, had miraculously won a position over them. He'd even managed to get her new boss to allow her to do much of the work in her own home so that she would be safe in the apartment he'd rented for them. Whenever he visited, he brought loaves of Judith's delicious bread, rolls, and pastries; as well as fruit, vegetables, candy, and bottles of wine. After all, Judith was the finest baker any man could hope to acquire in this turbulent day and age, and the Brouquens's vineyard was the best in all of France; Celeste should show her

2

appreciation instead of expecting more than he could produce. She did not have to wait in long lines to buy food when he came to visit. He came as often as he could, stayed a few days not daring to leave the house accept in the evening, and she had never questioned him about his lack of a commitment...until tonight.

He tucked his white shirt into the waistband of his pants and sat on the bed next to her so that he could pull on his boots. "Celeste! Why do you vex me so? Are you close to having your flow? Why tonight of all nights must you start this with me?" He reached for her, but she pulled away.

She shook her head in exasperation. "Why is it that when a woman makes a small demand of a man it must be because she is having her period? Is it your wish that I should bear an illegitimate child for you? Another mouth for me to feed? A baby to hinder my life if you should never come back to our apartment? Lest we forget that these are perilous times. I have joined no women's club because you asked me not to. Some wear the tricolored cockade proudly and wonder why I do not. The neighborhood is populated with revolutionary women. They bicker inside their own groups against their own kind. The king is dead, Phillipe. No one is sane. No one is rational. None of it makes any sense. There is talk of killing the queen. Why? What has she done? And there are those who wonder why I am not in league with the other young, unmarried women, les sans-culotte, les tricoteuses, les enragés. Wonder why I have money, and they do not. Why I have a good roof over my head and a comfortable job. Why I have decent clothes to wear yet do not wear the striped blue and white skirt of a good citizen of France. Paris is alive with the Republic, and it will be the same all over

3

France, even in Bordeaux; but here I sit, lover to an aristocrat whose life is in more jeopardy than he knows, hiding him here in this apartment for which he pays an exorbitant sum."

He stopped all movement and stared at her. He was listening now. "What do you know?"

She tossed her hands into the air as if to indicate that he had lost his mind. "Where do I *live*? I am surrounded by those who would have your head and that of everyone in your family too. Are you so vain that you think your comings and goings have not been noticed?"

Phillipe knew that he should not see her again. That this might be the last time they'd be together. He pulled her close to his body and kissed her tenderly. "Celeste, I love you."

"You must leave Bordeaux, Phillipe. We both must leave now if we are to make this love of ours last. You live near a port. There is transit, and if we are cautious..."

He raised his right hand to silence her. "I can't leave right now. I have no letters of transport," he said.

He thought of how awkward it would be to try to move an entire household to Germany or Switzerland. "My father lives in our country home far away from the turbulence. We live a simple life and are free from political attachments. We have not shown Royalist allegiance...or any allegiance to anyone for that matter and wish to be left alone."

"It won't stop what will happen, Phillipe. It is just the beginning. They think that killing Royalists will free commerce, and we will all eat, drink, and be happy because we are a Republic where all men and women have equal rights. At least the women of the newly formed Revolutionary Republican

Women's Club think they'll be considered equal to men once they have fought for liberty. There have been riots here in Paris because of the cruel price fixing by the idiot merchants who favor those who have the money to pay their high prices. But, the men who lead the people are greedy and only want what they can steal from the aristocrats—what they can get from being in power. For now, they are puffed up with their own importance and their lust for power, but it won't be long before the blood thirsty crowd, les enragés, will want their heads too."

He tilted his head in amazement at her words. "How do you know all this?"

"My cousin, Claire, you know the actress, is in the heat of it, yet evil gossip from her own friends touches her as well. Then there is her...friend, Leclerc, the editor of the newspaper."

She stopped in fear that she had said too much. "It frightens me when those who fight against the traditions of our country war among themselves. The Revolutionary Republican Women whipped Theroigne de Mericourt during one of the meetings the other day."

"You should have gone into politics, Celeste. I marvel at your wisdom and knowledge."

She shook her head slowly in frustration at his careless demeanor. "They will come for you, mark my word," she said sadly. "They say that there are some who are escaping by ship to America. Can you expect me to stay out of the political chaos that surrounds us both? Take me away to America. I am strong and can find work there. Don't you understand? You are a wealthy man, and I am your lover. God save us both!" She crossed herself as if it might protect her. "Mother of God, he does not listen to me!"

He gave her a bag of coins—her allowance he called it. "Do you think *you* are in danger?"

The coins would have to last her for some time to come. God help her, he thought, if she should use this tone with her employer. She would lose her only livelihood as well. What would become of his beautiful, sweet love then? He fancied he would lose a few nights sleep over the end of their affair, but then the memory of her sacrifice would be made sweeter in his imagination.

"We are *all* in danger, Phillipe!" she cried.

"Then I should not visit you again."

She was quiet when he glanced at her. She looked so deliciously charming when she pouted.

He said, "Ah, but, how can I not? I love you so."

She placed her arms around his neck, and he kissed her passionately, curving her body against his.

"You are my life, Celeste, and I will risk all that I am for you. I will never forsake you. Never."

"Take me home with you. I have one or two allies who might be able to get us passage on a ship to America."

"I can't leave my...family."

"You can't stay in France either. We must leave here—at once."

"Well...I will think upon your words. I best go now, but I will try to return if possible."

Celeste grinned wickedly, cocking her head to the side to show that she wasn't really angry with him. A way to say that she was sorry for her nasty words. "I do so love you, Phillipe, don't disappoint me."

"I pledge my honor and my name to your safety. I will speak with my father about what you have just told me."

"You promise."

"And return, or write, as soon as I can with my answer."

She left her bed, placed a thin robe around her body, and hugged him tightly.

He kissed her and smiled. "I love you beyond all reason," he said softly. "I cannot live one moment without you. Leaving you now is so difficult. I wish to stay in your fond embrace forever. You know that I speak the truth."

She smiled and held his face between her palms, "Yes."

"Farewell. Until we meet again."

Her lips trembled, and the tears came quickly. He hurried to his carriage—the one that bore no family crest. She stood in the doorway and waved to him. He took one last look at her. The sight of her standing there with her long, light brown hair curling over her shoulders, falling onto her breasts; the robe clinging to her luscious body; the smile of satisfaction illuminating her visage; the gleam of love that burned in her blue eyes, might be the last portrait he would have of his fair Celeste. It would have to last a lifetime for he didn't see how he could afford to come to this apartment again. He smiled at her and then entered his cab and left Paris for home.

A dark, shadowy figure stirred in the alley. One who watched. Neither Phillipe nor Celeste noticed. When Celeste shut and bolted the front door to her apartment, the figure moved to the window and gazed in at her. Just one swift examination of a woman in love crying. Then the stranger was gone.

7

Celeste sauntered towards the easel that stood in a corner near the window. The canvas that rested on it had been covered for two weeks. Funny that the man she loved had never shown any interest in what lay beneath the linen cover. She carefully pulled the cloth from the canvas and stared at the half-finished oil portrait of Phillipe de Brouquens.

"What's to become of us?" she whispered to the portrait.

Chapter One

May 17, 2000
Richfield Springs, New York
Cooper Cottages
7:30 A. M.

There comes a time in every man's life when he suddenly realizes that he's met the right woman. A glance, a word, a sigh, a smile, a touch, a name perhaps, and he knows. Over centuries they have met, fallen in love, married or parted; and in every time period, in each setting, he has recognized her. The woman in a man's dream comes to life before his eyes. Celeste Montclaire was that fantasy woman, and Jim Cooper had been lucky enough to find her.

"I love you," Jim said, as the muscles in his legs quivered all at once, and a wild display of fireworks exploded in his mind. It was the truth, and he said it as often as he could to Celeste. He had no intention of losing her.

Celeste softly moaned a form of his name as she reached her finest moment of pleasure. She held him tightly as the wonderful afterglow of lovemaking took hold of her body and mind.

Jim collapsed beside her and pulled his hair away from his strong shoulders and long, lean face. He smiled at the thought that making love to this woman made him happier than he had ever been. He wanted to please her in every way.

Celeste smiled dreamily, cuddled the comforter around her naked body, and let her focus rest on the timber roof of the old, woodland cabin that belonged to Jim and his brother Sam.

"You're incredible," she said, and then turned so that her lover could see her satisfaction.

The rays of the afternoon sun winked between the limbs of the trees. Alternating degrees of light green, deep chartreuse, and gold, swayed in the lazy breeze like an artist's watercolor brush on fine canvas. A light haze, created by intermittent beams of sunlight that streamed through the cabin's window, invoked a thin, mystical veil—like a surrealistic curtain—that had been drawn across the beams of the bedroom, and had magically transformed their moment in time into a romantic fantasy for two.

"May I return the compliment," Jim said. He reached for her hand, took it, and played with her fingers while they talked.

"I love it here," she said.

A tiny, yellow bird flew from tree limb to tree limb and regarded Celeste, tilting and twisting its head from one side to the other as if scrutinizing why the young woman existed in its world. Celeste could see it from the open window, and she fixated on its flight—its freedom—and the sheer exuberance of its song.

"Open invitation to come whenever you wish," Jim said, breaking into her thoughts.

She did not respond to his comment. The tone in her voice changed. "It's hot," she said matter of factly. "I'm going to open the front door." She looked at him for a moment. "That is if you promise we're alone."

She stood up completely naked, stretched her anatomy as tall as she could, tossed her long, brownish-blonde hair into the air with her hands, and strolled to the middle of the room.

"I told you that we're alone," Jim said, remembering that Sam was planning on going downtown early this morning to buy supplies. Jim rested on his side, let his index finger trace the design of one of the tulips on the antique tulip quilt, and watched her. He needed more of her. Now. Forever.

Celeste was beautiful. Her hair had an interesting hue to it that, in the sunlight, looked blonde, then brown in the shade, and light auburn in the nighttime hues. A man could just watch her hair alone to become totally entranced by the woman. Her eyes looked deep blue in the dim lighting of the cabin—like the color of Arctic water; then they'd turn sky blue when she was outside in broad daylight. Her skin was pale and blushed for any number of reasons. Her hips were smooth and rounded; her buttocks flat but muscular—taut like a runner's. Her waist was small which made her large breasts more obvious. Her complexion was prettier without makeup. Her lips were tinted with a natural pink shade and needed no lip gloss. Her neck was slender—a pedestal for the fine, classic, porcelain sculpture of her perfect oval face. Jim saw her through the eyes of a man desperately in love, and thought she looked like the Roman goddess of love. She was talented, confident, witty, sexy, lively, flirtatious, and perceptive. But right now, Celeste did not look like a woman in love, and that fact tarnished the picture for Jim.

"I can see why you stay here whenever you can." She walked to the door and let the cool air bathe her naked skin. "So much nicer than the hot city. Makes a great weekend retreat."

Jim winced at the subtle meaning of her words. Was he also 'a great weekend retreat'? It bothered him that Celeste had completely ignored his declamation of love. How could she have not heard him? He uttered the words often and at very appropriate moments. Perhaps he was expecting too much from the modern, sophisticated, business woman/attorney who ran, if not the biggest, certainly the most efficiently run legal firms in New York City.

Celeste and Jim met when he and his brother, Sam, traveled to New York to join their partner, Bruce Wainwright for the April board meeting of Time Travelers, Inc. With their earnings from the Dr. Templeton caper, Wainwright purchased an office suite in the heart of Manhattan. The office was decorated in a rich, classic style with clocks being the central theme in almost every room, and state-of-the-art computers resting on all three desks. The fact that no one went to the office or worked there but Wainwright did not dissuade Bruce from making it look like a thriving business to all and sundry.

The three experienced time travelers promised each other to meet once every two months in New York City—to keep up the appearance that the office housed the business—and to discuss their clients' travel arrangements. Wainwright still used his apartment in New York City but traveled to Cooperstown often to sit in Trudy's stone house and have friendly chats with Jim and Sam. The Coopers stayed in Richfield Springs or Milford and journeyed to New York City to meet with Bruce. A mutual agreement had been made that the three should share long distance trips. The office in the city gave credence to the bizarre business in case the IRS became curious.

It was Wainwright who first set eyes on the lovely Celeste at an art show. He asked her to join him for a drink afterwards. She agreed and drove them in her BMW to a high-rise restaurant with a great view of the city. Wainwright talked about himself most of the evening, but Celeste managed to tell him about her business, and he jotted down the name of her firm so that he could call her the next day. The "date" lasted two hours. She dropped him off at his apartment building afterwards. Before exiting the vehicle, he gave her his card and told her to look him up sometime; that they might see an opera at the Met together. Wainwright cleverly left his wallet that held two fifty-dollar bills, on the passenger's seat of her car so that he would have an excuse to call her the next morning. Celeste used his card to find his office and return the wallet.

The moment Jim Cooper saw Celeste slap Wainwright's wallet onto his desk, ask what sort of business Time Travelers, Inc. was anyway, and question if their business might possibly be some sort of cover up for laundering mob money; he knew he'd found the woman he would love forever. When she turned her head to get a good look at Jim and his brother, her direct stare told Jim that she was attracted to him as well.

Jim asked her whether he could walk her to the elevator, and she agreed. In the few minutes it took to get to the lobby of the office building, Jim managed to get her to accept a dinner date for that evening. He let her choose the restaurant, and she picked an expensive French one that had music and dancing. He let her order. He smiled and ate whatever it was without comment. She ordered too much wine and champagne, and he wasn't used to that much alcohol. The music was perfect for slow dancing; the room far too hot. While they were dancing—if that was what you could call holding each other tightly and swaying hips and legs provocatively close to certain erogenous zones—Jim kissed her. It was a deep kiss, and she parted her lips begging for more. She stopped dancing and looked at him. The invitation in her eyes was obvious; the intent unspoken. They went to her apartment and made love all night long.

Since Sam and Jim never stayed long in New York City, so Jim asked Celeste whether she would like to continue seeing him long distance. She smiled her approval of the idea, and he gave her his Milford phone number and his e-mail and home address. He invited her to the Cooper Cottages for the first warm weekend that spring and then waited. She didn't call until Thursday evening. She wanted to visit him and had thought of nothing but him since their one night together. The moment he heard that she would make the long drive to the cabins, he began cleaning, gardening, purchasing wine, food, a CD player, classical music CD's, and flowers.

This whole affair did not escape brother Sam's attention.

"I gather you want to get rid of me," Sam stated when the last bag of groceries had been brought from the truck. "Can that little refrigerator hold all this stuff?"

Jim gave a cockeyed smile to his brother and said, "Stay at my place, Sam?"

Sam grinned. "Sure. This thing for real?"

"It is on my part. I don't know about her."

Sam crossed his arms over his chest, leaned his back against the front door frame, and raised his right eyebrow. "She may be investigating Time Travelers, Inc. just as Wainwright said."

Jim shook his head. "Wainwright's just bitter because

she dumped him. If she wanted to find out about our business, why not stick with the president?"

"I can think of all sorts of good reasons," Sam said, making his own private Wainwright joke.

"What's she going to find out?" Jim asked.

"The truth."

"Good. I hope she does."

"Are you sure?"

Jim stopped long enough to stare at his brother. "I love her, Sam. That's all I know right now. I haven't felt this way before. I've been missing what Stephen, Trudy, Jessie and Matt, and Jane have had the good fortune to find. A soul mate. This is the first time in my life I've felt really good—happy."

"Might I mention that sometimes your heart gets broken in the final chapter?"

Jim stopped his activities in the kitchen and gave his brother a warm smile. "I know. I don't care," he said shrugging his shoulders. "You have to take risks, don't you?"

Sam watched his brother fluff up the couch throw pillows for the fifth time. He said, "Hope she doesn't get lost. Give her good directions?"

"From the Internet."

"That should do it. I don't suppose you've made up your mind about the New York businessman's Roman holiday."

"Do we have to get back to Wainwright right away on that?"

"Grant Tyrell has been bugging Wainwright once a day for two weeks. Squeaky wheel theory, I guess. Wainwright sent us e-mail about it this morning. What do you think?"

15

Jim paused and thought for a moment. "I just don't like the guy. He wants to go back to the Roman Empire to be his relative who was the emperor at the time people were being brutally murdered in the Colosseum. What kind of guy wants to go back to that? Why? The genealogical transfer is safe enough, but who's going with him?"

"He told Wainwright that he had no need of assistance."

"How does he know that his ancestor was an emperor?"

Sam shrugged his shoulders and put his hands in his pocket. "He had his family tree done by a college professor in Harvard. Considering how professional and powerful the man is, I wouldn't doubt he *was* a despot in another lifetime. Wainwright told me that he ordered his secretary around as if she were his slave the whole time they discussed his trip. Says he'll pay double, and we needn't do any research for him; he knows all he needs to know. Bought his own coins, some antique fibula and had a Broadway designer make his clothes. The college prof did the research for him. He's very specific about the time of departure too. 200 A.D. We have to tell Wainwright soon if this guy's going to travel this June."

Jim gazed at the floor and thought for a moment. "What do you think?"

"I think we have no choice really. Now that we're a business, and word-of-mouth is starting to build up our list of possible clients—not to mention the Internet junkies who play around on our web site—we have to think of the business first. A double shot of money could be most useful right now."

"I just don't like the guy, that's all."

"Yeah, I know. Even Wainwright thinks he's a donkey

16

vortex."

Jim chuckled and put his hand on his brother's shoulder. "It really isn't our choice anyway."

Sam moved away from his brother, walked to the cabin's window, stared at the sun peeking through the distant pine trees, and allowed his thoughts to turn introspective. "You still think we're not the movers we think we are?"

"Ever since I got home from 1066, I've been pondering Jessie and Matt's story. That shouldn't have happened, brother. They both shouldn't have transferred like that. They're together now when they were once enemies. And Trudy, Cuyler, and the baby that would never have been? The three of them are a happy family in that new Milford home Cuyler built for them. Tell me that what happened wasn't a life saver for two people. Remember all the pain you said Stephen was in when you first met him. Now he and Isabella's new life lady our planning their wedding. If Miss Jane could transfer from that little bedroom, why hadn't she done it before? It was only when that school board guy was totally shot down, and his son completely depressed about not getting Jane for a new mom, that she flew back to find out how much she wanted Garrett. That little boy, Trace? Praying for a miracle? If we could just ask Jane some questions, or have Matt and Jessie explain their thoughts on what happened to them, but they're all gone now. Why does the trigger work sometimes and not others? I know that the person has to be thinking about the time period and want to go back, but, Sam, I still think somebody else makes it all happen—pulls it all together. A higher power."

"Well, if that's so, why didn't the 'someone' tell me to

17

stop sleeping with my own great-great-grandmother?"

Jim flopped onto the couch. "I don't know about that one. You've always been the one dedicated to the genealogical search for our relatives. Maybe that's why. Maybe you'll always have the Cooper lineage on your mind."

Ever since Jim found the universal portals by using Trudy's computer, he'd been totally fascinated with time travel. He and Sam listened intently to Wainwright's explanations; he seemed to be the all-knowing expert on such matters; and almost everything Bruce said about time travel made sense.

Sam, Jim, and Wainwright decided to test their theories by taking vacations the summer Trudy slot transferred to Toddsville. Academic curiosity, however, hadn't been the only reason they'd left that season. Trudy had found something they lacked, and a certain amount of sorrow and time traveling envy had to be dismissed in some manner. Traveling far from Richfield Springs seemed the only option—the only sane way to grieve about her final departure from their time period and their lives.

When they came home that fall, Wainwright moved into Trudy's stone house in downtown Cooperstown, and tried to explain the loss of a friend, daughter, and well-known novelist to all who asked. The more he had to make up; the more imaginative his ideas became. The three men met once every two weeks, despite weather conditions, in the Cooper Cottages. One full year of brainstorming resulted in the creation of Time Travelers, Inc. Jim built the web site; Wainwright did the paper work. Their first client, Dr. Stephen Templeton, took the cyber bait. His trip was so successful that all thoughts of problems or new theories were discarded. The business was based on Wainwright's philosophy of time travel, the family journals they'd read, the stories they received from the global network of time travelers Jim had met on the Net, and their own personal experiences.

Sam had every right to dissuade his brother from questioning Wainwright's knowledge. One didn't discuss error issues now. But, in his heart, Jim felt that they were lying to themselves, and their customers, if they didn't have all the answers. Wainwright seemed to know everything, and Sam was dealing with personal issues that he refused to discuss with his brother. His brother was unhappy despite the jovial flair he showed the summer guests. His was a soul ache, deep in his heart, puzzling his mind, and one that may never heal.

"Well, don't let Wainwright hear you talk like that," Sam said, interrupting Jim's thoughts, "and never say it in front of a client." Sam looked down the hill. "I think your fair lady has arrived. Her carriage is chugging its way up our hill."

Jim brightened.

Sam grinned that wonderful Cooper smile they both seemed to have inherited from somebody and said, "Yeah, I know, get lost, Sam."

The two brothers walked to the edge of the path. As Sam stepped into his truck he said, "I hope this is the right one for you. You deserve it." There were tears in Sam's eyes that only a brother could see.

The two vehicles almost collided going around the final bend nearest the cabins. Celeste braked the car, waved to Sam, and then continued up the hill.

19

"I sure hope so," mumbled Jim.

Chapter Two

"Why don't you put some clothes on, and I'll take you to breakfast in Cooperstown? How about the Doubleday?" suggested Jim.

Celeste smiled wickedly. "What's the matter? Don't you like my cooking?"

"I love the way you cook, lady. I just thought," he said, coming close to her, his own body completely naked as well, "since it was our last morning together, I should play the gentleman and offer milady her final meal before she heads back to that nasty, noisy city."

"Oh," she said, throwing her arms around his neck, allowing her body to touch his, and kissing him. "I don't want to go back there."

Jim looked into her eyes and grinned. "Suits me fine. Stay here with me. Forever, if you like." He pressed his lips to hers again—a more passionate embrace than the first time. He pulled her body further into his, separating her long thighs with his foot, and slowly placing his thigh between her legs. She ignited all the fire in him, and the physical reaction to her nearness was obvious.

Celeste was everything to Jim. There had never been a woman who could press all the right buttons the way she did. It was hopeless to think there would ever be another one like her. He wondered if the attraction was because of a past life together. Everything rested on the two of them staying together, but Jim had yet to see a glimmer of love in her eyes. Don't press the issue he would tell himself, but he had already chosen a perfect engagement ring to buy her if she even remotely mentioned cohabitation. Every time she ignored his pronouncement of love, she chiseled another surface crack into his heart.

Celeste gently pulled her arms from his shoulders and stepped back from him but not away. "I wish I could," she said as she pulled her loose, blonde hair from her face. She refused to meet his stare. "We're having such a lovely spring. And it's turning warm so quickly."

Jim held her at arms length, smiled into her eyes, and said, "Come here next weekend?"

"I can't. We have a court date next Monday, and the trial could last a while. Why don't you come with me and stay at my apartment?"

Jim thought about the problem Time Travelers, Inc. was having with the arrogant New York businessman; he thought about the summer guests and how he'd be leaving Sam all alone to make the old cabins ready for another year of tourists; he thought of staying in her small, stuffy apartment bored out of his mind while she went about her business, and answered, "I have to help Sam get ready for the summer tourist season. When do you think you can get away?"

"In a few weeks probably. I can send you e-mail."

The computer wizard of Time Travelers, Inc. said, "You better, lady. In case you missed it the first time, Celeste, I love you, and it's not a line."

Celeste looked away. "I'll get dressed," she said, smiling so as to soften the fact that she hadn't responded, "and we can go down to Cooperstown for breakfast. I love the Doubleday. It will be a nice way to say goodbye."

Jim's heart ached at her words, and he tried hard to not show the tears that were forming in his eyes, but he dressed and shaved without saying anymore. He would try to get her to open up at breakfast. He needed her to confide in him. When he spoke of emotional love, she physically recoiled. Something was very wrong. Was it him? Or was it something from her past that made her such a wonderful lover, yet one who might never commit. He knew she liked him. Why else would she come to the cabins and give herself so completely to him? Maybe he was moving too fast—expecting too much.

"I'm ready, lover," she called to him from the porch.

They drove in Jim's new, white Malibu the short, curvy road to Cooperstown. They were early enough to pick any table they wanted, so Jim chose one in the back so they could talk. After ordering a huge breakfast of eggs, pancakes, sausage, and coffee, Jim took her hand in his. "Am I moving too fast for you?" It took courage to ask the question, but the man who killed Tostig and saved a king's life handled it deftly.

Her focus shifted; her lower lip trembled. She looked at the table. "Maybe. I don't know." Her eyes filled with tears. "It isn't you. I...I...do care for you. It's heaven being in the cabin with you. I can't tell you how much I adore what's happened between us."

It was as if someone had just poured healing ointment on Jim's wounded heart. "Then there's hope...for us...for you and me?"

She shook her head, and her hair danced around her shoulders. "I'm just starting a career. I have so much to think about right now. I've worked so hard to make a name for myself in the political arena."

"I know."

The waitress poured them both more coffee and smiled. "Your food will be ready shortly."

He said, "Thank you," to the waitress. Then he continued speaking softly to Celeste, "I don't want you to give up your job. I just know that I love you, and I've never said those words to any woman—ever."

"Really?"

"You doubt me?" He sat up straight, rested his back on the wooden frame of the small chair, and opened his hands wide in a gesture of openness.

"I doubt men in general, Jim, it isn't just you." She dared to glance once into his eyes. She knew he wanted an explanation. She sipped her coffee and started, "I was very much in love once...back when I was just a kid...eighteen-years-old and on my own in Paris."

"You never told me."

"Well, you might not believe this, but I never planned on being an attorney. My Dad wanted me to follow in his footsteps, but I wanted to be an artist. Because I won a scholarship, he let me go to Paris to study. What artist doesn't want to paint in Paris? It's expected that you should starve and create there...in Montmartre, at the very least. I had such romantic ideas. But, Daddy had no intention of letting me starve. I had plenty of cash. Then I met Phillipe."

"Another artist?"

"No, of all things. Should have been to make a better

story, right? Anyway, he was very rich and on a summer holiday when we met. We lived together for four months in a small apartment he leased for us in the heart of the city, and I was crazy about him. He promised to tell his family about me and return to Paris so that he could make an honest woman of me. He paid for my apartment for two more months and then, all of a sudden, the money stopped coming. He never returned. Never wrote. Never even tried to find me when I had to leave the apartment I couldn't afford."

"Did you try to find him?"

"Yes, but he must have given me a false last name because no such person lived where he said he did. I didn't try any other part of France. I was crushed. I never got over it, Jim. I was so ready to commit, so in love; and, since then, I've guarded my heart. I won my degree and came home to Dad. I told him that I would never paint again, and that, if he would pay the tuition fee, I would go to his college and take up law. He didn't understand the change in me and never asked for an explanation, but I knew he was watching me. He must have guessed. Fathers know things like that about their daughters." She shrugged her shoulders. "They just know."

Jim thought of his own father and mother who had died ten years ago in a car accident on the curvy roads that led from Cooperstown to Milford...their home. "I guess you're right. But, that was so long ago. You haven't painted since?"

"Haven't picked up so much as a pencil to sketch during a boring cross examination."

"Are you still in love with Phillipe, then?"

"I don't think so. See, there was never any closure. I

still don't know what happened to him. I mean, he might have been in a car accident or something. Still, when you get hurt like that, you sort of watch what you say and do. Watch letting your heart belong to anyone else. I think I want to love again, but I'm just so afraid I'll wake up the next morning and find he's abandoned me too."

"That won't ever happen with me, Celeste. But, now that you've told me the truth about this affair, I can understand why you have issues on the subject of a permanent love affair. Just know this, I have no intention of leaving you...ever. I'm not like that. Unless you tell me to go."

She reached for his hand. He took it in his own.

Jim continued, "I like what we have, and I won't push you into more until you're ready. Take as long as you want. I want you to be sure this time because I'm risking it all. I know how I feel about you. I know what I want. I've traveled and experienced life and love to the fullest, and it's time for me to settle down with the right woman. I want that one lady in my life to be you, but if that doesn't happen; I want both of us to be able to say that what we had together was great. No tears. No regrets."

"Then I can come back in two weeks?" She grinned and tilted her head quickly to the side and back like a small child asking whether she could have another chocolate chip cookie.

"I told you that you could come back whenever you wanted. Just don't expect me to hang out in New York City. Not my cup of tea." He lifted his coffee cup in a mini-salute and drank the last of its contents.

Their breakfast was in front of them, and they stopped

talking long enough to inhale their food.

"Love improves my appetite," Jim said, tossing his napkin onto the table.

"Mine too," she said and then leaned over the table and kissed him on the cheek. "You mean all that you say? That you won't press me for more until I'm ready—even if that's never?"

"Ouch," he said flinching. "Let's not go there, okay. We'll take one day at a time. I mean, we did just meet. It's just that I know a good thing when I see it. Phillipe was a fool to let you go. I'm not like him. Not at all. Some day you'll realize that."

"I'll e-mail you when I can come back to the cabins."

"Sure. Ah, but I have to make a small stipulation."

"What's that?"

"We have to be careful around certain dates in June, September, December, and March."

"Why?"

"*My* business."

"Time traveling business? Oh, come on, Jim, you don't really help people fly into the past?"

Jim kissed her hand. "My secret."

He stood to go.

She followed suit. "But, it isn't real. I know it's just a front."

"It's *not* a front," he said and laid several bills on the table that would satisfy the fee as well as a tip.

"Are you going to tell me about it? Huh?" she said grinning wickedly.

"Only if you come back next weekend."

"But...my work?"

"Can wait until the following Monday. After all, that's why you hired the other attorneys."

"You're just full of mystery and intrigue, aren't you?"

Jim turned his head to look at her and gave her his roguish sideways smirk. "I've been told that that's how to win a fair lady's heart. Especially one as beautiful and intelligent as you. Want a T-shirt?" he asked, pointing to a tan one on the wall. "That one would look nice with your hair."

"From the Doubleday Cafe?"

"Yeah, a huge one that you can wear when you visit the cabin. 'A drinking town with a baseball problem', " he said, reading the back of the shirt.

"Can't be naked once the tourists show?"

"Something like that."

He bought her the largest size they had; the waitress placed it in a bag and handed it to Celeste.

"Now I'm a real tourist! I have a souvenir."

He stared at her for a moment as if thinking on a subject that had nothing to do with T-shirts and everything to do with time travel, shook the thought away, and returned his wallet to the back pocket of his jeans before saying, "Congratulations!"

*

Chapter Three

Wainwright traveled to the cabins for Time Travelers, Inc.'s final meeting before the solstice of June 2000.

Wainwright said, "So his majesty the high emperor of Rome gets to travel then?"

Sam said, "I guess so. Only I don't like to think of anyone going back in time on their own. I mean, he is paying us a lot of money, and if anything would happen to him..."

Jim said, "I agree. If you think about the differences between Jane, Trudy, Matt, Jessie, and Stephen, you can see that things just work out better if someone goes along. I, personally, don't mind staying behind if one of you wants to become the emperor's right hand man."

"Because of Celeste," Sam said.

Wainwright cringed.

"Shall we make the 'buddy system' part of our contract from now on?" asked Wainwright.

"If one of these customers goes off on a trip, and Attila the Hun decides to test our client's manhood—or womanhood, aren't we libel?" asked Wainwright.

"I don't see how," said Jim. "We outline, in detail, the possible risks, and I doubt that anyone could seriously have a case against us who willingly puts his or her life in another time period. The whole point is to experience the time, and there's no script in the world that could outline what's going to happen in, say, 445 A.D. But, I do like the idea of sending one of us back with each of them. I think the client would feel safer in the long run knowing that an experienced guide is there if things go weird on them. I don't think the 'Being' would allow someone to be hurt, but, it would certainly make us all feel better in the long run."

Wainwright shot him a puzzled look. "What's that you say? Being?"

"He's going on again about a force behind the time travel mechanism. Jim thinks that there is an all powerful 'Being' that controls the time travel experience," Sam said.

Wainwright stared at Jim. "Well, I don't know about that, all I know is that we have clients who want to travel to the past; and if they have a good time, we will have more clients wanting the same experience. That means money—a lot of it."

"Then are we agreed?" Sam interjected, changing the subject, "that Grant goes back to Rome with an aid?"

"Yes. I'll go with him," said Wainwright.

"Poor guy," Jim mumbled under his breath.

Wainwright pretended that he hadn't heard the comment and continued, "I can learn about the time period and stay out of his way. Sam went the last time."

"That means Jim and I can stay at the cabins for the summer since Grant made a point of stipulating that he needed no one to watch over his modern life. That suits me. I need a break to sort out my thoughts on so many things. Maybe do a little research on Boston and girls who look like infamous pirates."

Wainwright wrinkled his forehead. "What?"

"Sam met the great-grand-daughter of Lady Jane and Captain Garrett Michaels, the pirate, when he was at the Mardi Gras Ball with Stephen. He's trying to find a way to get back to her before she gets married and can no longer be influenced by his charm," said Jim.

Sam gave his a brother a disapproving look.

Wainwright directed the conversation back to business. "Whatever. I'll tell Grant we fly June 21, 2000. He'll have to take me along, or the deal is off."

"Agreed," said Sam.

"What about a portal?" asked Jim.

"Let's find one now."

Jim clicked on Trudy's computer—that had been updated when the business became a reality—and went to his "Favorite Spots."

"He's in New York? But that's a trip for you, Wainwright. Let's make it nearer the business."

"We could use this cabin," said Wainwright.

"I suppose. That would be a Wednesday, and Celeste travels here only on Thursdays when she comes for the weekends. Not many tourists around just then. Sure. That'll work. Hopefully, he'll be so thrilled that we agreed to take him he'll agree to our terms. Better get a nice toga ready, Wainwright."

"Can I cruise the Net for a while to dig up some basic information on the time period? I know Grant supposedly knows all, but I need a working idea of what I'm getting into. I may have to purchase some books too."

Sam grinned. "Do you speak fluent Latin, Wainwright?"

"I'm somewhat versed in the language, yes."

"Then you need to get a CD on Advanced Latin and start conjugating your verbs because 'somewhat versed' ain't gonna cut it where you're headed. Remembering all that French at such short notice to be Emile's Creole cousin was *so* pleasant for me Wainwright that I'll be happy to find you a *nice* course at the local bookstore. Oh, *yes*!" he said with a devilish cackle, "this feels *so* good!"

"Advanced Latin? Well...yes...I suppose you're right about that. You know, we really do need a costumer too. Look into that while I'm gone, will you. Someone who can make authentic, historically accurate clothing for our clients. I mean, how many theatrical stores can one find at short notice?"

"Got a point. I'll look into it," said Sam. "We have some wonderful universities around here. Surely, one of the theater professors can point me in the right direction. Someone looking for a permanent job."

"Test them first on their knowledge. I don't want to go back in time in a satin toga or a cotton tunic!"

"Will do. Better get busy. You going to stay here until the travel date?"

"I thought I might. Can I take one of the cabins?"

Sam looked at Jim. A private message was sent between the brothers. "Why don't you stay at Trudy's house? I think it would be easier for me to help you get ready for the rise and fall of the Roman Emperor, if you'll forgive the pun, there," said Sam.

Wainwright agreed to stay in Cooperstown, then e-mailed Grant Tyrell that both of them would be leaving for Rome circa 200 A.D., June 21, 2000.

Jim sighed and collapsed next to Celeste on their bed in the Cooper Cottages. "So happy you could get away this weekend!"

She regained the normal rhythm of her breathing and then kissed him. "You just have this way about you."

"So do you, lady. Hungry?"

She giggled. "Not anymore, but if you mean food, it's clear you are. I brought *fudge brownies* with me. They're on the table in the great room."

"Coffee? Some coffee and brownies, I think."

"And conversation," she said as she slipped on her new T-shirt, panties, and a pair of jogging shorts. "You promised to tell me about the time travel stuff, or was that just a ruse to bring me back to your bed this weekend?"

"It worked, didn't it?" he said, pouring water into the coffee maker.

She laughed. "But, seriously, I'm curious. You said that time travel was possible, and I want to hear all the dirty details. Who wouldn't? Hand me one of those brownies."

Jim handed her a plate with three chocolate brownies on it. Her brownish-blonde hair was loose, and she waved it away with her hand so that she could watch him and munch on the brownies simultaneously.

"My brother and I come from a long line of time travelers. That's how we know so much about it. Bruce Wainwright is a researcher who stumbled onto the theory long before he met us. I think he was a teenager or something when he first flew back in time, but he's sort of tight-lipped on the subject. When the three of us met a few years ago, we were able

33

to fill each other in on all the different ways to travel, and, shortly thereafter, created Time Travelers, Inc. The theory is that one travels on the solstice and returns on the equinox. That means you can travel twice a year—once in June and once in December. You travel because the atmosphere around the earth shifts, and when it does that, tiny portals, or time tunnels, pop open. The person can travel only to the past—recorded time only—and then the holes shut until they reopen on the equinox to bring you home. Now, if the weather shifts dramatically, you experience some serious discomfort wherever you are; and, if you're near your home portal, you can flash back home until the storm subsides. There are five ways to transfer: general transfer—which means you are an average citizen in the past and not trying to be any particular person; slot transfer—which means you were born in present time but destined to live your life in a past time; death slot transfer—which is when you take someone's place as their soul is leaving the earth plane and live as they did for three months; reincarnation transfer—which is when you go back in time to live one of your past lives; and genealogical transfer—which is when you go back to live the life your ancestor lived. On these last three transfers, since you become one with another life force, we call the transference the Gemini effect. The best way to describe the Gemini effect is to picture two magnets who cannot find one another because they are in different time periods, but that when they are in the same time period—zoom—they bond and become one unit. Physically, they are two in one. It's mystical, I'll admit, but very real. Occasionally, we have spontaneous transfers too. A person just happens to be at the right place at the right time and thinking about a historic period, and they fly. See, Celeste, that's part of the mechanism. You have to be thinking, or have your heart set, on a time period at the time the portal opens. We have records on this going back to Egyptian times. And, of course, anyone who travels with us must write a page or two about the experience so that we can learn more about this natural phenomenon. It's real, my love. Wainwright and my brother and I decided we knew enough to start the business...but...I just don't know," his voice trailed off.

"Don't know about what?"

"When Sam visited 1722, and I was in 1066, some people traveled with us who had a very limited fix on the age. Miss Jane was reading a pirate book, and we still aren't sure about Matt and Jessie from 1871 Calhoun. Never had the time to discuss it much. Jessie was being hanged, and I have no idea what she might have been thinking about at that time. I know Matt was thinking about how he could stop her execution."

Celeste swallowed half of her brownie before saying, "This is true? Really?"

"I wouldn't lie to you. People who travel with us pay $150,000.00 to have us research the time, find them a portal, get them antique currency, teach them whatever they need to know in the time period they wish to travel to such as etiquette—dancing—how to cook, etc., watch their homes, businesses, pay their bills, water their plants, feed their cat, and lie to their friends and family about where they've gone. I would never have told you any of this if I didn't trust you completely...and love you."

"Has anyone *not* traveled who wanted to?"

"I don't think so. Almost anyone who really wants to, and is sitting in the right spot, will fly. It's the opposite that's the problem. Those who aren't planning on going who do."

"I see." She was quiet for a while. "What you are telling me is that if I wanted to go to 1993 Paris, France, and find Phillipe and straight-out ask him where the blazes he went and why he never returned, I could."

"You got it."

"This is just too incredible to believe."

"Got a need for a vacation and $150,000.00 handy, Celeste, you can give it a try. Or, if you'd like to make a trip with me, we can arrange a nice little vacation transfer to, say, a slow moving barge on the Nile. I'll feed you grapes, and you can feed me..." He walked over to her, set his cup of coffee down on the small table next to the couch, and slowly pulled the T-shirt above her shoulders. His lips touched her nipples, delicately kissing them with a reverent respect for her beauty. "These."

"You're incorrigible. Why'd you buy me this shirt if you're going to keep pulling it off?"

"Sorry. I can't help myself. I'm in love."

She pulled her shirt back on and sipped at the coffee for a moment before saying, "Can you...?"

"Die? Frequently asked question. If it's your time to die in the present then you will die during the three months you are traveling in the past."

"Well, what if you change something? Alter history?"

"If you are a slot transfer, it is expected that you *will* change history. That's its function, its raison d'etre. But, my family has found that if you change something that isn't supposed to change, within a few years it miraculously goes back to the way it was meant to be. It's a little weird. Almost as if...well, let me give you an example. Let's say you accidentally burn down a house in 1890 that still stands to this day, and, in fact, housed many families. So this house is the birthplace of people who would be shocked to visit their hometown and find a gas station there and people denying that the building ever existed. The time tunnel function kicks in after the fire, and the house is rebuilt exactly as it was right down to the fence around the garden within one to two years of your interference. Life goes on. The error is deleted. The same holds true for people. And the time travel mechanism won't let you alter major events no matter how hard you try. It's just like..."

"There's more. Why are you afraid to say it?"

"My brother has a theory that history hovers in the heavens above us like a large oval—a sort of record that keeps spinning around and around and can be accessed as easily as you place the needle of a record player onto any groove to hear only one song. Likewise, the needle can also be taken off, as well. Even if you make a small scratch on the record, the song will still play. But, I think there's more to it. It's hard for me to explain, but it's like there's a time travel angel, or something picking the songs for you based on what she or he thinks you need to hear."

"What's so hard to believe about that?"

Jim threw up his hands in desperation. "Because I'm the only one who seems to believe it's a possibility. See, Wainwright is very scientific, and we would know only a little bit about the five ways to travel or the Gemini effect if it weren't for his expertise. He doesn't like the idea that science—or himself—isn't running the show. And my brother Sam had a real bad experience. He made yearly visits to a woman he married and had a family with back in the 1790s, but when Wainwright told him that he was genealogically transferring to his own great-great-grandmother through the Gemini effect, Sam was heartbroken, and, of course, could no longer return to her, or his own happiness with his family."

Celeste summarized, "In other words, if something were watching over the process, why would it allow him to be his great-great-grandfather and he not know it? But, he found out in the long run. And his love for her was the same as his grandfather's because they bonded as one body. Right?"

"You've got it. But, he doesn't understand why he was allowed a fleeting glimpse of happiness. An immoral one to his way of thinking. One that was taken away."

"I see. If I wanted to go back to Phillipe in 1993, would I be able to change the course of my own life?"

"To do that would mean that you would alter the life of the man you saved from a guilty verdict back in January 2000, so I would have to warn you against it. See, if things went well with you and Phillipe, you'd be painting, or married with three kids, and not speaking in front of a judge in New York City."

"It would rewrite itself in one to two years, right?"

"You mean that you would eventually decide to take up law?"

"I suppose so. Why do people decide to time travel?"

"For many reasons but primarily to solve some problem they're having in this existence. Just like past life regression therapy works to help people solve their present phobias. And sometimes they end up dealing with issues they aren't even aware need healing."

"Another reason for your theory that someone else pulls the strings."

"Yes."

"And who do you think is the scriptwriter? God?"

"Maybe. Like I said, this is just a theory. Mine."

"I can't believe we're talking about this as if it were real. Just an hour ago, I thought you were making it all up as a tax write off."

"Can't. It makes a lot of money."

"So, I could go back to 1993 and solve my issues with Phillipe. Learn whether he died in a car crash or something, follow him when he leaves that last day. I mean, I can't even look him up on the Internet because I don't have his real last name."

Jim turned his head so that she couldn't see the expression on his face. "If that's what you need to do."

"Will it hurt you?" she asked.

"Yes, but we can't move to the future if you can't free yourself from the past. I do need to mention this, if you are serious about traveling, your travel plans have to be accepted by all three members of Time Travelers, Inc. And we have just made it a rule that we allow no one access to a trip without a guide. Wainwright is traveling this June; it wouldn't be right for me to help you with your old beau—I'd probably just punch him or something; so it would mean that Sam would have to go with you."

She frowned. "It was just a thought. Just a whim of an

idea. I might not want to know. Or I might wait until later—another year." Her blue eyes looked childlike and trusting as she bit into the last brownie on her plate.

Jim put his arms around her and looked into her eyes. "Whatever you have to do, Celeste, I'm behind you one hundred percent. I trust you. I love you. And...maybe the 'Being' wants you to find your heart. When you gave up your art, you lost your soul. That's pretty frightening when you think about it."

"I'm living a lie?" She pulled away. "Is that what you're saying?"

"I'll let you think that one through while I take a shower. I'm taking you to the 1819 House for dinner tonight. So, put on something feminine and frilly."

She smiled. "The 1819 House?" She wiggled her eyebrows up and down as if she had just won a major victory.

"I believe t'is one of milady's favorite restaurants. If you like, I'll give you a tour of Toddsville in the bargain and tell you the tale of Trudy and Cuyler. Without Trudy, we would never have formed TTI. Drink your coffee while I clean up, and then it'll be your turn to use the trickle of water, otherwise known as our shower."

She took her cup of coffee out onto the porch and sat in the old rocker there and stared at the squirrel who was staring at her as it crawled down the tree.

"What are you looking at?" she said, watching him with curiosity.

It chattered and looked sideways at her as if it were asking a question.

"Sorry. I don't know what you want. I don't speak

'squirrel'."

The squirrel seemed annoyed that she didn't understand his body language, that she had no sweet roll for him, and, after realizing that she wasn't Trudy, and tilting his head back and forth several times to dismiss her, darted up the tree chattering wildly. She watched him disappear. "I don't know what I want, either."

Chapter Four

"Too much champagne," Celeste moaned her excuse for being slow in her response to his sexual advances into Jim's ear as he gently massaged her right breast which was still trapped inside her bra. She slumped onto their bed and grinned.

He sighed, "Nuts and Berries too."

She giggled, and the sound was as pleasing as rushing water racing down a creek after a torrid thunderstorm. "Good coffee. *Good* coffee. What a name! Who came up with that one, I wonder?"

He tried to release the breast from its prison. "Someday I'm going to have to do a study on exactly how many ounces of liquor it takes to make a woman easy to seduce without nullifying her libido." The bra was unhooked gracefully with one hand.

"Good food, good drink, good storytelling, nice ride in the country, nice man," she said smiling; her whole face beaming with childlike happiness. She was beyond simple inebriation and focusing all of her attention on what her lover was doing with her clothing. "Who could ask for anything more?" she sang to him and snickered.

"Well..." he said wickedly, "I could. Now she's singing."

She laughed again and curled her legs under her hips. "Take your pleasure, man. The woman's mind is gone."

"As you wish."

He stood before her and slid his jacket from his shoulders, undid and tossed aside his tie, took off his belt and dropped it on the floor, sat on a nearby chair to take off his shoes and socks, stood up to unzip and discard his brown trousers, slowly unbuttoned his tan shirt and flew it into the air, and then smiled down at her.

She looked at him and chuckled. "I see what you mean."

He took his time sliding his underwear from his hips imitating what he thought were the actions of a male stripper. She giggled at his antics.

"Got to get you out of this dress." He unzipped the back of the peach floral, chiffon dress and placed it delicately onto a chair beside the bed. Then he gently tugged at the unhooked bra, carefully taking it from her shoulders, and then began to caress the tips of her breasts with his tongue while his hands massaged them into a point. She was a little, rag doll just rolling over helplessly and allowing him to do as he wished.

Jim suddenly stopped all movement and stared at her for a second. Then he let the back of his hand gently slide down the side of her face and pressed his lips passionately against hers. His fingers ran behind her neck and massaged her back and shoulder muscles. His lips kissed her cheeks, her throat, her neck, her stomach, her abdomen, hips, the inside of her thighs, and continued further down. He pulled off her panties. "You wouldn't!" she said.

"You said I could do as I pleased, didn't you? You're completely defenseless. Why not? Haven't you ever had a man embrace you there before?"

"No. I'm not sure I'll like it."

"Remember the part where you said your libido was dead, well there are ways to fix that problem. Relax. Let me love you."

"But I'm numb from the champagne."

"This area didn't have anything to drink."

His tongue moved with the rhythm and grace of a belly dancer as it pulsated, gyrated, and twisted in every possible way he desired to manipulate her most vulnerable erogenous zone. The result was an incredible orgasm. She called his name loudly when her mind burst with ecstasy.

Immediately, she was covering him with her body, pressing his hot skin close to hers and kissing him with fierce passion. Her hands went around his body and cradled him close to her. Her tongue danced across his chest kissing his nipples, his neck, and then slipped between his lips. She began to moan softly—a creature call from the depths of her most sensual nature. It was the sound of uncontrollable hunger, passion, desperate need, and any man would want to hear it from his lover. Beyond lust. An urgency locked away in some secret part of her mind. Desire beyond appetite. A craving that no other man but Jim could satisfy. Her perfect white teeth bit his lower lip.

"What do you want, Celeste?" he asked simply to hear her answer.

"You," she growled. "I want you."

He cuddled her in his arms and rocked her body close to his hips. "Just needed to hear you say it. You smell like warm coffee and vanilla. Sweet."

He spread her legs so that they could encircle his thighs, and she rested her buttocks in his lap so that he could hold her vulnerable softness above his manhood. His body slipped into hers rapidly once he realized how close she was. He rocked back and forth, holding her in this warm lovers' dance. His thigh muscles tightened and relaxed with each orchestrated move. He smoothed her hair with both of his hands, moved the strands from her forehead, looked into her eyes, and smiled. She stared at him and parted her lips. He allowed her body to fall back onto the mattress, and, with an assurance no glass of champagne could mask, and with no hesitation because they had already made love once today; Jim moved inside her with an almost reverent devotion for her femininity.

"You don't have to wait for me," she said. "I already..." but a new mind dissolving thrill stopped her words. "Oh," she whimpered, "who taught you all this? Did you learn this on some time traveling trip?"

"You could say I picked it up on my many travels, yes."

Jim could no longer allay his longing for his own pleasure. He closed his eyes to her beauty and began moving in and out of her with a ferocious need to find his own path to paradise. He didn't hear her sighs, her moans of pleasure, or her soft coos of delight. He wanted release. He tasted her skin which glowed with perspiration. He savored her breasts—soft mounds playfully rocking from side to side with every move. He detected her heartbeat. Feel the soft pounding of her pulse on her neck. Her hands tried to embrace him, but he stopped them with a gentle bite on her shoulder. Then he arched his back; the muscles aching to be stretched. He cried out unaware of how loud his voice might be, or how far it might carry in the woods. He opened his eyes and smiled at her.

His body still held the scent of his spicy aftershave; only now, like mulled red wine with cinnamon and cloves stirred into

45

it, his flesh had a deep, rich aroma. A masculine warmth all its own. "Hi," he said and grinned. Then they both laughed as he collapsed on top of her.

Celeste playfully swatted at his disheveled head of hair. "Cover me," she said cuddling into his side. The band that held his long, dark brown hair in place had pulled free a long time ago. His hair now rested on the nape of his neck, fell onto the top of his shoulders, and curled around his face so that she couldn't see his expression. "You're bad."

He rolled to her side and kissed her. His voice was a whisper. "Really. I could have sworn I heard you scream otherwise just a second ago. Now stay put, I have something for you." He put on his underwear and went to a closet in the bedroom.

"I thought you already gave it to me."

He looked at her and winked. "Cute!" Jim pulled a huge package wrapped in brown paper from the small closet in their room and placed it by her side.

"What is it?"

"Open it and find out."

She put on her T-shirt, which was hanging on the handle of the bathroom door, and walked over to the monstrous gift. She smiled and gingerly pulled the wrapping from just one corner.

"I hope you like it."

Then she tore one panel of the paper from the front section of Jim's gift. It was a professional artist's easel.

"There's more. He walked over to the closet and handed her a professional artist's tackle box. "Open it."

Inside were professional brushes, oil paints in every

46

imaginable hue, watercolors in every shade, sponges, everything a true artist would need from a hobby store.

"This cost you a fortune."

"I thought you might keep them here, and then when the spirit moved you; you could try painting again. Not trying to rush you into anything, but this woodsy cabin has many picturesque views. Please say I did the right thing, or I'll be crushed."

Celeste leaned over to him and kissed him on the cheek. "I love it. Not ready for it yet, but maybe someday I will be. Now all I need is a clean canvas and some paper."

"That's in the closet too."

"Thought of everything, didn't you?"

"Thought of you. I didn't know what to buy, but the guy in the hobby shop helped me. I just told them that you were a professional, and he did the rest. Didn't want you to have some paint by numbers set. And it *is* sort of our anniversary."

"Anniversary?"

"Yeah, we've been together two months now."

She kissed him again. "You're right. Scary, huh?"

He took her into his arms. "Not for me, lady. One month. Two months. A lifetime. One lifetime with you isn't enough for me. Let's try eternity."

"How did I ever wind up with such a romantic lover?"

He kissed her. "Lucky, I guess. Let's get some sleep now, lady mine. I'm taking you out in the boat tomorrow, and we're going to pretend we're fishing."

"Maybe I'll take that sketch book with me and make some pencil drawings of the lake, the boat, you."

"You draw people too?"

"Honey, I can draw anything."

Chapter Five

May 31, 1793

Paris, France

1:00 P.M.

There came a hard pounding, like the sound of cannon fire, on Celeste Lacombe's front door. Expecting to find Phillipe, she ran to open it.

Mademoiselle Claire Lacombe and Monsieur Leclerc burst through the door slamming it shut afterwards. They were breathing hard and were perspiring from the combination of the temperature of the warm spring day and their own intense emotion. Claire's dark brown hair was flying from its chignon, scrolling waves down her cheeks, streaming down her neck, and clinging to her breasts. She was a windstorm. Leclerc's clean shaven face was crimson with joyful exuberance. Though not as wild looking as his lover, Claire, he was a flame—a burning ember of passion.

Claire had a delicate figure as did her cousin, Celeste, and wore a bright blue dress. The alluring bodice of the dress was accentuated by a lace shawl collar and matching, detachable, lace cuffs and was quite tight. The sleeves of the dress came to her elbow, and the full cuffs assisted her exaggerated hand movements like a waving banner used to announce the beginning of another band in a holiday parade. The bodice was also quite low, as was the fashion of the times, and her corset pushed her breasts way above the neckline. If the shawl had not been there, almost all of her bosom would have been exposed. She wore blue brocade pumps with pretty ivory colored bows on the front of each shoe. Volumes of petticoats encircled the hem of the gown and made the skirt swirl alluringly every time she moved. Her eyes were the color of coal; her skin bore a vital peach hue; her cherry cheeks and lips allied her passionate nature; her tiny nose was almost too perfect; and her dark eyebrows and flirtatious eyelashes made those seductive orbs seem wide, expressive, and disarmingly beautiful. There was an intelligent, almost wickedly bright life force that emanated from and around Claire. She took your focus. Forced you to notice her. When she fixed her gaze upon you, you were trapped instantly. She was the sort of woman men adored. Witty, beautiful, sexually aggressive with not an ounce of fidelity in her bones. It was a challenge to a man to be the one who could steal her heart and loyalty. So far, no one had. It made her irresistible.

Claire's voice fluctuated to match her mood. Her theater training had nurtured that voice, and she knew how to use her vocal skills to perfection. Smooth like satin when she wanted something, harsh and cold when she argued, and soft like an angel's hymn when she spoke with a man about love.

Leclerc was the antithesis of Claire. Contrary to fashion, Leclerc wore no wig. His long, dark brown hair was tied away from his face with a black bow. He wore a burgundy velvet coat with rows of buttons down the front of one side, and slim gold slashes for button hooks on the other. His figure was handsomely attired in a long gold vest, burgundy velvet breeches, white stockings, and black leather shoes with a broad two-inch heel and brass buckles on the front of each. He wore a white lace shirt under his vest. The lace cuffs of the shirt dangled elegantly from his wrists so that when he waved his hands it looked as if he were waving a handkerchief through the air. A black tie, twined around his high collar, added just the correct stylish touch to his suit. The tie was torn from there because he needed to catch his breath, but the effect was not lost. His face was handsome in a strong, powerfully masculine way. His oval visage was accented by petulant full lips, dark brown eyes, a slender nose, a short but wide forehead, and high cheekbones. His eyes—like hers—were bright with life, energy, and internal fire. His long neck sat upon broad shoulders and a strong chest. He moved rapidly, as if he were trying to dodge a pistol ball, and gave the impression that he would never stay in one place for very long. He was a man of action and boundless intelligence. The constant animation kept his body lean. His thoughts were mirrored in his facial expressions which made him a delight to watch during conversations. His voice echoed like distant thunder when he spoke. In short, he was a man any woman would want in her bed, but one who might not be there when the rent was due.

Historic hindsight being what it's worth, one might remember Shakespeare's line about being wary of men who wore a "lean and hungry" look when one thinks of this intelligent, driven man; for such a dangerous look belonged to Leclerc.

"What a glorious day, Celeste!" exclaimed Claire as if she had just tasted the heady sweetness of ambrosia.

"I have stayed inside all day...working," said the artist with an uninterested, self-effacing shrug.

Claire swung her arms restlessly in short, punctuated

jabs. "But why? We've all waited for this day. The overthrow of the bastards who imprison all good citizens through famine are upon us today. Let them be imprisoned instead."

Claire's lips pouted, and her chin jutted forward as her index finger sliced the air. "Heads will fall, Celeste. No one who owns property is safe."

Claire gave Leclerc a meaningful and seductive look. "We thought we might find a resting place here with you for a moment. We are exhausted and hungry."

"There is some wine on the shelf, there, and some soup on the fire. Help yourself."

"She is good to me, my love," said Claire to Leclerc while kissing her cousin on the cheek.

Celeste watched as the two militants set themselves a place to eat at her table and waited silently for them to tell her all their news.

Celeste prompted her cousin with, "I thought you were going to act this year. The contract? With Mayerre? Three thousand livres a year is a good sum, Claire."

"Mainz is under siege; the company cannot begin rehearsals. It looks as if I am an out-of-work actress and maybe that is good, oui? It gives me more time for important things, eh, Leclerc?"

Celeste had not seen or heard from her lover, Phillipe, in two weeks. Not so much as a short note had arrived. She knew that the politics of the day was critically pertinent to her way of life, and yet all she could think of was making love to Phillipe.

Leclerc nodded agreement as he ripped a loaf of bread in half and bit into one side of it, and then handed the other half to

Claire. Then he poured himself a tankard of wine and drank thirstily. "God, I love passionate women! Claire says you're an artist."

"Yes. I have a job doing small sketches for a printer."

"I could use an artist for my paper."

"I have a job with his print shop."

Celeste's mood was far too tragic on what appeared to be such a joyful day. It disappointed her rebellious cousin.

"What's the matter, Celeste? You should be happy. Is it, Phillipe?" Claire asked while ladling soup into two wooden bowls.

Celeste sighed, pondered whether she should tell the truth then finally admitted, "I haven't heard from him in days. I'm worried about him. He's in Bordeaux."

"Yes, I know; but, Celeste, you warned him to leave the country. Why hasn't he come for you, then?"

"I don't know." Celeste fell silent.

Leclerc watched the two women as they talked. He stared at his soup, waiting for it to cool, and raised his eyebrow. "He's an aristocrat?" he whispered.

Claire turned and looked at him. "You must not say a word, love. He has been a godsend to my cousin. He found her a job, gave her this house, and treats her well. You must say nothing, do you understand?"

"I will say nothing, but, if you want me to find out how he's doing, it can be arranged. Anything Claire wants is my command to act."

"Could you do that? Without endangering him?" asked Celeste with sudden interest.

"I don't see how he can escape the Terror, dear cousin, but you have been kind to me and to Claire, and I would not hurt you for the world. But, you must join us in our fight, Celeste. Join our cause. Wear the cockade..."

Celeste's eyes widened with terror. "I dare not. My employer."

"Well, yes, of course, I see," said Leclerc after sampling a spoonful of soup. "Still, Claire can take you to the meetings of the Revolutionary Republican Women's Club—which she practically invented—and you should go to city hall with us and watch the course of liberty. Freedom from oppression. Equal rights for all."

Celeste thought about not responding, watched them savor the wine Phillipe had brought with him from his vineyard in Bordeaux, and then said, "And why are *you* oppressed, Leclerc? You have food on your table. You own your own business. And you," she turned to her cousin, "who will be able to afford your performances if the rich no longer attend? For how long will you act?"

Celeste stared at her fingers for a second before interrupting the silence, "I am in a mood, forgive me. Still, you will eat and drink and make merry in the taverns and fine hotels with your gentlemen, eh, Claire?"

Claire placed her spoon on the side of her dish and said softly, "You must be in a temper. No Phillipe to make you comfortable and happy. Are you jealous of my love for Leclerc?"

Celeste darted a wistful glance towards the window. "As dangerous as my love for Phillipe, as far as I can see. You speak of executing the aristocrats and then fall happily into bed with them." A tiny, whimsical smile crossed her face. It went unnoticed by her companions.

Leclerc smiled after a disturbing moment of silence and said, "You should go into politics, Celeste, you'd be good at it."

"That's what Phillipe said too."

"Commendable soup by the way. Good and hot."

"And full of the meat I bought for too high a price today with the pittance of money I get from my employer. I fear there will be no coal for the fire tomorrow if he doesn't pay me soon."

"And the gold you get from Phillipe?" asked Claire, giving a secret smile to her lover.

"When he shows, which he hasn't lately. I have to live. I do what I have to. So do you."

Leclerc stood with his wine glass and walked about the room in an attempt to lighten the mood. He noticed the portrait of Phillipe that stood on an easel in the corner of the small front room. "Is this the man you love?"

"Yes," she said sharply.

"I'll see what my sources can tell me about him. Bordeaux you say?"

"Yes. Thank you. I'm sorry for being peevish today."

"Can we use your other bed, Celeste?" said Leclerc suddenly with a glance to the second level of the apartment.

Claire stared at him in surprise and then smiled.

Celeste said, "Of course."

Leclerc dropped the glass on the table by Phillipe's portrait. "I'm heated from all that has happened today. And you, Claire?"

She swayed towards him, gazed adoringly at him, and then pulled at her blouse. "My love!"

He bit into the flesh above her breast and then placed his hand into her bodice and pulled one breast free. He began to pull on its tip with his lips and tongue. She growled her approval. The two fled up the stairs and began a long and very noisy lovemaking procedure.

Celeste tried not to notice and went back to placing a flesh tone oil based paint on Phillipe's sketch. As she was judging the color and its effect on her portrait, she caught a glimpse of a man in a cloak hurrying away from her apartment. Since she lived near an alley that led nowhere, she knew the figure was not an idle passerby. She hurried to the door, flung it open, and stepped onto the cobblestone street. She only viewed the back of the six-foot tall man and his fine black cloak and high hat. She had never noticed him around her house before, but she had the chilling suspicion that he was spying on her. Someone watching Claire or Leclerc or both no doubt she thought and went back inside closing the door behind her. Resting her back against its roughness, Celeste let her thoughts wander. Why was she being watched? And by whom?

Chapter Six

June 2000

New York, New York

"I didn't kill my husband!" demanded the woman seated across from Celeste Montclaire. "I need you to represent me."

Celeste examined some papers in a folder. "The evidence against you is very strong. The neighbor did find you standing beside your husband, who was lying dead in the bathtub, with a bloody knife in your hand. By the angle of the wound, and the way you stood above him in his bath, it looked as if you killed him. There is a hefty motive here too. Insurance policy of one million dollars, and, we have been told by an anonymous source that you had just been told a rumor that your husband was fooling around with his secretary."

Celeste looked into the woman's ice blue eyes. The only suspect in this murder trial was rather pretty though right now her face was ghostly pale. Her eyes were wide and expressive; her cheeks were high; her nose a bit too long; but, for her age of thirty-five, she looked as though she were twenty. The most intriguing aspect of the woman's appearance was the truth that rested in her eyes.

"You have to represent me," she said, clutching a tissue she had used to dab away her tears. "I came into the bathroom and found him dead. I froze. I saw the knife, and, without thinking, I picked it up. You don't think of fingerprints and homicide detectives when you're looking at the man you've lived with for thirteen years bleeding to death in his own bathtub."

Celeste sighed and doodled on a note pad. "No, I don't suppose you do."

"Please. I'm telling you the truth. I don't want to die for a crime I didn't do."

Celeste smiled and gave the woman a direct stare. "I'll speak with my associates today about helping you." But, she already knew that the others on her team thought this woman was guilty and should pay for her crime. It wasn't the need for work anymore. It was the law firm's growing reputation for integrity that helped each member of her team decide the fate of their possible clients. The woman's tortured expression, grief, and those incredibly beautiful eyes clung to Celeste's inner vision. Somehow she just knew the lady was innocent. Maybe she would have to take the case on alone if the others refused.

A female guard led the woman away, and Celeste took a taxi from the prison to her office.

It was a rainy morning in downtown New York City. Celeste read some briefs and tried to forget the woman accused of murdering her husband. She had a headache from the pollution, the overcast sky, or too much wine the night before, so she could not concentrate. She thought of a new twist to their courtroom strategy on an old case. Then she played on the Internet for a while and wrote an e-mail to Jim.

All she could think about was the peace and happiness she'd experienced in Richfield Springs last weekend. It was exhilarating to have a new lover, and, yet, quite frightening. Jim wanted more than she could give. He deserved it. Jim was a great guy, a fantastic lover, and an intellectually stimulating companion. They had some similar interests. He didn't seem interested in art shows, but he loved antiques. He had no intention of ever attending an opera, but he could be persuaded to go the the theater for other performances. However, his cabin in the woods, and the time she spent there, bonded them together despite any possible differences they might have had. It was spiritually refreshing to visit there, and reminded her of her forgotten talents. This was emotionally and psychologically beneficial for Celeste. Unfortunately, her renewed interest in art unearthed memories of France that had remained buried for several years. The whole love affair had become a double-edged sword. Joy and pain. Something new to remind her of something old. Freedom to be herself. To find the lost woman left behind in France. A chance to reflect on why she refused to let go of the past. Maybe this was good for her, after all. Jim seemed to be chipping away at the ice block that surrounded Celeste's heart. How long would he continue?

Celeste thought of the sketch she had made of him. Jim had been napping under one of the trees that bent its branches over the lake. He looked so relaxed—so peaceful. She sat there for an hour and traced his likeness on the new art paper he'd given her. Long lean face. High cheekbones. Shoulder length dark hair held back behind his neck with a rubber band. Strong arms. Long legs. Broad shoulders. Cute butt. She couldn't have painted a better portrait of a man to love. Considerate in a time when men seemed so self-centered. Mature. Witty. Deep. Yes, she liked that philosophical side of him. He'd turn his head towards her, give her that sideways grin he had, and then just knock her flat with a compliment or an idea that made her mind spin. And loving. Chiefly loving. He was wonderful in bed. No man, not even Phillipe, had ever loved her like that. And he was artistic in his own way. He liked beautiful antiques. Took time to make them shine. His collection was vast beyond words. And, of course, there was the time travel business. She found herself mulling over his words about traveling to the past all the way home Sunday night. Why was she coming back to New York? Well, to make money, earn self-esteem, prove to her father that she really was something special, and to make Phillipe, wherever he was, jealous that he hadn't returned for her. That was all, but it was enough to keep her from a happy life with Jim.

Thoughts of Phillipe fueled her bitterness. Why couldn't she get over it—him? The man screwed her—literally—and left her to her own devices. Yet, her mind kept replaying all these little vignettes that showed he'd had no choice. He'd had a good reason. He'd gone home and found out his family was bankrupt. His father had died, and he'd had to take over the family business and couldn't get back to her. He died in a car accident *before* getting home so his parents could not let her in on the news because he'd never told them about her existence. He'd received amnesia after falling from his polo pony.

None of the excuses worked at all and she knew it. Except for his dying in a car accident, which was the best of the lot. Phillipe's family should have been aware that she was living in a rented apartment that he was paying for with his family's money. Since the romance had lasted over the course of a year and a half, Celeste wagered that he would have told *somebody* about their heated affair. Surely that same someone would have called, written, or informed her that Phillipe wanted nothing more to do with her. She struggled with that theory. He'd used her, lied to her, and discarded her. He'd cut off the rent payments without a simple call or letter. He'd proclaimed his love for her on numerous occasions and taken care of her for many months. He'd told her that he would return for her and make her his wife. When you're in love, you believe all that a man tells you, and to make sure you never feel that much pain again, *you make certain that you never fall in love again.* Then a man like Jim Cooper enters the picture.

Maybe she should see a counselor, a psychiatrist, a past life regressionist, someone. Someone to talk to about her lingering feelings for the man who would always be her first love. Because if she didn't unravel her heart and mind on the subject, her future with Jim, or any other man, was doomed. Phillipe had broken her heart, but why should his influence destroy her future life as well.

Her secretary interrupted her thoughts with a knock on her door. Brenda entered when called and was carrying a uniquely wrapped box. "For you," said Brenda. "Just arrived."

"Is it from Jim?"

"No, it's from that client who owned the antique store. You know, the one with the fake Rembrandt."

Celeste chuckled softly. "Must be grateful. What do you suppose it is?"

"Opening it would just kill the suspense, wouldn't it?" Brenda said and smiled at her boss.

"You're right." Celeste carefully unwrapped, unraveled, snipped ties, and eased an old, golden brown, leather hardback book that looked at least a hundred years old, from its casing.

"Read the note," said Brenda.

Celeste read, "Just a token of my appreciation. This book dates back to 1797, Paris, France, and is worth a small fortune. It is the diary of a police spy named Jean-Jacques Coupier who witnessed all that transpired in the streets of Paris during the French Revolution time period of 1793 to 1795. He rescued his reports and printed them in manuscript form in 1797. Only a few were published at the time so that makes this copy, which is in excellent condition, all the more valuable. I would guess it's worth somewhere between $150,000 to $200,000 dollars. It's yours. You helped me win my reputation back. Accept this with my humblest gratitude.

Gratefully,

Clyde Desmond

The two women opened the old book carefully and when a few pages stuck together, Celeste rushed to close it. "I'd love to look inside but don't want to hurt it, and I know just the person who would love this book."

"Jim Cooper?" said Brenda.

"Won't it make a wonderful surprise gift for him? He bought me art supplies for our anniversary, but I didn't buy him anything. I'll sneak up there this week, buy a little champagne, and then call him in Milford and tell him to come up to the cabin to fetch his 'gift'. What do you think?"

"Sounds like a plan—but you're in court until Wednesday."

"Well, cancel all my plans for Thursday and Friday, I'll go Wednesday night."

"Whatever you say; you're the boss."

Brenda hurried to her office and turned the desk calendar's page to June 22 and 23. She started to call the clients listed there to tell them that her boss would be unavailable from *Wednesday, June 21* on.

Celeste stared at the book and opened it just enough to see the date. She saw the first few entries the man had made.

June 1, 1793, Rue Neuve-des-Petits-Champs/ Lepeletier, Paris

"Claire Lacombe, the French actress and revolutionary, and Leclerc, the editor of his own paper, stay at an apartment in this section of the city with a young woman whose name is unknown to me but is an artist of exceptional talent. I believe she has a job at the print shop for a man comes and gives her work and then returns at the end of the week to retrieve it. This artist is a very handsome woman and could receive the sympathies of any man. She rarely leaves this domicile. An aristocrat by the name of Phillipe de Brouquens must be her lover for he comes every two weeks and stays for one. The woman appears to have no political allegiance to the clubs, yet Claire is here a good part of the time. It would be difficult to believe this woman has no interest in the citizens' revolt. Leclerc is an enragé, so Claire, too, must be interested in the death of those one might call aristocrats. I think Phillipe is an aristocrat from Bordeaux. Claire Lacombe is reputed to be in love with Leclerc whom, some may consider by his choice of professions, to be an aristocrat. None of this makes any sense to me. The city is alive with rioting and the revolution today, yet the two who wish to 'put terror on the agenda' are harbored in this place free from all the violence that surrounds us. There is looting and destruction all through the town. The people have had enough of the price fixing merchants. It is rumored that the Convention will vote soon. I will continue to keep my eye on the apartment and the artist."

Celeste stopped reading and perused the book for a picture of the man who wrote about all he saw. There was none.

She smiled a self-satisfied smile. "Oh, Jim, have I got a wonderful surprise for you!"

Wednesday evening was a fine night to drive the long distance to Richfield Springs. Celeste's first glance at the parking area confirmed her fears that the cabins were full to capacity, and parking would be impossible. She parked her car on a grassy hill behind the cabin and carried her packages to the door of "their" cabin before remembering that she had no key. If she called Jim to get the key, the surprise would be ruined. Since there was a small light burning on a table inside, she chanced a turn of the knob and the door opened with a small shove.

"Jim?" she called to no answer.

She put her suitcase in the bedroom and brought the antique book to the round table in the great room. She had covered it in a special mauve colored velvet cloth, tied it with a white lace bow, and hand painted a card that had a French flag on it which said: Happy Anniversary. Chilled bottle of champagne and warm cuddly lady wait in the bedroom!

Then she returned to the bedroom, shut the door, and

changed into a cool, white, cotton nightgown with eyelet lace, pearl buttons, and no sleeves. She took her sketch of Jim from the closet and began to finish it. Celeste smiled and hummed with delight at the way his features came to life under her skillful pencil markings. Then she remembered that she hadn't called him yet. She reached for her cell phone and hit all the buttons on her call book until she came to his name. She pressed the talk button and waited. He wasn't home. That was odd. It was twelve o'clock. She left a message on his answering machine that he should come to the cabin, and that she had a wonderful surprise for him. She hoped he would get the message soon, or she would have to open the champagne without him. She hadn't had much to eat in her rush to get to the cabin so that she could play this trick on her lover, and she was starting to feel hunger pangs. She knew there would be no point in looking for supplies in the vacant cabin, and she was starting to regret that she hadn't eaten some fast food hamburger before she left for Richfield Springs.

"There's no point in you or Sam coming with Grant and me when we go to the cabin," said Wainwright in his most professional and businesslike manner. They were at the Trudy/Wainwright house in Cooperstown. Sam, Jim, Grant, and Wainwright had eaten dinner in Tunniclif's pit, sampled a bit of gourmet coffee at The Stagecoach, and were now sipping Wainwright's imported sherry back at the stone house.

Grant mentioned that it was a satisfying way to start a vacation. He said, "I'm not putting this toga thing on until we're there."

"Well, if you think you can handle things without us," said Sam, "I suppose we'd better go. It's getting late, and Jim needs to get back to Milford. I'll drive you to the cabins. I'm the resident manager of the Cooper Cottages this summer, and we have a slew of guests right now. I was in the cabin earlier tonight, left the light on for you, and the door open. It's better I don't go inside. Don't need to travel tonight."

"I must admit that this whole time travel business is thoroughly astonishing. It's difficult for me to believe that by tomorrow morning I shall be Emperor of Rome. The omnipotent ruler of all around me."

Sam winced. "Just make sure you have the research tucked away in your bag just in case you get into any trouble."

"He has me to guide him," said Wainwright, swallowing his final taste of the sherry.

"I know," mumbled Jim, "that's why Sam's worried."

"And we'll return to the cabin in September? Correct?" asked Grant.

"Getting a little worried?" said Sam.

"Not at all. Three months is not enough."

"You can always go back," said Wainwright. "I mean, later if you decide to return that is."

"I intend to. Often. I plan to reap all the inherent benefits of being the man who holds the power of the known world in his hands."

"Right now I think you and Wainwright better get a move on if you want to hit the solstice by two. My chariot," he pointed to the old, worn truck that sat by the curb in front of the funeral home, "awaits. Night, Jim."

Jim watched as the three men left the house. Then he locked Trudy's house, found his car parked on the next side street, and headed for home.

The busy week and the long ride to Cooperstown had taken its toll on Celeste. She took her sketch book over to the bed, dropped her weary body onto it, cuddled the picture close to her chest, curled into a ball on top of the tulip quilt, and fell asleep. She was deep into a beautiful repose when Wainwright and Grant entered the great room and put on their Roman attire. She dreamed of Jim and how much he would treasure Jean-Jacques's diary.

The portal opened at two in the morning, and Wainwright and Grant, as well as the fair Celeste, time traveled.

Chapter Seven

June 21, 1793

Paris, France

"Wake up, cousin. Oh, how you sleep like a dead woman! I told you that we'd have to get up early to get in line. Look at her," said Claire Lacombe to her lover. "Where did you get this gown? Did Phillipe give it to you? Is it from America?" Claire turned her head to see whether Leclerc was watching. "How he dotes on her." Then she looked at her cousin closely. "What's that you have in your hands?"

Celeste woke on the word "Phillipe."

"Who are you?" she asked, her mind and speech instantly transferring to French—the language she had used so well during her studies in Paris—as she focused on the room, the furniture, the woman with the pretty 1790s dress, the man with his full lace shirt opened to expose his attractive physique. She smelled chicken soup, fresh air, wet horses, and mud. Her first physical sense was that of urgent hunger. "I'm hungry."

"Get her some wine and soup," ordered the woman. "Were you dreaming, mon petit cher? It took me so long to wake you; I thought you might be dead. Is something wrong? Don't you remember me? Are you ill?"

Celeste became conscious immediately. Her eyes flashed with sudden awareness of her situation. There was no question in her mind what had happened. She remembered the date. So that was why Jim told her that she couldn't be in the cabin at the end of June. It was one of the primary portals. Well, he had to keep *some* things secret from his new love. Business secrets. She thought of her plan to surprise him with the book and her unexpected visit. Well, at least she had left the book behind and the message on Jim's answering machine. Then she thought about her clients, and the fact that for the next few months Jim would be on the spot to explain what had happened to her. Not to mention the fact that he would be frightened for her safety. She would be able to ascertain where she was within minutes, but he would have no idea what year or what location she was visiting. If he had heard her message, he would have been able to call Sam and tell him to get her out of the cabin or come there himself and travel with her. It had been so late, and he must have not checked his messages before he went to bed. Apparently, fate had decreed for her to fly alone, and, she ascertained by the look of her sparse surroundings; she had traveled to the time period of Jean-Jacques Coupier's book...June 21, 1793. If all that Jim had said were true—and by the looks of things it was—she would be here for three months.

Celeste's cross-examination skills would have to help her now. The sketch in her arms and her own nightgown was proof that she had brought two items from home with her. She looked at her drawing of Jim and burst into tears. "Oh, Jim, I need you. I don't know enough to do this without you," she whispered to the picture.

The man handed her a goblet of wine which she drank down in two fast gulps. He asked, "Who's Jean?"

The woman winked, made a clicking noise with her tongue

and teeth, and said, "Probably a new lover. It's those eyes of hers, mon cher. You did say Jean, didn't you, Celeste?" She gave a questioning look to the man and tilted her pretty head. "*I thought she said Jim.*"

Celeste's mind spun. "I said...Jean. Of course, you are correct." She prayed for the two to call each other by name. The man handed her a bowl of steaming broth and a spoon. There was something incredibly sexy about the way he moved, the turn of his hips with the stiffness in his back, the way his broad chest towered over his slender form, and the movement of his arms and chest that dictated self-assurance combined with a cavalier air. The woman was as beautiful as Elizabeth Taylor was at this lady's age. Celeste swung her body to the edge of the small bed and sipped at the nourishment while her mind sought ways to get them to tell her who they were, whom she was, and where she was.

"You need to get dressed, Celeste, or you two will never find bread today...or meat for that matter. I think I may be able to get you a card for that. The soup might taste better, no offense, Celeste. You better buy soap while you're at it, Claire. The prices will be unbelievable in a few days, I fear. They say there is a shortage, but who believes anything they say. What will they take away from us next? Didn't you say your employer was picking those prints up this afternoon, Celeste? And Claire and I were planning on revising our speeches for the next meeting of the Convention, so she can't spend twelve hours in line waiting for what probably will be 'section' bread at best. I wouldn't feed it to a dog. I promised to help Jacques prepare his manifesto of enragés tonight. There's another meeting the twenty-fourth. Now that the Girondins have fallen, it is time to strike."

The man finished dressing right in front of Celeste. "I thought I might come along with you two—keep you safe as well as get a story for my next edition. Literary bread, n'est ce pas?" He chuckled at his own joke which was good since neither of the ladies saw the remark as amusing.

Celeste's mind was spinning. The moment she pondered what one sentence meant, the man was onto another subject; she was having a horrible time keeping up.

He continued, "If I go along with you, the bakers will pay attention to you. Heaven knows what will happen if Claire gets into it with one of those street bitches."

"I'll behave myself. I have no intention of ruining our plans by opening my mouth again...until the convention meets that is."

"A good time to do it, love. Your cousin's speech will be quite good, Celeste; you might want to come and hear us. That is if she ever gets a chance to speak."

Claire shrugged and mumbled, "Equal rights is what they say they want...but not for their women." She gave her cousin a knowing look. "Oh, no! Those bastards want the women to fight for the cause as long as their mouths remain tightly sealed. What a surprise we have for them, eh, my love?" she said to Leclerc.

Celeste tallied the sum. Claire must be Claire Lacombe the actress, and this man was the editor mentioned in the police spy's diary. By the looks of Leclerc's disheveled appearance, he and Claire had been pleasuring themselves while she slept. If

71

they are in this house with me, then she—or rather I—must be...must be the mystery woman, the artist who has the job at the print shop and who is in love with Phillipe de Brouquens who lives in Bordeaux. The aristocrat. Screams reincarnation, she thought. And the soup was not satisfying her because the woman, the other Celeste, the one who now lived within her body was hungry...incredibly and insatiably hungry. The thought of fresh baked bread encouraged her to rise, but, where the hell were her clothes?

She looked at the chair beside the window in her room. There, waiting for its mistress, were her clothes: a deep mauve colored dress, white bonnet, white undergarments, black stockings, and high-heeled shoes with a wide buckle in the front. Having no clue how to put them all on, she made her way to the chair.

"Can I help?" asked Leclerc in a wicked tone. Celeste almost agreed to let him until she saw Claire's look of agitation.

"Don't be vulgar to my cousin," demanded Claire. "It's immoral."

"Oh? And since when has immorality stopped any of us? Besides," he paused and gave Celeste an approving glance, "she's different some how."

"That's silly. How can she be different? You've had too much sex."

"As much as I have always admired you, Celeste Lacombe, and respected your beauty and talent and occasional fits of temper; I must admit your general behavior has always seemed rather...passive to me. The way you let Phillipe run your life for you has always irked me. But this morning, there's a look in

72

your eye I've never seen before. It's an intelligent sparkle that's most attractive. Independent. Passionate." He flirted with her by turning his head so that only she could see the wry smile on his face and the secret message in his look. "I like it."

"She's finally taking after me," Claire said, reminding him of his allegiance to her by smacking his arm with her right hand as she crossed the room to help her cousin dress. "Turn your head."

They began with the undergarments which hurt so much that Celeste almost cried with frustration as her breasts were cinched into a modest corset. The stockings were short; the pantaloons felt strange because the seams at the crotch were too high on her; the bodice of the dress was too low. The petticoats fit, and that was only because they gathered at the waist with a drawstring. She thought that she would expire on the spot for lack of oxygen. The shoes were the wrong size. The clothes were too small and too tight, the armholes of the top all wrong, the sleeves too short, the shoulder to shoulder material in the back almost ripped apart when Claire tried to lace her into the dress. Claire had to leave some of the strings open in the front which made Celeste look like a prostitute showing her wares.

"Are you gaining weight or are you pregnant?" was all Claire could say to the frustrating situation.

Celeste closed her eyes to the thought that her alter ego might be with child. That was just not what she needed to hear right now.

"Are you?" demanded Claire.

"I don't think so," said Celeste trying to breathe.

"When was your last period?"

Celeste stammered, "I don't remember."

"Did you and Phillipe have sex on his last visit?"

She couldn't very well answer that one so she said, "Of course."

"Well, if you have gained a little weight, it might be that you are pregnant. Isn't that a fine situation? With him abandoning you and all."

"Abandoning me?"

"Well, he was supposed to be here two weeks ago with money and food, and he never showed. What sort of man is he? Comes for one thing, if you ask me."

Celeste replied sharply, "Well, I didn't ask you, Claire!"

Claire stared at her as if she were looking at a ghost. "Leclerc was right," she whispered. "It is as if a new woman rose from this bed today."

"I think you'd better get used to it, cousin," said Celeste with a rising sense of confidence.

"I'll find you a tailor to let out your clothes. And I'm pinning this to your bodice." She placed a red, white, and blue cockade on Celeste's dress. Put on your other shoes," she said to Celeste, pointing to wooden shoes that looked as if they came straight from Holland.

"I don't know about this," said Celeste, staring at the rosette of ribbons while finding the wooden shoes to be a satisfactory fit.

Leclerc scowled at Celeste. "Claire won't be dissuaded on the issue of the cockade. As her cousin, I'm afraid, you must." Leclerc had finished dressing and held out his hand to her. "Coming, mon Cheri? The two most beautiful women in all of

Paris shall be first in line today."

Celeste allowed herself to be escorted to the streets even though she truly wanted to stay in the apartment and pull herself together before attempting to exist in another time period. Her head felt heavy from the wine, and her heart was pounding with the excitement and knowledge that she had time traveled. Her mind spun with worry that Jim would be terrified when he came to the cabin and found she was gone. She knew he couldn't come to her—the solstice had passed. There was no one to help her through this, and two people who weren't about to give her time to adjust.

As they emerged onto the wet, smelly streets of Paris at the indecent hour of two-thirty in the morning, she noticed a figure dressed in dark clothing draw himself into a stairway. She smiled and thought to herself, "Ha! I know who *you* are. If you hadn't written that book, I wouldn't be here, because I certainly did not wish to come to 1793, so this is all *your* fault. However, I wouldn't know who these people were if I hadn't read that excerpt. Come on out, little spy. You're not fooling anyone, Jean-Jacques."

They walked rapidly through the streets until Celeste could smell the wonderful aroma of home baked bread. A man was yelling from a window, "The bread is still cooking! Enough of this noise! My wife and family are trying to sleep. Why must I live next to a baker of all things? I shall call the police."

"Oh, shut up," said a woman who would be later identified by Claire as Nanette Du Bois. "It isn't our fault that he sets his prices so high that only the wealthy can buy his bread, or that he makes us wait for hours to get a small loaf.

Then you cry because we speak with one another? What do you expect us to do? We have the right to gather and gossip, fat fool. Go back to sleep."

Claire sat on the curb of the street, and Celeste did everything her new cousin did. Claire immediately started to talk with those around her while Leclerc waited over to the side watching everything that transpired.

A woman, trying to gain a better place in line, pushed ahead of Claire, Nanette, and Celeste.

"Hey, what do you think you're doing?" said Nanette angrily. "Go to the end of the line."

"This is my place in line. I was here before you," said the woman with an impertinent turn of her head.

"I have been here since midnight, and I've never seen you," cried another woman who was ahead of the line jumper.

"My sister saved my place for me because I had to go home and nurse my baby," said the liar.

"And which one is your sister?" asked Claire, looking around at all the women thereby pulling them into her play. She casually waved her hand towards the line of women and raised her right eyebrow. "I don't see anyone here who resembles you or is eager to hug you to her breast."

"Leave me be, *whore!*" said the hefty woman who ripped Claire's cockade from her blouse and threw it into the gutter.

Celeste saw fire in Claire's eyes.

"*How dare you!*" screamed Claire, "I should kick your ass!"

"Revolutionary puppet, I'd like to see you try," cried the woman who turned to face Claire.

76

Claire stood to meet the challenge. Celeste thought about fetching the poor cockade from the mud but thought better of it when the women's arms started to fly.

Nanette, who also wore a bright cockade, stood to back Claire, and Celeste followed suit but was secretly hoping Leclerc would do something to stop the inevitable.

The nasty woman noticed Celeste's glance towards the editor. "Is that your man over there? Is he waiting to see who you will sell yourself to tonight? *Whores!*" said the hefty attacker.

Celeste joined in just for something to do. She screamed, "You can't call my cousin that." It seemed the right thing to say since there was obviously going to be a fight.

The fat woman's eyes narrowed, and there was a nasty expression on her face. "Ah, the little artist whore who lives in Lepeletier with her actress cousin and the man they call Leclerc. I've heard of you. You took the job my friend wanted at the print shop. You make good money sleeping around, eh? You and your whore cousin. And Leclerc is your owner who mounts you both." She motioned her chubby fingers towards Leclerc. "I hear you make love as a threesome. Is it true? You think you can kick my ass, shy one, *do it!*"

Nanette entered the argument. "You get back to the end of the line where you belong, or we'll all beat you to a bloody pulp. What? Your husband leave you to go to the front, and all you have is a soldier's pay in your purse? Ah, no that cannot be, who would willingly sleep with you, you fat cow?"

Leclerc was not entering the fight on Claire or Celeste's behalf; he was chuckling at the drama.

77

"Get back to the end!" chanted the mass of women in the bread line.

"Will you bitches shut up!" cried the baker's neighbor from his window. A head of lettuce was hurled at the window, and he disappeared rapidly.

While the foul mouthed "cow" watched with delight as the lettuce smashed against the window pane, Claire squared off and hit her across the face with her right fist and knocked her to the ground. A young girl who was half-sitting half-lying in the street beside the bread line, whose legs were slightly separated as if waiting for something special, and whose right breast had fallen from her blouse so that her pimply faced boyfriend—whose face had been happily buried in the girl's bosom during the whole argument—could suck her nipple at his leisure, suddenly pushed him aside roughly.

"Take her, Claire! I'm with you." She pulled her breast back into the blouse, closed her legs, straightened her clothes, and came to stand by Nanette and Celeste. "Kick her ass!"

Claire had done damage to the woman's mouth and smiled victoriously. •

"*You whore!*" screamed the unknown woman while spitting blood into the palm of her hand. "I'll kick your ass all the way to Orleans. Your pretty face will be fractured for life, and no one will come to the theater to see you." She stood up and rushed towards Claire.

The fight was on. Claire was knocked down by the power of the woman's amazing punch; but, after checking to see whether there was any injury to her jaw, the actress stood, and, with both hands, swung her fists into the woman's face. She

78

dropped her attacker to the ground, sat on her stomach, threw the lady's cap into the street after waving it as if it were some sort of winner's ribbon, and then dug her fingers into her opponent's hair, grasping it tightly, and pulling strands of it out in huge fuzzy clumps.

The crowd was alive with the thrill of the drama that had been set before them. No one was on the line jumper's side, and Nanette frequently kicked Claire's opponent in the abdomen or thigh whenever she found an open spot. The nasty woman's face was bleeding, her lips were cut, and her eyes were swollen; but Claire's cheek was bruised only slightly. French curse words stung the air.

Another woman, who found disfavor with Nanette, decided to hit her for no reason but that there was a fight going on. Nanette turned and punched that woman in the stomach and then hit her over the head so that she fell. Then she started to kick her and dropped on top of her just as Claire had done with her assailant.

"You think you can whip me?" squealed Nanette to her attacker.

Fists flew for about five minutes until a man pulled Claire off the fat woman with one arm thrown around Claire's waist while grabbing Nanette's hair with his free hand thus pulling her from the wailing woman who wasn't half the fighter Nanette was.

"Stop this!" he screamed.

It was the cloaked man from the alleyway. He was about six one in height and approximately one hundred ninety or so pounds. His shoulders were broad and strong looking behind his suit and cloak. His long legs bore most of his height. His tall black hat flew into the air when he grabbed Claire thus making his head and face visible. His long, dark brown hair fell from its tie and settled on his shoulders. He wore a mustache and small goatee on his long face. His cheekbones were high; his eyes sky blue. There was a nasty expression on his face. It indicated his complete revulsion to the fight and the bother it was to stop it.

"You," he spoke with the bothersome woman, "get to the end of the line."

She did what he said immediately. Celeste thought that they did as he said because they knew him, but she was wrong.

Claire Lacombe screamed, "Stay out of this! She called me a whore. I'm going to kill her for that."

He wouldn't let either of them go, so Claire kicked him in the shin, and he dropped her. Nanette pulled free when he bent over in pain. The women in line shrieked Claire's name as the victor of the fray, and Claire smiled her acknowledgment and then did a fancy bow.

He told them softly, so as not to disturb the baker's neighbors, "If you cause any more trouble tonight, I'll take you all into prison. And you," he looked at the teenage girl, "if you must make love to your boyfriend, do it in a private place. That's disgusting."

Then his focus fell on Celeste. Her words caught in her throat, and she couldn't breathe for a minute. She just stared at him and him at her. The tightness in his jaw relaxed. His eyelids widened, and the expression in them softened. His right eyebrow lifted. His lips parted. No words were said. This was the faceless man who had written the book in 1797. Jean-

Jacques Coupier. This was the spy who kept a record of all Celeste, Leclerc, and her cousin, Claire, did in that apartment. This is the man who survived the Terror and was probably reporting every word and action that Leclerc and Claire said and did to the police, and whose data could get them all killed or imprisoned with a flash of his quill pen. He was the one who had said that he would discover Celeste's identity. This man was their worst nightmare. His eyelids squinted slightly in a disapproving glare, and a sideways smirk crossed his lips. His confident smile attached itself to a memory—and that memory to an emotion. He was, feature for feature, an exact replica of Jim Cooper.

"Get back in line, girl," he spat the words directly to Celeste.

It was and was not her Jim in so many ways. Not Jim's way of talking. Not his attitude or manner with women. Not the way he would have broken up a female fight. But, if one could believe in reincarnation, this police spy, Jean-Jacques Coupier, was the past life persona of her present day lover, Jim Cooper.

Maybe she wasn't alone after all.

Chapter Eight

June 22, 2000

Cooper Cottages

Richfield Springs, New York

"*Where is she*?" cried a worried Jim Cooper as he raced through the cabin looking for Celeste.

Sam was frightened as well and watched his brother search for Celeste with no idea how to keep his brother from the horrible truth.

"As soon as you called this morning, I came over to hunt for her. Her belongings are in the bedroom, her clothes on the chair, a bottle of champagne is chilling in the fridge, and..." Sam said.

Jim let his fingers run through his untethered hair and then rubbed his forehead with the back of his hand as if this action would help him understand what to do. There was nothing he could do, and it frustrated the hell out of him.

"I didn't get her message until I woke this morning. If I'd just checked last night when I got home, but I was so tired. She wanted to surprise me. Well, she did that all right. What am I going to tell her secretary and business partners when they call Monday morning? What will happen to her clients? Without her to guide them, they'll probably get life with no parole."

"You'll think of something." The look on Sam's face was not reassuring however.

Jim's hands stretched out towards his brother in a

pleading gesture. "*What*? How am I going to explain that an attorney can't speak with anyone for three months?"

"Ah...she has laryngitis?" suggested Sam.

"*For three months?*"

"Scarier thought still. *Where* did she go?"

Jim gave his brother a stern look. "Do you think she's with Wainwright and Grant? Oh, God, please not Wainwright or the Roman Empire!"

"She is a good orator," Sam said, trying to be reassuring before he noticed the dangerous look in his brother's eyes.

"Well, she must be, Jim. Stands to reason. They were thinking about the Roman Empire. She must have been asleep in the next room not to have heard them. Her car's still parked out back, and you would think that if she heard someone coming into the cabin, she'd call to them or leave or something."

"Not only has she left me, but she's with Wainwright and that pompous ass, Grant Tyrell? For three months? Can things get any worse?"

"She's a smart girl; I'm sure she'll survive."

"But why? I don't understand why she had to come up so early," Jim said.

"This might have had something to do with it," Sam said while pointing to the gift on the table.

Jim slowly opened the card and read the sentiment. He touched the handmade art lovingly, and tears formed in his eyes. "Happy anniversary. In 200 A.D.?"

Sam's voiced was soothing. "Open the gift."

Jim carefully unwrapped the ancient book, rolling the ribbon around his fingers and setting it aside, and then folding the soft material and placing it beside the book with the ribbon so that he could save them. He looked at the book in complete bewilderment.

"How did she get a hold of this?" He looked at the copyright page. "The copyright date is 1797. Jean-Jacques Coupier? This is a one of a kind copy of a famous police spy's records of the French Revolution of 1793."

Sam watched as his brother smoothed his hands over a few of the pages. "Wonder where she got the idea to give you this?" he said.

"More to the point, where could she even find such a treasure? I assumed that the books from that time period had been destroyed or just deteriorated over time."

"Is it worth much money?" asked Sam.

"It's almost too valuable to suggest a price, but I'd say it might fetch $150,000 or more. She must have spent a fortune."

"And was so excited to give it to you that she canceled all her appointments, made a card, and wrapped it in this fancy way just for you."

Jim sank into a chair and rubbed his hands before his eyes to prevent the flow of tears. "Celeste!"

"Maybe she isn't in Rome," Sam ventured to suggest. "Maybe she read some of the book before she wrapped it and fell asleep thinking about France in 1793."

"Well, she did study in France for a while and would have been intrigued enough to read some it. She's fluent in the French language."

Sam smiled and shrugged his shoulders. "Jane was

reading a pirate novel before she flew."

"Yeah, maybe you're right. But, I can't get to her. I can't guide her through whatever it is she'll encounter—keep her safe."

Sam placed his hand on his brother's shoulder. "You're the one who believes in the 'Being'. Maybe *It* wants her back in time for some reason. Think on that."

"Why didn't I tell her that the cabin was a portal?"

"Did you tell her anything about time travel?"

"Everything *except* that."

"Well, then she'll be clever enough to survive. Maybe you weren't supposed to go back with her. She'll be okay, Jim. And it's kind of weird..."

"In what way?"

"If you're right about the price of the book..." he said grinning, "she's actually paid for the trip. Which means that your 'Being' honors our time travel business contract and price."

"But not our new rule about always sending a guide?"

"Well, we don't know that she's alone. Trust in the time travel gimmick, Jim. Have a little faith. There is one consolation, little brother."

"I'm dying to hear it."

"Only a woman in love would have planned such a surprise or given her lover a gift she knew he'd cherish. You know it's the best treasure you have next to the dueling pistols from Stephen and Emile. She chose it for you and sat half-naked in that bedroom waiting for you to come and enjoy an evening with her...a weekend of love with her. That's important, little brother."

Jim fondled the bow. "All I want is her. Now she's lost in time somewhere. What if she doesn't...make it back to me?"

"She will. Even if she's with Wainwright, she'll make it back. He'll catch on to what has happened and watch out for her. He's very professional, you know."

Jim suddenly smiled. "But you think she's back in the French Revolution and not with Tyrell?"

"Have a gut feeling about it, yeah."

"But the French Revolution is such a dangerous time period. What if she's the genealogical descendent or reincarnation of Marie Antoinette?"

"She's only going to be there for three months."

"Three months is an eternity."

"And it will test your theory and her love. Besides, how much can happen in three months?"

Jim looked at Sam who winked and smacked his brother on the thigh. "It's going to be okay, Jim. Remember Stephen Templeton. No matter what any of us said to him, he stayed true to his belief that Isabella Durell was innocent and that he could save her. Celeste is in the hands of destiny now, and both of your lives hang in the balance. Pray for her to come back...to you. Oh, yeah, I'd read the book if I were you. Might help."

Chapter Nine

June 23, 1793
de Brouquens Vineyards and Estate
Bordeaux, France

Phillipe de Brouquens and his best friend, Guy de Saige, spent the early morning hours hunting in the woods that belonged to the de Brouquens family. Phillipe flushed a pheasant from the bush, aimed, fired, and the bird dropped to the ground instantly.

"Your turn, Guy. We shall have a feast tonight," said Phillipe.

"I so miss these early morning hunts with you, my friend," he said, motioning to the boy they'd brought along that he should retrieve the dead bird. "I think you got him in the head. Magnificent shot."

"Merci, but, let's face it, pheasants move rather slowly."

"We haven't had much time to talk." He gave him a secret smile. "You've been in Paris so much this spring."

"Well that may all change. The riots in Paris will keep me on the estate this summer. The place has gone mad with politics. There's another bird. Must be his mate." Phillipe shot but apparently only winged her for she kept moving; so he reloaded, raced after her, and when she fell he finished her. "I'm the only one working here. Guy?"

"I'm inclined towards conversation this morning. Sorry.

87

Are you breaking off with your mistress, then?"

"Just cooling things down a bit. Until they stop all this discussion about independence."

"I don't think they will. Personally, I've been thinking of moving to Spain. You should think about it yourself."

"She mentioned moving. You know her cousin is Claire Lacombe."

"Good Lord, man, are you out of your mind? Claire Lacombe? The actress? She's the ringleader of all the women in Paris. They idolize her. They say her lover is Leclerc, one of the enragés. She'll have your head! Does her cousin know about you and...what's her name?"

"Of course, and her name is Celeste. Celeste Lacombe."

Guy made a mental note of the name. "I was thinking of accompanying you the next time you went to see her. Purchase new clothes, maybe some gambling, and a woman for myself."

"You're thinking of taking a mistress, then?"

"I have the money now that my uncle died and left me—his only surviving nephew—a fortune and his estate. Ah, there's mine," he said, aiming at a small bird and firing. When the smoke cleared, it was obvious that there wasn't much left of the bird to eat, but he summoned the boy to fetch it anyway. "Perhaps we should try for larger game."

"We agreed that small birds were all we could manage after drinking all that wine last night." He returned to the subject at hand. "You shouldn't have any trouble finding a pleasant woman to keep."

"How did you snag Celeste?"

Phillipe grinned. "Actually I was taking my mother's

poems to be published in Paris. You know what good friends we are with Tallon. And Celeste was waiting in line to apply for a job. I went ahead of her into the office and suggested that he hire her on the spot so that I could date her. She was wearing soiled clothes and looked as if she hadn't eaten for weeks. I must say, when they're hungry, their waists are so tiny and their faces so thin that they actually are lovelier in that frail state than when they've been well-fed. Those high cheekbones and her beautiful eyes drew me to her. I waited until she was told the good news and then walked with her for a while introducing myself as a young aristocrat from Bordeaux who was in Paris to do business with Tallon. I offered to take her to a fine restaurant for dinner, but she said that she had no clothes for such a date. So, I took her to my mother's dressmaker and had two gowns made for her. Since neither would be ready in time for an evening on the town, I borrowed a gown your sister was planning on fetching the week after."

"You did not!" exclaimed Guy.

"Yes, Celeste has warmed your sister's new pink and teal gown," he said laughing. "But don't you dare tell her, or she'll kill me."

"Not a word. Go on."

"I took her back to my suite at the hotel and sent for hot water and a tub. I left Celeste to wash all the filth from her hair and body and then sent a dresser to do her hair for her and help supply whatever undergarments she needed to make her ready for a night on the town."

"This works?"

"You cannot believe how well. The thought of a hot meal

89

encourages any of them. Looks as though I am the only one clear-headed enough to bring home dinner tonight," he said as he aimed and killed another pheasant. "The cook will have to get the pellets out of that one, I'm afraid." He motioned that the boy should reload his gun for him and then fetch the dead bird.

Guy rubbed his head and eyes. "Sorry. Please continue. I haven't had a woman in a month, and this tale is...quite...stimulating."

"I found all that she said that evening to be ever so intelligent and witty. When you want to bed a woman, you must be agreeable to everything that first night. Celeste is wonderfully gifted in so many ways. She can paint, sing, dance. I think she and Claire must have grown up together and studied with the same tutor."

"She has aristocratic blood in her veins?"

"Probably. I don't now; I never asked. When I found her, Celeste had just lost her job and her apartment, was living on the streets, and her cousin was not in Paris. Celeste owed money to everyone. I took her back to my hotel and made love to her all night long. The champagne was not as good as ours here, but heady stuff none-the-less, and it worked perfectly on a woman not used to such intoxication."

"You seduced her?"

"It was not difficult. That's the trick. I am aware of my immense sexuality and incredibly accurate knowledge of women and the ways to get them into one's bed; but if I had been old and ugly, she would have gone home with me after that little display of comfort and attention. The clothes, the warm suite, the job, the seven-course meal, the wine."

"I see."

"And she was so beautiful in your sister's dress, witty, charming in every way. Especially after she'd eaten. With her stomach full and her head spinning, she became chatty and amusing. I decided that very night, that it was worth investing time and money into the affair. I spent the week joyously creating our little love nest. It's not that expensive, Guy, to have a nice townhouse in Paris furnished with basic necessities."

"Yes, chiefly a bed."

"That and more. I was hoping this affair might continue for some time, and then the bloody bastards started all this craziness."

"You won't go back?"

"She warned me to protect myself. She loves me so. She's frightened for me." He stopped walking and whispered, "I think there's another nest close by, perhaps we should be quiet, or they'll notice us and take flight."

"But how shall I ever take a woman in Paris if you don't explain?"

"We'll go again, together, and find you a lady, Guy, if you insist. Of course, I'll have to stay with Celeste and you in a hotel. I'll make excuses and join you often, though. Perhaps she has a friend."

"I don't want a soldier's widow or one who has a child."

"Not to worry. The young ones are just as compliant."

"Sans mother and siblings?"

"It can be arranged."

"What if all the women in Paris are following Claire

Lacombe and her treasonous allies?"

Phillipe smiled. "Dress well, mon ami, and they'll find you."

"I don't want a prostitute."

"Celeste was a virgin that night. No man had ever touched her before me; that's why it's critical that she has my child. My son, hopefully."

"And how does she feel about motherhood?"

"Not interested in it at all. But, she won't deny me our bed for fear that I may suddenly abandon her. Do you have any idea what would happen to her if I am displeased?"

"You would do such a thing?"

"If I don't pay Tallon to keep her, he may hire another more desperate woman who might not be as talented as Celeste but in such dire straights that she'd sleep with that fat pig for the job. Celeste won't touch him, of course, because she is so in love with me and so very loyal. If I am late with her rent, she'll be tossed to the streets. She'd have to sell all of her belongings, including her art supplies, to pay any debts."

"Maybe Claire could help."

"Claire's savings will only last so long. With no job, no housing, no way to work, and no food, there will be only one thing Celeste can do to earn a living besides begging."

"You wouldn't do that to her."

"Of course not, I am very fond of her. But, I am explaining to you the way to trap them so that they do anything you want them to. Anything at all."

"Do you think she's with child?"

"I hope so. I'll buy her a small house in the country

outside the city if she is. Can't have her in the heart of the city with all this trouble. It would be too dangerous. I'll hire some servants for her and my son."

"Does your father approve of all this?" Guy saw his chance and killed one fat and slow pheasant with one shot. "There. I am worthy of the feast tonight." He handed the gun to the boy and continued walking and talking with his friend.

"He's so very pleased. After all, he has a mistress of his own in Chartres. Had her for years. She's as old as he is now, but, still, he visits her, and they share happy moments together even at their age. He even took me to meet her once, explaining the whole time why a poor girl turned mistress is every man's dream. They cannot displease you or get peevish, or they'll lose all they have and starve."

"What if something happens to you, Phillipe? Have you thought of what might become of Celeste if you should die, God forbid such a thing would happen?"

"If she is with child, and I can set her up in a small cottage in the country; I shall pay in advance for all she needs. I'll give her an account and tell the servants that a fund has been set up so that they may always be paid to take care of her. Then, of course, I will buy her so many jewels that she will always have security and can pay her way in the long years ahead. Then again, she may find a new benefactor after I am gone. With housing, a ready-made family, and security, many men might find her a good prospect. A merchant, perhaps, who is down on his luck."

"Yes, I suppose." Guy's head began to ache from the party the night before. "What if she isn't pregnant?"

"I have no reason to take care of a woman who isn't willing to bear my children. I will eventually get old and weary of her charms and the long trip to Paris."

"But your father? He's loved and protected his lover for years."

"And she bore him a bastard son. Celeste must do the same."

"And if the problems in Paris continue?"

"I can't risk my family's name by going to her when the citizens are rioting in Paris. Do you think we have enough game? Should we head for home?"

"Perhaps four more. We have servants to feed."

"I don't hunt for meat for my servants. Do you?"

"Of course. We always provide game for the whole household."

"I have a baker who makes excellent bread. And, of course, we make our own wine and cheese. They eat that. But, you may be right." He motioned to the boy. "We'll hunt until we have meat for the household."

The boy's arms were full with feathers, but he smiled immediately at the news.

"I am anxious to meet your Celeste. When may we go to Paris?"

Phillipe smiled. "I suppose I should see how she's doing. I had vowed to stay away from the fracas there, but, maybe she has some good news for me, and I can get her out of the city at last. You must tell her nothing about my life if she asks. She's very clever with questions. She thinks I will some day make her an honest woman."

94

"I see. Another lie to keep her?"

"She's worth the lies. Lord, man, you do need me to help you. You've not a shred of an idea how to keep a woman, do you?"

"I have no lady of my own. I would like one. None of the girls here please me though my mother keeps introducing me to them."

"I know how you feel. I think there's a nest up ahead. Quiet now."

A mother bird was resting close to her new brood. Phillipe captured her without wasting a shot and broke her neck before she could warn her children. The babies were left for the boy to kill. The two young men walked on through the woods.

"We have enough now?" asked Phillipe.

"Your household is full."

"Correct. Perhaps you are right about larger game. I know where we can find some rabbit. It's early summer, and they have finished mating. They leave the young to their own devices. One of the few mothers in the natural world who leaves her children after delivering them into the world. And, of course, the young ones are so easy to catch. I'd set up some traps to make hunting easier for us, but the servants' children play in the woods, and I'm afraid of losing a potential stable boy."

"You let your servants breed, then?"

"Of course, don't you? We have a small church on the estate and encourage lawful matrimony. Since they have no one else to sleep with except those on the vast property; they soon see the sense of marrying. We are very religious and allow no sex play without a bond so that we can create whole families and give them small houses so that they feel as if they have a family of their own. I can't believe you'd allow it any other way. Once they become part of a family, and see they have a permanent role in ours; they breed and teach their young the skills they have. We never have a servant shortage."

"But then you have to feed them all."

"And look at the forest land around us, Guy. We bake every day. But now that you have given me the notion of seeing that they have meat, I'll teach some of them to hunt, and then my job will not be as great. I'll make hunters of them."

"I'm not sure that's a good idea, but suit yourself." He gave a quick glance at the boy who was not listening.

"Let's go in a week's time," said Phillipe.

"What? Oh, to Paris? Splendid."

"It won't take you long. Make sure you like her first. There are so many women starving in Paris, that you can have your pick. They give their hearts to soldiers who leave them for war, a very intelligent way to get rid of a lover, eh, war? Some of them aren't aware that they can have a share of the soldier's pay, provided there are marriage bonds attached to the affair, and a child or two."

"I want a pretty one. Smart and clever like Celeste."

"Not too smart, mon ami, or she'll guess what you're up to. You'll find many pretty ones on the bread lines."

"But I need an in like you had with Tallon."

"Not really. We'll get you some cards for meat and bread before we leave. They honor them everywhere, and, of course, since you have money, you can get the best of everything they have to offer. Trust me, when the ladies of Paris see the way you're dressed, they'll hover around you like bees to honey. Get a nice suite at a good hotel."

Guy smiled broadly. "I can't wait."

"Take lots of money, but I'd suggest real gold and no Louis. Remember, you care nothing for the royal family. Complete disinterest in Marie and her children's future."

"Of course, poor butchered king. Will they harm the queen, do you think?"

"No. She's done nothing wrong."

"Should I take Charlotte's new dresses, then?"

They laughed so hard the game ran for cover miles into the bush.

"Well that ends our hunting today, I fear," said Phillipe.

"Better game in Paris?" said Guy.

"Much better, mon ami."

Chapter Ten

The look that passed between Jean-Jacques Coupier and Celeste Lacombe froze time. He scowled at her, and, because she had so many more years of philosophy, history, and evolution in her head, and knew that he would be returning to her in her lifetime as her lover, Jim Cooper, she surprised him with an innocent smile. The real Celeste Lacombe would never have done that. Of course, her reaction only made Jean-Jacques scowl more and that made her giggle. She tried to stifle her grin but couldn't help the emotion because she had never seen Jim look that way, and the expression just seemed comical under the circumstances.

The whole affair between the two did not go unnoticed by her cousin. Claire said, "What is wrong with you? The man is insufferably impolite, and you are laughing like a little girl."

Celeste placed her hands over her mouth to compose herself. After a moment of trying to stop, gasping, giggling, and trying again, she said, "He broke up your fight. That was worth something, wasn't it?"

Claire smiled and said, "I suppose. Is he the Jean you were thinking about? In your dream? Is he Jean?"

Celeste made direct eye contact with her new cousin and said with complete honesty, "Yes."

Claire shook her head sadly and said, "Oh, Cheri, he is a dangerous one to fall in love with. Stay away from him. What will Phillipe think? I don't think he likes women anyway, look at the way he stares at us. Has he spoken with you?"

"No, but he has been snooping around the apartment lately. Probably watching you and Leclerc," she said truthfully, and praying that it was all right to blow the police spy's cover. The thought made her uneasy. Should she tell her cousin more and harm Jean-Jacques, or be on his side and help him uncover Leclerc's plans? In that one second, she understood the other Celeste's problems. She was employed by a man who was a merchant who would not like the plot Claire was weaving, and was the lover of one who would be in danger if Leclerc's petition for the arrest of all aristocrats was accepted by the committee and had to live with these two revolutionaries in the apartment meant to be a love nest for her own affair. And Leclerc's plans would succeed, wouldn't they? Celeste knew that much about the time period, but—in her present predicament—she wished she'd paid more attention to her world history teacher in high school.

Claire straightened her disheveled attire. "I kicked him good and hard for you," she said and then laughed and hugged her cousin. "I'm sorry. He's not interested in you, Cheri."

Celeste turned her head to see whether Jean-Jacques had given her a second look as he limped over to a side street. He was staring at her again. "Oh, I don't know about that." Celeste made direct eye contact with him and smirked.

Claire waved her hand as if to discard the man. "Ah, forget him and think about how we shall make it to the baker's door when he opens it at six."

The crowd became unruly and quite loud when that happened. There was too much pushing and shoving to the extent that someone could get killed. Celeste looked at Jean-Jacques who seemed more interested in his bruised shin than the silly women who mobbed the baker's door.

Leclerc intervened. He walked to the front of the line, pushed a few women aside who cursed and spat at him, and paid for two loaves of good white bread. He came to them in the line and pulled the two women away from it. "I've had more than enough of this waiting. Let's have some breakfast so that you and I can get back to my office."

They were not stopped as they made their way back to the small apartment. The coffee they had left to brew on the coal stove was overcooked, but they drank it anyway. Celeste smiled when she saw the coffee beans lying at the bottom of the pan. "We aren't grinding them yet," she thought to herself.

They ate some cooked sausage with their bread, and then the two rebels left her in peace. "I'll send a tailor to the house so that you can get your gowns widened. You looked positively scandalous out there today," Claire said as she closed the door.

"At last! Thank God they're gone!" Celeste said aloud. "Now what am I going to do?"

She looked at the apartment. It was plain enough. One big first floor decorated sparsely with sketches the other Celeste had made over the months she'd lived there. Small coal stove at the center of the room. Two bedrooms upstairs. Rather like a modern day townhouse. Some thin lace curtains on each of the windows. Nice touch and probably very expensive for the time period. She stared at herself in a mirror by the door and saw no difference in her face. Her hair was now pinned to the nape of her neck, but it was still brownish-blonde. Her eyes still quite blue if not a shade bluer than before.

"I suppose I need to learn more about whom I am or rather was. Reincarnation? Maybe after all."

The first thing she did was find her picture of Jim which was still buried in the quilt on the bed. She found Celeste's art supplies downstairs by a covered easel, took one of the other Celeste's charcoal pencils, and etched the mustache and goatee onto her portrait of Jim Cooper.

"Except for darker and wavier hair," she changed the hair on the picture, "and the fact that Jean-Jacques doesn't tie his hair back; the face is identical." She stared at her rendition, smiled with satisfaction, and then went back upstairs and placed the portrait under her bed.

It occurred to her that an easel was covered downstairs, and that she had not even looked at it. A covered portrait meant a special masterpiece that would help her determine something about her new persona. She raced downstairs, and, after giving herself a moment to prepare herself, lifted the white linen that rested over the oil painting. She gasped when she uncovered the portrait of Phillipe. "This is a really bad dream. Come and get me out of here, Jim."

She thought about what he had told her about the Gemini effect. Two magnets connect and become one unit—one body. "So, I'm you, and you're me for three months, girlfriend. I must be the assertive one, because I don't feel any different now that you are inside me, and Jim said the more aggressive personality becomes dominant. But, you're going to have to help some, okay? Will I hear you talk to me in my head or will you just keep quiet and let me sail the course? Can you send a message to my dreams? Hey, in there, I'm talking to you! I don't know what to do. How to make coffee. What to say to Phillipe. Who to trust and whom to avoid. What to say and what to keep a secret. Maybe he left you just as he left me, huh? And your cousin? I don't know. What's this business with Leclerc? He's kind of hot, if you know what I mean. Does he always come on to you as he did this morning or is this the first time? How does your boss treat you? When will he come for the work? Where do you put the stuff he brings? How can I draw like you? Tell me will you! Because if you don't, they'll think I'm mentally unstable. Put the notion in my head or something."

Just then three stitches on the right side of her gown popped open. "Great! Pregnant? Ha. That's a laugh. I'm just so much larger than you are in 1793, right, or...? Are *you* pregnant? How am I going to get out of this one? Will my body know? You poor kid. How are you and I going to know whether I'm...we're 'with child'? Three months? I know I'm not pregnant because I'm on the pill. I guess we have until September twenty-something to find out. Three months! I may never know, but you will, won't you?"

She sat down on one of the tiny chairs by the window. "Oh, God, Celeste, do you love Phillipe as much as I did? Seems we never get away from this heartache." She stared at the painting. "Well, at least we have one other thing in common. Let's have a look at your stock."

She examined the other woman's art supplies. "This is pathetic. How am I to finish his face with almost no color left?" She found a small amount of clear oil. "I suppose I can stretch this."

Just then a figure darted by her window. "Probably,

Jean-Jacques snooping around. I look indecent in this gown. I'd better find something you use for those *puffy* days." She slapped her hand to her head and groaned. "Okay, now I'm talking to myself."

She looked in the woman's closet and found two dresses and four blouses and one skirt. The skirt was blue and white striped and had a drawstring. "This'll work."

The blouse wrapped around her breasts nicely, tied at the side, was very frilly, and matched the skirt. Then she found an apron and tied it around her waist to make it look as if she were wearing a belt. It also covered the fact that the skirt was snug.

She had no idea that it had been a gift from her cousin, that the other Celeste never wore it because it was political, and that if she wore it, she'd be marked as a revolutionary.

Celeste took the small chair and set it in front of the easel. She sat there in the light offered by the window and worked on the portrait. "What a handsome devil you are Phillipe de whatever they said your last name is. Look at those strong shoulders surrounded by that blue velvet jacket. And how that white shirt and scarf around your neck highlights your best features. Same aristocratic cheekbones, same sweet, delicious red lips, same big, blue eyes, same darling, bitable earlobes, and those extra-long eyebrows...so bushy. Here, let's make those lips glisten the way they used to when you were hot. I wonder if you're still a scandalous kisser. And a dot of white and silver in the eyes to make them sparkle. You need more color in your cheeks, Phillipe. You look sort of thin too. When we were together in Paris, your face was full, and your cheeks were like small plums when you smiled."

She rested the paint brush on the palette and examined her work. "I want you," she whispered to the face on the canvas. She felt the erotic hunger grow inside her body the moment she touched the paint to his lips. "Oh, God, Phillipe, I'm still in love with you, aren't I? I still want you!"

Her intimate memories were interrupted by a loud knock at the door. Celeste felt suddenly weary, as if her entire source of energy had been depleted, but she answered the door hoping that it was some door-to-door cockade salesman. It wasn't.

Jean-Jacques Coupier, with his stern visage and machismo attitude, fretted on her doorstep as if he were about to tear the door from its hinges if she did not answer immediately.

His arms were crossed in a defiant manner, and his right eyebrow was raised imperiously. "Where's your cousin?" he asked.

Celeste rested her hand on the door frame so that her body could block his entrance and relaxed her weight to one side. "Good morning to you as well, Monsieur. Is it normally your habit to force your way into a household, or do you have a search warrant?" she said this without realizing that it was the right thing to say in the wrong time period. "I mean...by whose authority do you come to my house and make demands?" Then she mumbled under her breath, "Better."

"I want Claire Lacombe and the enragé, Leclerc. Rumor has it that they intend to ask for the imprisonment of all aristocrats at the meeting on the twenty-fifth of this month. I want to ask them a few question."

Something surged forth from beneath her own personality and screamed, "Who are you to come to my house

104

with no introduction and demand that any of us should be interrogated? Are you a police spy?"

He didn't answer her question. "After that display of pure idiocy in the streets, I feel your cousin and her friend are a threat to public safety. I'm simply here to ask some questions."

"Then ask me for they are not here."

He stared at Celeste for some time before saying, "What do you have to do with it?"

"Perhaps nothing. Perhaps a great deal. Come inside. Close the door, Monsieur, or all shall hear you. What is your name?"

He did as she asked and introduced himself, "Jean-Jacques Coupier, and you, Mademoiselle? Your name is?" He took off his hat and rested it under his arm.

"Celeste Mont...ah...Lacombe."

He tilted his head as if he had heard something suspicious. "You hesitate? Are you lying to me?"

"I don't think so," she mumbled softly and grinned. "No, it's Celeste. Come in and sit down."

"I am here to speak with Claire and Leclerc," he said, but his eyes said that he wanted to talk to Celeste about anything but politics.

"Besides, I know all I need to know about you." He appraised her apartment with one quick and effectual glance.

Celeste saw a perfect opportunity to find out something about her new situation. "Oh? And what do you know about me, Monsieur?"

"I know that this is your apartment but that Phillipe de Brouquens pays the rent; that you are his mistress when he comes from Bordeaux to sleep with you; that you have a job that other women would kill you for because he knows Tallon who owns the print shop where you are employed; that your cousin is a hot tempered actress turned would-be patriot-bitch; that she has started the Revolutionary Republican Women's Club, a club to which you refuse to belong; that you wore the cockade today but do not as a rule take sides on issues; that Phillipe has not come to see you for weeks; that all moneys have ceased to come your way; and that very soon you shall be forced to use your cousin's savings from her past acting jobs as well as her lover's friendly aid to assist you as Tallon will soon be around to take advantage of Phillipe's sudden disinterest. Unless I miss my bet, Tallon will want something more from you than sketches; and if you refuse, you shall have no income at all. If anything should happen to Claire or Leclerc, you will be forced to go begging for bread. I also know that Leclerc wishes the execution of men like Phillipe de Brouquens, and that Claire supports him. She is his mouthpiece...nay puppet. She says what he coaches her to say. If you wish them to continue to help you by living here with you, you will have to follow a path that will surely destroy the man who has, so far, kept you from the streets. They won't stay with you if they think you cannot help them in some small way. Bitter still, you will soon have no choice but to believe as they do, for anyone who does not agree with Robespierre is doomed. Tallon finds you very attractive and will leap on your helplessness as soon as he is sure that Phillipe has left for good. But, Tallon will not approve of your playing politics with Claire and Leclerc. So, if you are nice to one, you lose the trust of the other, as well as the so-called love of the man who keeps you as his sex slave. Does that place a frame on your portrait, Celeste Lacombe?"

Celeste couldn't breathe, lost the ability to speak for a moment, and then said, "I'd say that rather ties it up nicely, Monsieur. Except for one thing."

"And what is that?"

"Phillipe will come back for me."

A ghost of a smile flickered and then faded on his handsome face when he said, "No, he won't. He doesn't dare enter Paris with all that's happening here. His father was one of the king's men. One of the first who'll feel the axe. Although, they say there is a charming new piece of equipment that is much faster, cleaner, and more humane than the executioner's tools of the past. It's called the guillotine. At any rate, Phillipe's father will be one of the first to be taken."

Celeste said nothing.

Jean-Jacques gave her a long, slow, up and down appraisal, "And now you wear the skirt!"

No response from his suspect again.

He moved close to her and gazed into her eyes. "Will you tell me where the rebels are?"

"I don't recall." She turned away from his steady gaze.

"You're lying to me." He turned her around by the shoulders so that he could look at her. "Is Phillipe de Brouquens in Spain?"

"I don't know. As you yourself said, I haven't seen him in weeks."

His voice softened a fraction. "Are you a member of the women's club?"

"Why would I be?"

"A question for a question?"

"Why? Do you think that I am?"

"The cockade you wore today."

"Claire made me wear it."

"I'm taking you to prison."

"Why?" she gasped and pushed him away.

"I think you know more than you say. Besides, if you aren't home, if they return and can't find you, they'll have to come for you, and that's when I'll snatch them. I gave you a chance to tell me where they were, to stay out of it."

"I have work to do," she said, having no idea where her work might be.

He touched her chin with his gloved hand. "Tallon will be here soon. Alone in the house is just what he'll want. What will you say to him, Mademoiselle, when he gives you but one choice?"

Celeste stammered, "I'll tell him to go to hell!"

That comment seemed to please the police spy. "Will you then?"

When he smiled at her, his eyes sparkled, and it was difficult for Celeste not to see the resemblance between Jean-Jacques and Jim.

The color of Jean-Jacques's eyes suddenly turned ice blue. "You didn't say that to Phillipe when you became his whore." His resemblance to Jim faded on that line.

Celeste slapped his face, and it must have stung quite a bit because he held his hand to his cheek for some time without saying a word. It wiped away his smile.

His gaze scanned the room, and he noted Phillipe's portrait. "But then you are in love with him, n'est ce pas? It isn't security; it's passion, eh, Mademoiselle?"

The tone in Celeste's voice changed to an aggressive 2000 A.D. female. "I'd say it's none of your *damn* business!"

The police spy was angry with her but doing a fine job of hiding it. "All right. Get your shawl, it's very cold where you're sleeping tonight. Disturbing the peace, fighting in the streets, rioting, wearing the cockade *and* the skirt, striking a man of the force; I think that should be good enough to drag you to prison for a long day and night of interrogation. I want to know their plans, and how they effect the citizens of Paris; if you are not willing to help me, then I must be more insistent."

"I'm not going anywhere with you!" She stood her ground with her arms crossed, and her legs firmly planted on the wooden floor of the apartment.

He picked her up in his arms and hurled her body over his shoulder as if she were a sack of flour. "Oh, yes you are."

"*Put me down!*" she screamed.

"No!" he said as he slammed the door shut behind him with his foot, turned into a lane, and headed into the busy streets filled with citizens walking to work.

Celeste saw a crowd of neighbors, mostly women, gawking at the two of them and was instantly inspired.

"What about my rights! I'm a good citizen of France!" wailed the humiliated artist at the top of her voice.

"Citizen, indeed. Pretend all you want, you're nothing but a woman of France, and you have no rights," Jean-Jacques mumbled.

Celeste looked up and over his back to see the crowd of women who stared helplessly as the man trudged into the midst of them with his prize. She couldn't let the moment pass. Celeste arched her back by pressing her one hand against his back, lifted her head high into the air, and raised her fist in defiance. The women imitated her and began cheering.

"Men are all *bastards*!" she declared in her finest French.

"Vive la Revolution! We will be *equal* when we are all free. *Both* men and women. Citizens of France!" cried Nanette.

Jean-Jacques wasn't irritated with her yet but said, "That's completely absurd no matter what they say to you. Lies. And you believe them," he said, jostling Celeste on his shoulder to a more comfortable fit. "Stop wiggling!"

"Tell him nothing, Celeste!" one woman shouted to her.

"He has no right to take you away from your home," said another.

"Shut up all of you and get out of my way, or I'll take the whole crowd with me." The police spy was angry but remained in control of his emotions and continued to carry out his duty.

A woman spat in the street in front of Jean-Jacques. "Your mother be cursed for having a son like you."

At this point Jean-Jacques ignored the small riot surrounding him and headed with a confidant stride to the nearest prison.

"Stupid women," he grumbled under his breath. "Why do they think things will change for them? They declare their love for justice while showing they are equally inhumane. They think they make a difference to this revolt. Rubbish. Men will always want their women to be submissive. That is the way it was meant to be from the beginning. Why do you females think it will change?"

Celeste pressed her lips together, scowled, and took the toe of her wooden shoe and jammed it into his stomach.

The women cheered.

Chapter Eleven

Jean-Jacques managed to carry Celeste all the way to prison, threw open the gates with just one hand, pressed open the door with his hips, stormed up one flight of steps, and tramped into a room above the cells that was apparently his office.

Celeste fell from his arms. "Is this your office?" she asked straightening herself.

"It's *our* office. We all use the same room for interrogating suspicious characters."

"Zut alors! I'm not a suspicious character. I am a quiet little artist who minds her own business and who just happens to have a long distance lover. I live alone except when Claire stays with me; I have an income; I wasn't fighting in the street, Claire was; and I didn't kick you in the shins Claire did. I giggled. Is that what this is all about? Because I giggled at you when you got angry. And I don't know anything about Claire and Leclerc's plans. And even if I did, I wouldn't understand any of it nor would I tell you about it even if you locked me up until—say—September twenty-second." She smiled ruefully at the exactness of the date she'd used and her own private joke.

The police spy was glaring at her while she spoke, so she continued, "I think you've been mighty rude to me too. You haven't even read me my rights. Considering that you assaulted me by hurling me over your shoulder and kidnapping me from my home, I could see my way clear to letting you off with a financial settlement to soothe my wounded pride instead of hauling your ass into court and seeing that your badge is suspended indefinitely."

She began laughing uncontrollably until the tears streamed down her cheeks. "Oh, my God," she said to herself, "I'm losing it now."

At first, Jean-Jacques pretended to understand what she was saying. He glowered and paced a bit pulling at his goatee and glancing at her occasionally. "I might very well keep you in this prison until that date you mentioned if you don't take my questions seriously."

She tried to speak, but it was difficult. The moment she could formulate words, she'd start laughing again. "You're not at all like my Jim."

"Who's Jim? Another lover or a rebel leader bent on killing the queen."

His words took hold of her, and she stopped laughing. The seriousness of the time traveling experience became apparent; she remembered how Jim had told her that a traveler could die in another time period. "Kill the queen?"

"The king was executed January 21, as you no doubt know; now they plot to kill the mother of his heirs as well as his innocent children, and for what reason? Your cousin's friend wants the death of all the royal family as well as every aristocrat in the nation, or hasn't he mentioned that to you? Aristocrats like Phillipe de Brouquens."

Celeste's entire mental and emotional state shifted. Every instinct she had as a caring attorney who had dedicated herself to fighting injustice in her time period sated her heart and mind. What she knew of the revolution raced forward in her memory to help her understand what was going on right now in 1793.

Her mind raced, "The queen does die, doesn't she? Let them eat cake—no—she never said that. The rich were guillotined. And after they murdered them, they went after anyone who crossed their path, or with whom they found disfavor. Costumed masked men saved people in prisons according to fiction. 'T'is a far, far better thing I do now, than I have ever done before.' Something like that. The three musketeers? No, wrong time period, or was it? Napoleon is having a war, right? Where's Josephine or has he dumped her for the fertile chicky?" She said nothing to Jean-Jacques as her mind whirled with the facts, and her vacant expression must have seemed curious to her interrogator.

Celeste stared at Jean-Jacques. She now had a chance to find Phillipe and settle the score. And in one brief tally of all that she knew about the French Revolution, she knew that this man was right and her friends were wrong. How could she continue living with people who planned to sit at the foot of the guillotine and knit into scarves the names of those who would be butchered? Women who had no food, torn clothing, and no roof over their heads; who died daily because they had no warm fire to ward of a winter chill, no medicine to save them when they became ill; who watched as their best friends threw themselves into the Seine so that they might end their miserable lives and thus finalize their despair; who watched their emaciated babies shrink into nothingness and die; and who fell into immodest behavior, allowing men to pleasure themselves with their thin bodies, so that they might obtain enough money to buy food for

114

their starving children.

Celeste fought to remember Robespierre, "Didn't he get his in the end? Yes. What about Leclerc and an actress named Claire Lacombe?" Her history books never discussed the editor or the actress. "Who was right; who was wrong?" she wondered.

Those women in the bread lines, who were starving to death, would soon wait in the courtyard and watch gleefully as one by one, men, women, and innocent children's heads were severed swiftly from their necks and held high above a dismal scaffold for all the crowd to see. Those same women would smile and cheer as a cruel and all-too-real drama was enacted upon a worldly stage. No one would ever forget the melodrama.

Celeste felt ill. She tasted a bitter, sour taste coming into her mouth. "Oh, God, I...I can't," she said out loud. She looked for a sink and, seeing none, vomited on his floor.

Jean-Jacques's concern was obvious. "Are you ill?"

"No...yes...I might be pregnant and all that jostling around on your shoulder—right over my stomach—has put me in a state."

"Let me get you some water." He raced from the room and entered with a chair and a cup of water. "Sit down. Drink this. Are you really pregnant?"

"I don't know," she said while sipping the cool water and easing herself into the chair. She dropped the cup suddenly and placed her hands over her face. "You're not Jim!" she moaned. "I thought maybe he'd come too. That maybe he'd managed to get to the cabin in time to come with me; and you—like Emile and Stephen—and Jim had Geminied, or whatever it's called, to be with me here. Magnets. Two in one. I think I could handle that. But you didn't. You aren't. You're Jean-Jacques Coupier, and I have your book. Well, I mean, I gave your book to Jim for an anniversary present. The cabin—don't you see—the cabin was a portal, only you...he...never told me that part. Kept it a secret. Told me not to go there at the end of the month, but I was so excited about the gift. And the light on in the cabin was a clue that someone else would be there that night. They were. Only I was asleep and didn't hear them."

"You haven't eaten for a while, have you?" said Jean-Jacques, gazing at her in bewilderment.

"No," she said as her only defense.

"Let me get you some of my breakfast," he said and left her in the room alone. When he returned, he had two rolls in his hands which he offered to her. "Better not drink the coffee, it'll make you feel worse. The bread will help ease your stomach."

Eventually, she could control her tears. "I'm sorry. I didn't mean to become so emotional—or sick."

"Well, it's understandable; you're a woman."

She looked to the ceiling to keep from screaming. "I think you and I will have some trouble over this male chauvinism issue."

"I beg your pardon?"

"Never mind. I'm delirious. What did you want to know?"

"You'll be compliant?"

Celeste waved her hands left and right, and her head shook back and forth as she rattled off the few details she knew. "I know little except Leclerc and Claire are writing some speeches they plan to give before the Convention in a few days. Someone named Roux, and a man named Varlet will ask for," she stopped suddenly and looked at him. "What's an enragé?"

"Someone who wants the heads of the wealthy on a pike."

"Yes, well, that's what they will do, and you can't do a damn thing about it so don't waste your time trying. Just keep walking your Paris beat and writing in your journal. You're going to make it. Now, may I go home?"

"How do you know I write in a journal about what I see in Paris?"

"Ah...er...doesn't every police spy record what they see?"

"Yes, it's mandatory."

"Well, then, call it a good guess on my part."

"What do you know about Phillipe de Brouquens?"

"He's my lover, and he lives in Bordeaux. Am I supposed to know more?"

His eyebrows came together in an expression of concern. "No, I suppose not. Will you tell me if he comes to see you?"

"No. You'll be snooping around anyway so what's the point?"

"Do you have his child in your belly?"

"That's a cute way of putting it. I don't know for sure, but after that display of nausea, I'd have to say that it's a good possibility she's...I mean I'm...pregnant."

She bit into the second roll and scrutinized the police spy for some time. "He's in love with her...me," she thought. "You can see the worried, pained expression in his eyes and across his face. It matters to him what Phillipe did to her...me. He hates

117

Phillipe even if he hasn't figured it all out yet. I bet Jim does too only he's too sensitive to admit it."

"Are you going to take me home?" she repeated her question.

"Probably not. If Claire comes to the apartment and finds you're not there, she'll be told by your neighbors that a policeman took her cousin to prison. She'll come and make a fuss, and that's just what I want her to do. Then I can ask her what's going on, and, after she's told me, I'll let you go."

"You're going to lock me up in a dank dark cell?"

"I'm thinking about it, oui."

"I've done nothing wrong."

"That doesn't matter." Then he went to the door, opened it, and called to a prison guard. The man came into the room. "Take Mademoiselle Lacombe to a cell with a view of the city streets."

The prison guard spun her body around and tied her hands with rope.

"Am I under arrest?"

"Oui," said Jean-Jacques as he smoothed his mustache into place with the back of his hand.

"What's the charge? I've told you all I know."

"Rioting in the streets, kicking and slapping an officer of the law, resisting arrest, and...ah...vomiting on my floor. Take her away."

"I want my one call! I want my attorney! You never read me my rights. I get one call!"

He smiled innocently at the guard who tied the rope around her hands tighter when she became enraged. "Ignore

118

what she says," he said with a shrug, "she's having a feminine fit." The guard shook his head, winked, and took her away.

Chapter Thirteen

Hell hath no fury as a female enragé scorned, and that's exactly how Claire Lacombe felt when she was told by a neighbor that her cousin had been taken away by a police spy. She rushed into the apartment, tore off her dress, pulled on a pair of men's pants and one of Leclerc's shirts, pinned her hair up and under a red bonnet, affixed her cockade to the bonnet, placed a pistol in one side of her belt and a dagger on the other side, then slipped her dainty feet into a pair of boots. Nanette entered the apartment dressed in like manner.

"Are we going to take Pauline with us? She's at work, isn't she?" asked Nanette.

Claire's ferocity rivaled a man's intensity and direction. "We'll go by the candy store on the way and see whether she can come. They usually cook the chocolate in the morning, so she may be free to go with us. I bet it's the bastard who broke up the fight by the baker's. The one I kicked." Then she smiled flirtatiously. "The cute one! He was cute, don't you think?"

Everything was a play to Claire Lacombe, and all that she did, she did for the role she felt required to play at that moment.

"Oh, yes, indeed," said Nanette. Then they both giggled.

"I'm not wearing a corset. Men don't strap themselves in, why should I? Do you have the others ready?" asked Claire.

"About fifty-some are waiting for a signal. She's not far."

"This police spy better not give me trouble," she said

patting her pistol.

Nanette shrugged her shoulders and shook her head.

"What's Celeste done? Why her? I could see if they wanted you, but Celeste just sits inside all day and night and draws pictures."

"It's those blue eyes. Her mother's blue eyes. Didn't you see the way they stared at each other? She told me he wanted her. She was dreaming about him last night. His name is Jean-Jacques."

Nanette made a clicking sound with her tongue and shook her head. "Then you better not shoot him, or Celeste will be angry." Both women laughed at Nanette's feminine take on their plans to storm the prison and rescue the damsel in distress.

"Where's your man?" asked Nanette as they raced through the streets. They would fetch Pauline from her workplace before storming the prison.

"Back at the office. We have to give our speech in three days."

They hurried into the chocolate factory and found Pauline carefully molding the cooling chocolate balls.

"Pauline! they have taken Celeste to prison for questioning and refuse to let her go. We have fifty-some soldiers ready to storm the prison and take her out of there. Are you with us?"

Pauline looked at her boss who waved that she could go. It was only a few hours until closing time.

"But I have nothing to wear but my skirt. I have my cockade, but no pistols, mes amies."

"The skirt will have to do, and you can use my pistol if needs be, but I think that this man is in love with my cousin and simply wants a reason to have her in his presence."

"Why not ask her to dinner?" Pauline asked with a coquettish smile on her face.

"He's a man and a police spy. This was quicker, and of course, Leclerc and I are asking for executions and for the rights of all French citizens. The Convention meets on the twenty-fourth and will probably vote on the Constitution then. Soon, we will all be free from oppression. But on the twenty-fifth Roux, Leclerc, Varlet, and I will tell the Convention our plans to annihilate the evil merchants who choke the life from the people by not giving us *le price juste*."

Pauline moved swiftly to keep up with the two women who were gradually becoming a crowd as one by one others joined the march to the prison. Some were dressed in peasant skirts; some dressed just as Claire in the garb of the sans culottes; all were armed and buzzing like disturbed hornets flying from their broken nest.

"This price fixing so that only the rich can afford common necessities must stop," said Pauline.

Nanette explained, "I work all day to get enough money to buy food for my two children, then wait in a long line half the night to buy it, and then when I finally make it to my turn in line there is nothing but black bread. All the good bread has gone to the wealthy who came before six—even though the authorities made it clear that no bread would be sold before that hour—to the baker's back door and paid the higher price for the best bread. Or the price is so exorbitant, when my turn finally comes around, that I can't possibly pay it. And when I do finally get my turn at the door, some man pushes in front of me and buys it for his wife; or worse yet, there's no more bread to be sold because they have already sold it earlier to those who have the money to overpay the baker. It is a circle that never ends. And it is my children and I who suffer."

"Now it is soap," said Pauline as she marched. "I heard my boss talking about that this morning. The soap makers have decided that if the bakers and butchers can get away with it, why not soap as well?"

"Common necessities. That's is all we're asking for. If they want to fix the price on wine or lace, who would care? We would go without, but have you seen Nanette's little Francois after he's been playing in the mud. His face? His clothes?" asked Claire with a smile.

Nanette raced to keep up with Pauline and Claire, "I will have a small pig for a son with no soap. They know how to hurt us. The greedy bastards. Well, people can only be pushed so far and then they will revolt. Will they never learn their lesson?"

"Apparently not, but we shall teach it just the same, eh citiyennes? We shall teach them. Ah, here's the rotting hole in which they have dared to hide my cousin."

Claire stormed the door shouting, banging her fist, and cursing. The other women joined in, and even some of the younger girls took part.

One of the guards came to the door and spoke with Claire.

"I want to see my cousin!"

"Who is that?"

"Celeste Lacombe, the one your bastard pig police officer took from her home this morning. If she is not freed immediately, the women of the revolution will cause a riot in the streets and take her by force."

"One moment," the man calmly said.

"That's telling him," said Pauline.

Nanette said, "He's definitely frightened now."

The guard returned. "I regret to inform you that the man who took her from her home refuses to give her her freedom until you have an audience with him and answer some questions."

"I do not dicker with dogs. He refuses, does he?" she said, drawing her pistol and aiming it at the guard.

The women chanted, "*Liberty!*"

"Shall I tell him that you refuse his kind request?"

Jean-Jacques Coupier pushed the man aside. "Do you want to speak with me, Claire?"

"Let my cousin go. She is innocent."

"Yes, she is. Completely. But, you and your friend are not. And I want to talk with you. Will you allow me a few minutes of your time?"

"Will you set her free if I speak with you, though why I should talk to a policeman, I don't know?"

"Yes. She can go home with you Amazons as soon as you answer a few questions."

Someone from the back of the crowd, who hadn't heard all that had transpired and thought Claire was winning through intimidation, screamed, "That's telling him, Madame President."

"I will tell you nothing," she said with a shrug, tossing her head to the side so fast that her bonnet almost fell from her head. She straightened it.

Jean-Jacques folded his arms over his chest and said,

"Then Celeste Lacombe will live on black bread and water in her cell for the rest of her life."

Claire shouted, "You can't do that!"

"Oh, yes, I can; I have; and I will. I rather like having little chats with her. She's ill, you know. Or maybe you don't since you seem to care more about your lover's welfare than your cousin's."

After a moment's silence Claire said, "All right, I will speak with you but only to free my cousin. Ladies," she said, turning to talk to her club, "I will go with this dog. Wait for me. If I am not out of there in thirty minutes, storm the walls, and free my cousin, Celeste."

Celeste heard all the commotion and saw most of it from her cell. She wondered if Claire would tell Jean-Jacques anything important and hoped that whatever she did tell him would be enough to set her free.

In about thirty minutes, Jean-Jacques came to her cell and unlocked the door. He untied her hands. "You're free to go. I have all I need to know now."

"Does that mean you won't be snooping around my apartment anymore?" she asked with mock respect.

He seemed to be deliberating his next move carefully. "I don't think our business is over just yet. I'll be back."

"Well, next time, knock on the door," she said and winked.

He appeared surprised at her response. "Are you telling me that you won't turn me out if I come to visit?"

She tossed the rope into his chest. "You wouldn't stay away if I told you to, would you?"

125

He thought about her comment and then said, "No. I think I would come around to see how you were doing despite your ire."

Celeste smiled coyly and tilted her head so that her eyes and hair caught the sunlight that beamed through the barred windows. "I thought as much." One long, blonde tendril that had fallen free from her chignon, draped over her eye, and she gracefully pulled it back in place with a loose hairpin.

She moved too close to him, but he did not back away. It was an intimate moment. Her voice was soft and seductive. "And you will for all eternity Jim-Jean-Jacques Coupier."

"You are a fortune teller, Mademoiselle?" he asked in a low raspy voice that hinted of a burning sexuality that had not been satisfied for some time if ever.

"I know you," she said and then smiled at the double meaning. Her mind flipped to the page where she and Jim had made love the night they'd dined at the 1819 House. How Jim had made her experience happiness beyond her wildest fantasies. "Oh, yes, I know what's going on inside that devious mind of yours."

Celeste stood on her toes, leaned her face close to his, and kissed him lightly on the mouth. Her eyes remained open to watch his close.

Jean-Jacques tried to speak, coughed, and then stammered, "I am still an officer of the law, Celeste Lacombe. If you break it again, you will pay."

"Are you coming, cousin?" cried Claire.

"Oui, merci, Claire. I am with you."

Celeste darted away from the police spy and into the crowd of happy women who claimed victory over the authorities

126

and hailed Claire as a true Amazon—a warrior heroine for all time. There would be a celebration that fine, hot, summer day: wine, cheese, bread, and chocolates for all.

Chapter Twelve

"Why are you dressed like Leclerc?" asked Celeste.

"You've seen me dressed like a sans culottes," said Claire who seemed puzzled that her cousin had suddenly gone senile on her.

"I got you out of prison because I was more intimidating to that police spy dressed like a man," Claire said as she and her friends practically danced in the street with glee over their presumed victory and the headiness of too much wine.

"What did you tell him, Claire? Tell me exactly what you said," said Pauline.

"Oh, nothing much. I did tell him that if he didn't let Celeste go I would gather more women and storm the gates."

Celeste pressed the issue, "You must have said something else to him, or he would never have let me go."

"He just wanted to pull me in for questioning so that I might think twice before I created another riot. Plus, I think he likes you, Cheri," she said to Celeste.

Nanette burst into laughter. The others, caught by her hysterical joy, followed suit.

Celeste smiled. "I think he's rather good looking, don't you?" she said, feeling comfortable with her new friends. Then she moved closer to her cousin and whispered, "What did you really say to him?"

"Later," was Claire's quick reply. "When Leclerc is with us. Just us three."

Celeste and Claire saw that everyone found their way

home safely, took an alleyway route to their own apartment, and discovered Leclerc staring at the portrait of Phillipe when they entered.

"The whole neighborhood is buzzing with news, but they were chatting away so fast; I couldn't understand a word of it. You were in prison, Celeste? Why?"

Claire, in her own theatrical style, told the tale of the wronged peasant artist and the arrogant police spy.

"But, I *did* tell him something. I told him that you were preparing a speech," admitted Celeste.

"And nothing else? And he believed that was all you knew?" asked Claire matter-of-factly.

Celeste thought it rather amusing that Claire was proud of her for not telling all that she knew. How could she tell what her other half knew but she didn't?

"I don't understand. You and Leclerc want to imprison the rich? That's what he said." This seemed a perfect time to play dumb.

"Well," said Leclerc slowly, "admittedly, we have not shared all our plans with you as you have shown no particular interest in our political philosophy thus far."

"I think you had better tell me everything. I'm up to my chin in all this and so is Phillipe." Celeste stared at him and waited.

A blush of crimson crossed Leclerc's face. "Phillipe's father, as far as I've been able to ascertain, is a Royalist, and that doesn't bode well, mon petite cousin. I'm sorry. We will speak the manifesto of enragés June twenty-fifth. Roux feels we'll gain support. If Phillipe cares about you, why hasn't he come for you, Celeste? I could see my way clear, only because of you, for I love you as Claire does, to forge a passport for him to take you from Paris and smuggle you both out of the country...say to Spain. That is our secret gift to you. I told you that I would try to find Phillipe, but I've had little success. Perhaps he has already left the country."

Celeste noticed a meaningful look pass between Claire and her lover.

"He would never leave without Celeste," said Claire, trying to be supportive of her cousin's feelings.

"If he knows you and I are staying here with her, I doubt he'll come within a mile."

He turned from Claire to Celeste. "You have no idea what families like the de Brouquens have done to the good citizens of France. They prey on the helpless poor as if they were simply stones in a stream to step upon so that they might not soak their dainty shoes. You should hear some of the stories Jacques Roux has told me. They bleed the good people of France for their own sport. Yes, sport, Celeste; a writer does not use words idly. None shall survive; Claire and I are in agreement on this. We understand why you've stayed out of the political discussions so far; but we want equality, and you can no longer sit in your private painting prison and ignore what is going on all around you. Women with starving children at their breast are taking up arms against tyranny, and you cannot..."

Claire interrupted, "Cher..."

Leclerc turned to her and gave her a harsh look. "She must not hide behind these walls, living side by side with us, without knowing that we mean to execute every bastard whose eccentric way of living is nourished by the lives of the men, women, and children of France. Women and children—the heart and soul of our country, our future, our salvation and our independence—it's all for them...for you, Celeste. If you are with child, will Phillipe take care of you? Why hasn't he married you if he loves you so much and wants a family?"

"Well, I..." Celeste was feeling a bit nauseous again and sat down on the small stool by the stove.

"Exactly. A woman needs to have a husband and a father for her child and not be some weekend retreat for some bored aristocrat."

"You have said too much," cautioned Claire.

Leclerc's voice softened. "I apologize for being so opinionated on a personal subject that is none of my concern, but I hate to see a beautiful woman like you, who has so much to offer a good man, pining away in her lonely room while he dances another waltz with some skinny debutante whom his father thinks would make a good catch. Tallying the sum of the lady's wealth and having her mother for afternoon brandy, or some such thing, to speak of an engagement. I know something about such things, Celeste. He'll not come for you. I'll wager he won't. If by some miracle he does, I will see that the two of you make it out of France. But, if he doesn't, I will show him no more mercy than I would any other leech. You shall be the princess of my soul, and I shall protect you, as I do Claire, with my very life."

"Well said," said Celeste, placing the back of her hand over her mouth at the moment she tasted bile rising in her throat.

Claire noticed. "I'm sorry. Leclerc gets too wound up

with his ideals and sometimes doesn't think before he speaks."

"He thought a great deal before telling me the truth," Celeste said while keeping direct eye contact with the editor.

His focus on her expressions and general reaction to what he'd just said never varied. Some sort of silent understanding passed between them. An affection. An intelligence. A bond of friendship that would last beyond their time together.

"It hurts me to hear the truth," Celeste said after a moment, "but it's far better than living with lies...empty promises...and senseless hope."

"You will break it off with him, then?" asked Leclerc.

"Hasn't he already broken with me as evidenced by his absence?"

Leclerc gave a knowing glance to Celeste. He tilted his head sideways as if thinking of another question to ask her, closed his lips tightly as though he were preventing that question's utterance, and raised his eyebrow thoughtfully. "You are so different, shy one. Shall I sign you on as a new member of the women's club?"

A soft, feminine smile crossed her face. "I won't go that far, but I will ponder all that you've said. You have to understand one thing though, Phillipe de Brouquens owns my heart, and there is nothing I can do about it."

He whispered, "I understand. I would hold you in low esteem if you did not listen to your heart first. If you followed me blindly from this moment on and tossed aside a man who might be the father of your child...well..." He shrugged his shoulders.

"I'm not sure I'm pregnant. Why must we all assume

that I am?"

Claire interjected. She had been watching the two and needed to be a part of the discussion again before she was forgotten completely. "The clothes. And that police spy said that you were ill when he brought you to his room," she said. "Were you sick?"

"Yes. He didn't lie; I was."

"Then what else could it be. Phillipe's wine is the best, and there was nothing wrong with the bread you ate this morning."

Celeste wanted to say that her illness could be attributed to jet lag from time traveling, but then she had to give her alter ego credit for having some say in the matter. Maybe she *was* pregnant, and if so, it was up to Celeste to help her keep her body healthy and safe for the baby's sake.

"I need to get back to work; my boss will be here soon," she said suddenly.

"I thought he came only on Mondays?"

"Ah...yes..well...he's given me much work, and I am behind."

"Oh? Yesterday you said," and Claire pointed to a large chest, "that you had most of it done and wondered if you were losing your touch because he was bringing you less and less."

Celeste walked to the chest and opened the lid. There, hidden underneath some white linens, were the small papers that made the plates for a book—a memoir of some kind. The pictures were portraits of aristocrats, possibly a family. "Ah, yes, the memoirs. I have one or two more portraits to sketch."

Then Celeste noticed the small caricatures of the original

family portraits she was supposed to sketch for the printer, and some floral designs the real Celeste had made to go around several chapter headings of what appeared to be a book of poetry.

"Almost but not quite done," she said, thinking that she would have no idea how to complete them or what the required task might be. She learned one thing about her other persona, however, she was an excellent artist. Perhaps better than the 2000 A.D. version would ever be. The 1700's Celeste's pencil drawings were impeccable, and that bookbinder should be grateful to Phillipe for getting her the job.

She mumbled, "I must get back to my work. Leave me now."

"Have I hurt your feelings? I am sorry," said Leclerc. He moved behind her and placed his hand on her shoulder.

"I am wounded, but I shall live. I am grateful for your candor. Now, leave me with my thoughts."

She did not see the look they gave one another before they left, nor did she care that they had nowhere to go but this home, and that it was getting late. They obeyed her without a word.

"I only need you," she said to the pictures in the chest. Her fingers embraced each drawing. "You, Celeste Lacombe, in whatever deep part of my soul you abide. I am here for you. I will help as much as I can. You're not alone." The word 'alone' brought tears to her eyes. She used the back of her hand to brush them away.

"Not alone. I understand how it is now with Claire and Leclerc and Phillipe. You don't know where you belong, or if you will soon be a mother like the ones out there starving in the streets. I'm from another time period, and I will help you. You

will survive no matter what I have to do to make it happen."
Then she smiled, "And I think you can help me too."

Chapter Thirteen

Celeste continued to learn more about her new intimate friend and past life personality, Celeste Lacombe. She didn't feel the woman's presence in her thoughts as she assumed she would. She felt no change in her attitude towards food, wine, love, or life. An occasional outburst of extreme emotion came upon her—volatile mood shifts which one might expect from a pregnant woman. She was, however, seeing a change in her own art skills. Her careful scrutiny of the other woman's immense talent was having an effect on her creativity.

The more she traced over the other woman's sketches; the more she learned. Celeste couldn't remember being taught anything like this in her art history classes in Paris. Now it seemed as if she were relearning everything about painting and drawing. It excited her. She found the whole experience enlightening, and it stimulated her to practice constantly. She ignored the intemperate summer weather of Paris, France, and the fluctuating moods of Claire and Leclerc. She almost forgot about the snooping Jean-Jacques Coupier. More extraordinary still, she wasn't thinking about Phillipe anymore. She wondered if that was why the other Celeste had never spoken with Claire and Leclerc about politics. She had been engrossed in her art.

The sociological atrocities of the time period piqued her interest on those few occasions when she did move away from her easel. It was impossible to forget what was about to happen in France. Celeste Montclaire found the revolution the most intriguing and frightening historic arena known to human civilization; and, as an attorney who believed in truth and justice, Celeste couldn't resist the classic time traveler curiosity of learning the truth about the politics. She watched from the sidelines, and wondered how long it would be before she was caught up in the play.

On June twenty-fifth, Jacques Roux read the Manifesto de Enragés to the Convention with Varlet, Leclerc, Leon, and Lacombe by his side. Their ideas were accepted. In that one speech, this man condemned thousands of men, women, and children to their untimely deaths. Claire was infuriated that she was not permitted to read her speech. The three men seemed only slightly upset about that fact, and told her that she would get another chance.

The merchants, as Leclerc had prophesied, raised the price of soap. In their defense, there truly was a shortage of soap; the subsequent rise in price would have happened anyway. However, in the course of these unfolding events, it made matters worse for the well-to-do. The fact that there really was a flour shortage was also an unfortunate reality that none of the citizens were about to believe, either. Rather like the tale of the boy who cried wolf—since the greed-driven money-grubbing merchants had told lies previously—when they finally spoke the truth about the shortage of supplies and earnestly needed to demand a higher price for their wares—the people assumed they were lying. The merchants—just like the boy who cried wolf— would eventually be slain by the very beast they had lied about earlier.

On June thirtieth, Jean-Jacques Coupier, and other police authorities, gave fair warning to the Revolutionary

Republican Women about their disruptive public behavior. Claire grumbled about the edict for days.

Celeste hadn't noticed Jean-Jacques near her apartment for many days. She really hadn't been thinking about love or the men in her life at all until July first, the day Phillipe de Brouquens showed at her door. He had an armful of gifts for her, a smile on his face, a twinkle in his eyes, and obvious expectations.

"My dove, I have missed you!" he exclaimed like a husband just back from a long trip.

"Where have you been?" said Celeste, who made a mental note that she would have asked the same question to her own Phillipe.

"This craziness...utter foolishness of the revolution...has kept me away. I wanted to see you again; but, I admit, I was wary of venturing to Paris again." He dropped his packages onto a chair, threw his arms around her, and kissed her fervently.

Celeste reacted in a way that told her a great deal about herself and her feelings for her own Phillipe; she pulled away and automatically wiped his kiss from her lips with the back of her hand. She wondered why she had done that because her heart was racing and her physical reactions to his closeness contrasted mightily with what her mind was thinking.

"What's wrong, Celeste? Oh, I know, I've been gone too long and now you don't think you love me anymore. Well, dispel that idea, for you adore me as I do you. Here, I have many gifts for you, plus an entire week of lovemaking planned that will take care of your ire. I know a woman gets irritated when she hasn't had sex for a while."

"What makes you think I have longed for you in that way?" she asked.

He kissed her again, and she pushed him away again. "I know you!" he said. "I know how you turn hot when I kiss you, and you cannot deny that you're feeling that way right now. You want me, and heaven knows I want you. I risked my life to return to you."

"If you want me so much, why don't you marry me? We could be together forever, and I should never miss you."

"What? That again. Celeste, I adore you; I treat you quite well, giving you all you want and need; why ask me such a silly question?"

She turned from him to check her emotions and take a deep breath before continuing. "If I am pregnant, the question is not silly. It's about a name for my child and a future family for us."

"Do you think you're pregnant?" he said with true joy.

"Claire thinks I am. I might be. What will you do about it?"

He placed his hand in the fold of her skirt correctly targeting her crotch. "If you are, indeed, with child, my love; I will find a lovely cottage for you that is closer to my estate and take you out of Paris once and for all. I've wanted to get you away from that cousin of yours for some time. I don't like her influence on you. You will not have to work for Tallon ever again. I will see that you have servants, and that you are given all you need forever."

"But not a marriage certificate?"

He turned away from her. "My father would never allow

it."

"I see," said Celeste.

His voice softened, and he approached her with his arms outstretched, ready to enfold her into an embrace. "Look. I love you, and you love me. We can be happy for the rest of our lives if not constantly together. Perhaps in the long run, it will be a better life. Husbands can be tiresome, you know. But, lovers are always exciting. We'll have many children and drive each other to new heights of joy when we are allowed time together."

"I see," she said.

The tone in his voice grew heavy and dark. "It is the best you can manage, my dear, considering your state. I'd prefer you never ask me about matrimony again. You have no right to complain; you're treated better than other women—much better. Now take off that dreadful peasant's skirt and try on this new gown I had made especially for you."

"I don't feel like it."

Celeste felt like a peevish little girl; the behavior being brought on by his sudden presence in her 1793 life. Perhaps she was sensing the other woman's personality after all.

"My skirt suits my humble state which you have just described to me ever so vividly. We are both peasants."

He laughed and tried to cup her face in his hands, but she pulled away. "Oh, yes, I understand that women get edgy when they are pregnant. I can take care of that too."

He placed his hand softly on her breast. Celeste closed her eyes and abandoned her body to the sweet sensations her old lover created in her. She felt overcome with sexual energy. Her body didn't care what her heart and mind were thinking at this point. It only knew that this hand was the same one that had taught her body how to make love, and it wanted more. She moaned deep in her throat.

He began kissing her neck, her throat, and gradually pulled the blouse down from her breasts, freeing them from her corset. Alternating between biting and kissing, Phillipe could enjoy himself. Then he pulled the blouse off entirely and undid the corset completely, and Celeste, whose mind had gone totally blank, was not stopping him.

Phillipe said, "Now, oh, my love, now is the time to make me happy. Thrill me with the sweetness of your body. Your lips are more luscious than wine. I can smell the fire burning within you. Your heart is racing. I can hear it inside your breast, pounding life like a baby bird crying for food from its mother; I can satisfy that passion. How you have hungered for me. It was unfair of me to make you wait this long. Unforgivable. Before I leave France, I shall buy that cottage for you whether you are pregnant or not. Outside the city limits so that it is safe for us to meet. Away from Leclerc and Claire. I only want *you*, Celeste. You are all I need in life to make me happy."

Celeste's mind told her that this was a damn good line, and she shouldn't listen to him; her body, however, wasn't interested in what she thought in the least.

His hand pulled up the hem of her skirt; his fingers found their mark. He looked at her while he massaged her body. "You like that, don't you? Oui. I am here for you. Take me in your hand and feel how much I want you. Take it."

Celeste had to stop this immediately. "No, Phillipe. Yes, I am very happy you've returned, and we have a great deal to say

141

to each other, but I don't like it when you rush me like this. You make me feel," she fought for the right French word for sex object but could not, "like a whore."

He stopped all movement, stared at her, and said nothing in his defense.

Celeste felt empowered. "You buy me a townhouse, bring me gifts, food, wine, say you love me; but the moment you are in the room, you expect me to service you immediately like a woman of the streets. It's the same as being paid, you know. I see nothing romantic about the way you're acting. I am here to fulfill your hunger, and you bring gifts to pay my way in life. You grab me as if I were a whore and ask me to say nothing about a name for the tiny one growing inside my belly."

Celeste was surprised by her new speech. Her words seemed more like Celeste Lacombe's than hers. Maybe she was allowing the woman to speak her mind.

"I have missed you so much, my love," he continued, "why do you argue with me? You know how in love we are with each other. You know I will always take care of you. You are my lady, no whore. That is a dreadful thing to say."

Celeste felt warm tears clinging to her eyelashes. "Well, why must I sit lonely in Paris with no clue where you are? Why did you abandon me if you care for me so much. I was worried sick, have been so for years...I mean weeks...wondering if you were killed, if you took another lover, if you were told by your family to leave me once and for all!"

He cradled her in his arms. "Hush, now, shy one. No, no, don't cry. I am sorry for the way I've treated you. I am a beast, and you have every right to hate me."

Celeste relaxed in his embrace. "Oh, I don't hate you, Phillipe. I was just so worried. Not knowing what was to become of me...us...ah...the baby...our life together. You could have written a letter."

"I couldn't risk anyone else intercepting or reading it. Here, you are correct; I have behaved badly. Stoke up the fire a bit, and we'll have dinner. I have roasted chicken, bread, cake, fruit, cheese, and, of course, our finest wine."

It was the first time in her life that the thought of food outweighed her desire for sex. She was so hungry the thought of delicious warm rolls and sweet cakes became more erotic than the fact that he had kissed her and opened her mind to the touch of his skin.

"Coffee? I'll make some so that we can drink it later. Here, let me set a table for us. How much cheese did you bring? Is that *real* chocolate?" Her lust for sweets had grown since her arrival in 1793.

"You must be pregnant. Your appetite has blossomed as well as your breasts?"

"You notice the difference, eh?"

"Immediately. Much bigger. Here, let me feed you."

Phillipe did just that. He ripped the chicken into small pieces and placed them delicately into her mouth. It had just been taken from the hot skewer of a tavern and tasted divine. The warm potato and hot rolls tasted better than any she had ever experienced in her whole four years in Paris. He opened the wine and brought two crystal goblets from a linen sack. "These are for our new home. My first gift to you, but not the last. I have new oils for you, canvas, all you need to paint."

A memory raced into her thoughts, and she heard nothing else he said as she broke the crust of the hard rolls with her hands and then placed the tasty Parisian bread into her mouth. Jim had given her the same gift—painting supplies to make her want to be creative again. Here she was with her old boyfriend drinking wine and breaking bread while Jim Cooper was probably worried sick about her. She was homesick all of a sudden. Her stomach was feeling queasy too.

"You look a little pale," Phillipe said as he poured himself more wine. "Maybe you shouldn't eat so fast, love. Is the wine not to your liking? I brought the best."

"No, I was just thinking. Thinking..." She had no sooner spoken the words when the figure of Jean-Jacques passed her window.

She darted a quick glance at Phillipe. His blue eyes were so merry, so eager to love her. Believe him again? Why? Jean-Jacques had been watching them just as she had been thinking of home and Jim. Both men were here, together, in the same time period, and now she had to decide. Two men. Two lovers. Two memories. Two time periods. Same problem.

"It isn't fair to keep Phillipe alive in your heart when Jim's with you," she thought. "And unfair to your memories of your first love to have never searched for Phillipe or brought closure to the affair. It isn't fair to yourself not to move on with your life. Well, now you can decide once and for all. And then, when you get home, make the most important decision of your life. But for right now, Celeste Montclaire, the play isn't being directed by you anymore. You're on a stage with no script, and you have another character within you who may want to run the

144

course of this production for her sake as well as yours. It's her life too. This time, don't play the child, let your heart improvise the scenes and watch the plot unfold. It's only act one, after all."

As the wine began to make her thoughts turn to love, Claire and Leclerc brushed into the room. Their arrival couldn't have been timed any better. Leclerc seemed surprised by Phillipe's visit. Did he think that the man in the portrait was fictional? Claire, in her usual way, curled her lip and tightened her eyebrows into a thin line.

"Ah, you! At last, you've come to make an honest woman of my cousin."

"This is my house, Claire. What are you doing here?" said Phillipe with a bitter tone in his voice.

Celeste corrected him. "This is *my* house, for I am the one who lives in it all alone while you're away. It's depressing without you, and these two are my only companions while you're gone."

"The man?"

"Is Leclerc—editor and publisher of his own newspaper."

"And no doubt a conspirator with Claire."

Claire said, "If you want us out, we'll leave. But, how are you going to help my cousin if you live in Bordeaux, and she has your child in Paris?"

Celeste made a mental note that Claire Lacombe was not a woman to have against you; that she would fight to the death to save a friend.

"I will move her outside the city limits, as if it is any of *your* business. Out of respect for my love for you, Cheri, I shall let them stay here with you while I make the necessary arrangements for the cottage."

"When did I say that I would leave Paris for a place in the country?"

"I...don't believe I asked your opinion."

Claire's facial features relaxed, and she smiled a sign of private approval.

"You just told me that you would *not* marry me. You will *not* give my child a name but cast him into this world as the bastard son/daughter of some aristocrat he/she doesn't even know, and you expect me to do what pleases you. To move away from the only family I have—the only friends who might help me if you suddenly decide to never show at my doorstep again? How utterly selfish you are. I want to be with Claire—not alone in some cottage close to, but not a part of, your estate. I don't want my only companions to be a bunch of servants whose daily hobby is to gossip and laugh about me. If something happens to you, who will give me the family unit I'll need to raise my child? If I am pregnant, I want Claire with me when I give birth. If I'm not, then why would I want to leave a city that holds my job, my only source of financial support if anything happens to you, and all my friends?"

"Oh, my, how Claire has changed you, my dove," Phillipe said. He paced and gave short fast looks at the people in the room. For a fraction of a second, it seemed as if he were losing, and Phillipe didn't like to forfeit control in any situation. "Do you want me to leave, for I will not stay if they are here?"

Celeste looked nervously at Leclerc.

"We can stay elsewhere if it bothers *his lordship*." He

said the words bitterly, and Celeste hid her smile. Leclerc was watching him as if the man were his prey, and his eyes shot invisible daggers at Phillipe. He would take Celeste's side no matter what Phillipe did.

"But we'll not desert you, shy one," he said. "We'll wait until he leaves for his father's estate. Until his money is gone, and he has to hurry home for more cash—cash which can be filtered as quickly through his fingers as water pours down a stream after a stiff rainstorm. You can trust *us*, Celeste."

Phillipe was a hunter, and he had his victim marked. In a fight, Leclerc would win, but Phillipe would have to wait until another time to take care of this man. "I think that might be suitable. I want to be with my love for as long as possible."

"Marriage has that quality too," said Claire.

"Leave us now. Stay far from this house until I'm gone."

Claire and Leclerc left without a word, but as they walked into the street, Celeste thought to call them back. She felt ill at ease with the one person she had always hoped she'd meet again. He wasn't her Phillipe. Not really. He was cruel, self-effacing, arrogant, and pushy, and her Phillipe had been witty, warm, charming, and loving most of the time. He never opposed her ideas and always took whatever she said to heart. If she wanted to cook, they stayed home and snuggled; if she wanted to go out to dine, drink, and dance the night away, he agreed and paid the bill. That was what she had loved the most about him. He was always on her side...just like Jim.

"The food was wonderful; I'm filled." He took her hand and kissed it. "Now? May we love again and make the heaven bright with our joy?"

"I...don't want to right now, Phillipe. I feel uncertain about so many things. About us. About your ideas. About the scene with Claire and Leclerc. It's gone awkward all of a sudden."

His jaw went forward, and he grit his teeth together. "You turn me out?" There was a dangerous edge to his voice.

"I don't want you to leave. Stay. Let's work out our problems together."

"I didn't come here to talk; I came to make love to the only woman who means anything to me!" His eyes were rimmed with angry tears. "Do you realize what I have risked in coming to you today?"

"Yes, I do, perhaps more than you. And I'm glad you've come. But, I've been getting...morning sickness. When I went to prison..."

"You were in prison?" He stood up. "What happened?"

"Nothing really." She was surprised by his sudden movement and tried to soften the tale. "I was questioned about what Claire was planning. It wasn't about you and me, and I wasn't in trouble or anything like that."

"Who dared this imposition?"

"Just a police spy. I..." she looked away. "I don't know his name."

"Do you see why I must take you out of this unsafe area?"

She stood and walked towards him. "I do understand." She thought how difficult it would be to explain to him that she wasn't his real love, Celeste Lacombe, and that she could not leave the only place in 1793 she knew. This whole thing was troublesome enough without being relocated to some cottage. A little cottage in Cooperstown was all she wanted right now. In addition, she didn't want to leave Jean-Jacques. No, she couldn't leave Paris. She'd lived here for four years when she was a teen and could do it again. She was amazed at how much of the city seemed so familiar to her even if there were a few hundred years difference, and she couldn't readjust to another setting now.

She stammered, "But, I just can't leave right now."

"But it has to be soon, Celeste. I might not have a chance to return to Paris to see you again, but I *could* get to the cottage without being noticed."

"I'll think about it this week while you're here. Meanwhile, we have a lot of catching up to do." She kissed him on the cheek. "I want to know everything about you...and why you left me for so long."

Chapter Fourteen

Celeste slept with Phillipe by her side, and it felt like old times. She held onto her story of abstinence. Phillipe didn't like it much, but he kept quiet. In fact, he did not leave her side; he clung to her like an extra appendage during his stay. As the days and weeks lengthened his visit, she realized that he adored her.

Despite his attitude and manners, the man really had risked all in returning to her and was thrilled that she might be having his baby. He watched her every move and helped her with chores in the small apartment. He told her to sit still while he fetched food for them. He surprised her with small gifts for the house: a new chair, a better mirror, a vanity set of a comb and brush, a new cover for the bed and finer linen sheets—the sort of acts a husband would do for his wife if he'd just discovered that she was pregnant. His voice softened when he spoke with her as if the loudness might bother the baby. He became more interested in her artwork, making comments about her many talents and her obvious beauty.

They only left the apartment at night to dine with his friend and that man's new lady in a quiet restaurant in Montmartre. They sat cloaked from public eyes by a curtain surrounding the area.

There seemed no recourse but to drink wine as it was the only thing they had that was safe to drink at the restaurant or at home. She didn't like the idea, but her lover owned a vineyard and seemed insulted when she refused. It was 1793, after all, and no one thought about prenatal precautions.

Phillipe bought her a lovely dress for the occasion—which didn't fit until he made the dressmaker redo the bodice and the waistband. The poor woman had to guess about the size from Phillipe's description, and a piece of string he had used to size her at home. Celeste was not permitted to go to the shop.

Phillipe's friend, Guy, seemed completely bedazzled by Celeste. His lady, who was quite pretty, couldn't compare in conversation. Celeste was witty, flirtatious, interested in all they spoke about, smiled, laughed, her eyes sparkled with the glow of the candlelight when she giggled, and she was more intelligent than either of the men. She cautioned herself repeatedly not to allow that fact to spoil the evening.

Guy's date sat silently and listened with a faint smile on her face. It wasn't her fault. After all, the men were spending the evening with an educated, talented, opinionated, independent, business woman from 2000, who was living with the hottest political couple since Caesar and Cleopatra.

After sipping the last of the champagne, Guy began to seduce his woman in the restaurant. He occasionally patted her hand during dinner; the action reminiscent of the sort of pat one gives a canine companion to remind it of your affection. Obviously, the two were going to make love right there in the restaurant, and it was equally apparent that she and Phillipe were expected to do likewise.

"Did you tell him that I might be pregnant?" she whispered as Guy's girl raised her head so that Guy could kiss her neck.

"Yes. And I told him that we were abstaining for the

baby's sake, but I don't think that's going to stop them."

"Can we leave then?" she said as Guy fumbled for his weapon, and the lady undid her petticoats.

Phillipe placed some bills on the table. "Assuredly."

After they had exited the rear of the restaurant, Celeste made a suggestion. It had rained, and the streets glistened in the moonlight. It was a cool summer's eve, and the temperature was perfect. The scent of rain washed roses filled the air. It was the perfect Parisian backdrop for a portrait of two lovers. She and her own Phillipe had walked these same streets often in the early 1990s. They had been inebriated and happy as they ambled jaggedly down the hills.

She smiled at the memory and said, "Could we walk a bit? Talk and walk?" she said, giggling for that had been the phrase her Phillipe had liked to use.

"I'd like that. It is a fine summer's evening in Paris, and I am with the woman I love." He said it as if he truly meant it. It stopped her.

"You sound as though you mean that." She looked at him, searching his visage for the truth.

"I do." He looked at her, and his smile faded. "Can't you see it in my eyes, feel my lips quiver when I kiss you?" He pulled her close to him and kissed her. He was correct. The emotion was in his lips. Her knees weakened.

He didn't move his lips very far from hers when he murmured, "How could you ever believe otherwise? Oh, I play the womanizer to my friend," he titled his head in the restaurant's direction, "it's what he expects from me. He thinks I am using you as a vacation. I told him so, so that he would come to Paris with me. So I would have some protection by my side in case something...happened."

He stared directly into her eyes. There was honesty, affection, and pain hidden there. "Celeste, I do what everyone expects of me. My father. My family. I have to be as they see me. But, when I am with you, it is so different. I can talk with you about art—something I love so much but cannot do. You can draw—paint. You are so talented. I even like it when you get cross with me. You are so quiet most of the time, and compliant to all my wishes; and then like a bolt from the blue, I see this burst of temper and energy. It is so very sexy. You are sexy, my love. A man can have sex with many women. As you know, I can perform quite rapidly and with little provocation—a half-exposed breast can launch me into activity. But, with you, it is so very different. Full lust and passion when we are coupled. Oh, my God, Celeste the thought of you arouses me even in my dreams."

So, here he was, abstaining from his erotic dream come true because she had asked him to. She said nothing as she walked beside him. The wine and his words were enough to make her mind think how sweet his body would be. Those legs. His kiss covering every inch of her flesh. His hips. And more. Oh, yes, she needed that. Baby or no, Celeste Montclaire needed passion. Her libido was positively screaming for sex. Did she owe it to herself to find out if this Phillipe was like the other? Should she see whether even the most intimate details of his anatomy were similar to her past lover's? She was single. Confused. Drunk. In Paris. It was wet, warm, the air was perfumed with the aroma of refreshed roses, and summer. A dangerous combination.

Phillipe had to know he was close to victory. Her eyes were telling him so. He made his move.

"When I am at home, my mind wanders to you. I'd love to have you by my side. I love you in case you ever doubted it. But, Celeste I can't marry you. If that doesn't suit you, then tell me to go and I will. But, you said that you loved me, and I am here to tell you that I will adore you until the day I no longer breathe and probably beyond it. No matter what happens to me...to you...you must forever know that my life is not orchestrated by my own actions or desires but by the expectations of my family name. I am a de Brouquens and must do as that name suggests. I must know the correct way to kiss a hand, to taste a new wine, to hunt, to bargain a price, to dance, to appreciate fine music, to be a brilliant conversationalist. Carefully taught from a small age. But, you, growing up in the house of a merchant with your cousin, abandoned by your mother and father to live on the streets, and then thrust into a new life by the death of the Lacombes and Claire leaving you for her career...well..."

Celeste didn't hear his last few words. So, she had been *abandoned* as a child, and even Claire had left her to her own devices. No wonder Phillipe had been unhappy with Claire's sudden arrival. Claire had been using her too.

"You had nowhere to live and nothing to live for. And then that day I saw you, standing in that line, waiting for a job with Tallon, talking to...Nanette I think that was her name. You looked so thin so pale. As if death had marked you for his lover. Nanette gave you some money so that you would not have to sell yourself to the sailor who had been stalking you...circling you like a shark. Our eyes met. Must I tell the story again for you, my dove? Well, then I will. I will tell it again and again until you see that I love you and want you as my lover forever even though I cannot make you my wife. It is all I have to give you besides money. Love is rare to me, indeed. Don't push me away, Celeste. You're all I have to love in this world."

She let him hold her in his arms and rested her weary head on his chest.

"And I am ecstatic about the possibility of you having our child. I will do anything I can to support our tiny family. This is what I can give. This is the true reality of our situation. Not a dream world or one you can paint on your canvas, but the very heartbeat of a man who has loved you since he first saw you at the printers. And when you drew that sketch of me..."

He reached for his billfold. "I still carry it." He unfolded an old worn piece of parchment. On it was a hastily drawn sketch of a smiling young man. No doubt drawn during dinner on a scrap of paper. He looked thrilled to be her model; you could see it from the expression on his face. Phillipe de Brouquens had always loved her. He had been Celeste's first love just as her Phillipe had been hers. She started to swoon as the realization that she had lived the same script of her present life in 1793. With very few variations, Celeste of 1793 would be abandoned soon by her lover and Jean-Jacques Coupier would come into the picture. She was getting to view her own future by way of this past life experience. At last, she would discover what happened, and what the other woman decided. Then this could mean that the little artist was not pregnant, because she had been on the pill in Paris, and had never worried about becoming pregnant. Was that the modern twist to the old story line? Or a precaution she had somehow remembered to take from a previous mistake?

She sighed, "Oh, Phillipe. I remember it all. You're correct, of course, we have always loved each other."

He kissed her again in that same way. Lips full of hunger and love, no woman could resist those lips.

"I want you," she said truthfully.

"The baby?"

"I can't think straight when I'm near you," she answered truthfully.

"Let's go home."

She kissed him. "It's been too long."

"I know. I shall make love to you all night long and continuously for the next two days I'm here."

"You'll leave in two days?"

"I have to."

"Then let's not miss a moment in each other's arms," she whispered.

He held her tightly and kissed her neck. "I was hoping you'd say that. I will make you very happy."

He looked for their carriage. Was it an accident that it was not far from where they'd been walking?

As they drove through the city streets, Phillipe asked, "You haven't mentioned Spain once."

Now she was lost. "Spain?"

"The last time I was with you, you mentioned that I should abandon my father's estate and take you to Spain."

"Yes, oh, yes, of course, I remember. Ah...Leclerc told

me that he would get a passport, or something like that, for us if I wanted it. He knows some people."

"I may need that eventually, but, for right now, I need to remain with my family. I don't think this political upheaval will last long."

Celeste felt an odd sense of emotion. The thought of people being guillotined, came to her mind; this man had just said that it would all go away. Swish. Gone with the wind? But, of course, it wouldn't go away. It was about to become the most catastrophic historic event of all time, and she was powerless to tell him how she knew that.

"Phillipe, don't worry about me if things go wrong in Bordeaux. I can take care of myself. I have Claire, and she will affirm to one and all that I am loyal to the cause; since I am a peasant, it will be easy enough to believe her testimony. But, Leclerc told me the other night that your father is a Royalist. You have to get out of France immediately. With or without me."

He took her hand in his. "You are so sweet, my dove. Worrying about me above yourself."

She wasn't sure how to protect the other Celeste, but she knew that she wouldn't be around come September twenty-second. "Keep her safe until then," she thought.

"Why don't we stop at the hotel, instead. I know a back way to the suite, and Guy will not be there for some time to come, I think."

"A French hotel?"

"Much nicer than the apartment, and we can order food and wine and spend our last few days in my room."

"But my work."

"Can wait."

The thought of sleeping in a 1790 hotel was too tempting for Celeste, so she agreed to being treated like a princess.

Unfortunately, there was a young man from the hotel waiting for them when they came up the back stairs of the third floor.

"Monsieur de Brouquens?"

Phillipe appeared nervous. "Mais oui, what's wrong?"

"A man delivered this for you while you were dining out."

Phillipe opened the door to his suite and gave the boy a tip. He ushered Celeste into the room and lit a small candle, then used it to light a few of the candelabras in the lavishly decorated suite.

"Mon Dieu, c'est ma mere. Elle est tres malade."

"Your mother is ill? Has she been sick long?"

"She is constantly ill, but I had no idea she was close to death. I will leave a message for Guy and send you home in another carriage. I'm sorry, Celeste. I will make this up to you. I promise. But it is my mother. You understand. I must be with her."

"Of course."

"I will discover what is wrong and come back to you as soon as I can."

He took her in his arms. "Celeste. I love you. Never forget that. You are the woman of my dreams."

She kissed him on the cheek. "I know. I know. I'll be waiting for you."

"We must go quickly."

The candles were snuffed; the door closed; the bill paid; and a woman deposited in the darkness of a small street in the Lepeletier section of Paris, France.

Celeste sighed. "Alone again," she said to the stars.

Had the other Phillipe left because of a sick relative too? Were they following the plot written for them, and were they destined to reenact it ad nauseum? Would she never discover the truth? She reached for her key which, besides a handkerchief, was the only other thing she had in her tiny purse, and opened the door to her apartment.

A figure stepped away from a darkened corner. It moved shapelessly in the bleak blackness of the street. She was startled and involuntarily jumped.

"Well, you told me to knock the next time. May I come in? Or is young de Brouquens returning this evening?" said Jean-Jacques Coupier, tipping his tall hat in a gentlemanly manner.

Chapter Fifteen

Celeste was startled by Jean-Jacques's presence and simply stared at him for a second saying nothing. Her mind had been on Phillipe, and, now, the other love of her life stood before her. Without batting an eye, she said, "Is it any of your business if Phillipe is here or not?" Her tone was assertive and defiant. She had to at least give the illusion that she did not welcome his stalking her.

Jean-Jacques moved very close to her, almost to the point of stepping on her toes. "Yes, it *is* my business. May I come in, or are we going to stand out here all night and converse for the delight of the whole neighborhood?"

Her lips pressed together suppressing a grin. She kept saying to herself, "He isn't Jim. He's a past life caricature of Jim. Though there may be some similar personality traits, don't drop your guard."

Celeste motioned with her head. "Come in." She turned the key in the lock, and the door opened to darkness.

"Allow me," he said while lighting a candle that sat close to the still burning embers in the stove.

"Would you like something to drink?" she said, far too weary and drunk to play hostess but trying to be courteous none-the-less. "A cup of tea, perhaps?"

An odd expression crossed his face. It was difficult for Celeste to understand this sudden shift in his countenance. The jaw line softened. The lips weren't as tense. The worry lines smoothed on his forehead. His focus strayed to the burnt red coal in the stove, as if he were meditating on them. It was the pained facade of a man who wanted to be home. A man who wanted a woman to be waiting for him with a cup of hot tea and a kiss. Wanted to sit next to the stove and feel its warmth. It was a lonely, forgotten, rejected, left-out-in-the-cold look.

"I would like that, yes," he said almost too softly to be heard. "I've been out all night and something warm to drink might be nice even on such a lovely summer's evening. May I help you?"

"I can manage," she said with secret pride that she had learned how to do many domestic chores in the 1793 style. She hurried about and placed tea leaves in a small pot, filled the pot with water, and placed it on the stove, then kicked up the embers with a poker and tossed a lump or two of coal on the fire.

"Was there a reason for your visit besides tea and talk?" she asked.

He eased himself into one of the chairs and said, "Nicely put. I suppose that was why I stopped."

"Phillipe isn't coming back."

He scowled. "You expected he would?"

She shot a glance his way and it said, undeniably, that he should mind his own affairs.

He looked away. "Sorry. Of course, you're correct, none of my business. I just hate the thought of a lovely lady such as yourself pining away for a man who doesn't have the decency to marry a woman who's bearing his child. Hits me wrong. I apologize."

His voice even sounded like Jim's right now. He continued, "Well, one thing has changed...no Claire. What happened?"

She shrugged her shoulders. "Phillipe wouldn't let them stay here."

"That was nice of him," he said sarcastically.

Celeste tilted her head towards him in a way that could easily be construed as flirtatious. "She'll be back though," she said smiling, "as soon as she realizes that he is gone, they'll both come home."

He dropped his eye contact with her. "Maybe not."

"What do you know?"

"Some women from the Droits-de-l'Homme section spoke with the Revolutionary Republican Women the other day. Claire and her newly formed Amazon club want to speak at the Convention tomorrow. They plan to accept the new Constitution. What a joke. Women accepting the Constitution as if their approval was something that mattered to men."

She felt her blood pressure rise and reminded herself that, in a later life, this man would be Jim Cooper who was more open-minded. "You are a...a..." She fought hard for the word for sexist, obtuse, male chauvinist, and then remembered that all the words she had learned for those terms when she was in France were ones that meant something different in this time period. "A man who does not believe in equal rights for women. One who does not see females as being citizens," she finally managed to say.

The side of his lip dimpled into his cheek, and his forehead crinkled. "Of course not. Why would I? Why would you?" He stood close to her. "I think your tea is done, Mademoiselle *citizen*," he said, taking the pot from the stove with a cloth so his hand would not be burned, and pouring the liquid into two nearby cups. "And I'm thinking that the sugar is...here." He pointed to the right spot. "Correct?" He opened a fat little jar, took a lump of sugar from it, and then let it dissolve in the amber colored hot water that rested in his cup. "For you?"

Celeste thought of the wine inside her stomach. "No, I'll drink mine without sugar." She didn't know how to manage him. He was completely in control of everything—her—the tea—history—the conversation. The candlelight flickered across his forehead, and he was so handsome that she forgot about Phillipe's sudden departure, or how close she'd come to loving him that night.

They both sat and sipped the hot liquid. Silence for a moment, and there was nothing awkward about it, either. Two old friends who didn't mind the calm, relaxed feeling of just being together. She should have felt nervous, but she didn't.

"And the Convention accepted their help?" she asked after a few minutes.

"Oh, yes, they played the game," he said, placing his cup onto its saucer and swallowing the burning tea.

"Why do you think women are inferior to men?" she said, tasting her flavorless tea as if she were playing a part in a Pride and Prejudice movie.

"Who said I think they're inferior? Women are wonderful, but they shouldn't try to be men. That's my point."

He placed the cup on a nearby table so that he might use his hands while he spoke. "Look at you. The way the candlelight highlights your facial features," he said, circling his hands in the air as if he were using a paintbrush to place her features on canvass. "The way your blue eyes sparkle; the way your lips press together when you're angry with me—hinting that they might want me to kiss them; the way your hair glistens with the color of honey; the way your body moves gracefully about the room while you make tea; the way you paint. You're incredible. I would never want to see you in the streets with pistols at your side looking like Claire. She is so unfeminine."

"You don't think Claire is attractive?"

His words had had the same effect fire has on wax. Celeste tried to fight her reaction, but all that was female inside her was rising to the surface right now, and she wanted to hear him say that she was prettier than her cousin.

"There's fire in her and spirit, no question about that." Celeste frowned.

"But that voice of hers is damned irritating. And what sort of lady fights in the streets like a sailor having a night on the town? I like a woman to be a bit tempered sometimes, but Claire makes it an occupation to bother as many people—especially me—as she can. No, I don't find her attractive in the least."

Should she ask the obvious question she wondered? "And me? You don't think much about me either, do you? Because of Phillipe."

"How can I condemn a survivor?"

She was surprised by his response.

"You are making do as best you can. I've been walking these streets long enough to know how hard it is for women, such as yourself, to keep body and soul together. Who am I to judge you? I think *you* think you're in love with Phillipe, but it's a girlish crush, built on nothing more than a vain hope that he will some day make you his wife. But he won't. Men like that never do."

Celeste felt a cold chill climb her spine. "You are blunt."

"In the time we live in, it's best to be, don't you think? Our lives have changed considerably in the last few days. If things progress the way they are right now, you will have to make some tough decisions, Celeste."

She was suddenly frightened. "What do you mean?"

"Do you have de Brouquens's heir in your belly? An aristocrat's child? You are living with people who may be arrested any day now for exclaiming publicly that 'terror is the order of the day'. I have been ordered to watch Roux, Valet, and Leclerc closely."

"And why are you telling me this?"

His reply was swift as if he had thought about it for so long that the answer needed no pause to weigh the outcome of his words. "That's simple, I like you. Somehow, and I'm not sure why it's so; I trust you. I watch you in my free moments because I find you extremely beautiful, talented, intelligent, and, above all, feminine."

She wasn't sure how to answer the comment, and he used that moment to stand and walk towards her. He pulled her from her chair so that she was close to him and looked into her eyes.

She said, "You're interested in a woman who is in love with a wealthy man you say will never marry her even if she is pregnant with his child?"

165

He watched the movement of her lips as she spoke. "Can't help myself, I guess."

He pulled her closer to his body so that she was cradled against his chest. "Absurd, isn't it? Why did you kiss me the other day, Celeste?" He whispered the words into her ear and then moved a loose strand of her hair with his lips.

His warm breath against her neck sent shivers down her spine. Her arm muscles lost their strength. She didn't resist his caress because her whole body was alive, responding to the man who had loved her after a nice dinner at the 1819 House restaurant. Her mind thought about how wonderful that man was, and all thoughts of Phillipe de Brouquens left her. She couldn't breathe; her heart was beating too fast. The wine was flooding her mind and making her dizzy. The tea was warming her body.

Jean-Jacques's body carried a wonderful smell of the rain and wind from the recent rainstorm—of the roses and the heat of the streets after a summer's shower. She closed her eyes and thought of Jim's scent—like the woods—fresh and clean when they made love in the Richfield Spring cabin. That cold fragrant blend of thawing winter chills and warm teasing breezes of spring that surrounded his clothes and hair. It was something one noticed on a purely subconscious level, but now it was too obvious to miss. She let all these sensations envelope her. Her lips parted, and Jean-Jacques took it as a reply to his question.

"I see, Mademoiselle." He wasn't a man to miss an opportunity. His kiss was long, desperate, passionate, and hot.

"Oh, God," she whispered, her voice trembling with emotion.

His arms moved around her waist and tugged her closer to his body. So close, in fact, that she could actually feel his heart beating next to her breasts and something else pulsating against her thigh.

"What are you going to do now, Mademoiselle?" he said in such a soft sexual tone—a tone Jim had never used.

"What am I going to do?" she said to him and then cursed her lack of an original response.

She wanted him. No question about it. Her mind told her body, "He isn't Jim." Her body told her mind, "Who cares?"

"Oui. What now, Mademoiselle?"

"I don't know what you mean."

"Your lips have told a tale for you, Mademoiselle."

"A tale?" She prayed for something more original to say.

"No woman who is in love with one man, could kiss another like that. Not that way."

"The wine?"

"Non." He pressed his body into hers, and she could feel his manhood stiffen next to her thigh.

"What am I to do?"

"I am not married, Mademoiselle, neither are you. There's nothing stopping us, is there?"

Celeste was positioned too close to the fire. Her whole body relaxed next to him. "But...I might be pregnant."

"Do you know for sure?"

A tiny foot kicked her abdomen just then. Her eyelids opened wide. She pulled away quickly and gasped out loud. The whole matter was unsettling. She was most *definitely* pregnant, or rather Celeste Lacombe was, and not just a little bit, either.

"Oh, my God." She placed her hands on her abdomen.

"What's the matter?"

"I am. I really am!" She started to cry. "This can't be happening to me. I don't want this. It isn't fair. I never meant to travel; now they want me to live for two other lives as well as my own. What's going on? I don't think this is amusing in the least. How did this happen?"

"Well," he smiled, "when a man and woman..."

"I know *how* it happened!" she screamed. Then she realized she was speaking out of character. She was being herself, and it wasn't what he expected to hear. It was confusing him. She had to think fast.

"The baby just kicked me—you—us."

"Then you are with child." He backed away from her.

"And more than a month, I should think."

"You didn't know this before?"

The real Celeste Lacombe must have known.

"I...ah...wasn't sure. Oh, Jean-Jacques, now what do I do?"

"Leave France immediately."

"But..." she fumbled for words, "my cousin, my friends, my job."

"None of that matters now. Your life, and the life of your child, should be your primary concern."

Celeste touched her abdomen and smiled sweetly. "I'm pregnant!"

"We've acknowledged that."

She sat down gently in her chair.

"A woman in every way. The blush of motherhood is on your cheeks, and it's most becoming," he said.

"This doesn't change how you feel towards me? Another man's child?"

"He will not marry you, Celeste. My suggestion is to leave France while you're only a few months pregnant."

"How?"

"I have friends all over France. I'll see what I can do."

"Leclerc mentioned something about getting me papers."

"They'll be noticed as a fraud the first time someone at the border sees them."

"What do you suggest?"

"I'll get back to you on that. Meanwhile, keep this as a memory of me." He took her back into his arms and pressed his lips hard against hers.

He took his hat, which he had placed on a table by the stove, and walked to the door. Before he left, he turned to her and said, "Phillipe de Brouquens is the past, forget him. The baby inside your body is your future."

He placed his hat on his head, tapped the brim with his index finger in gentlemanly fashion, winked at her, then grinned a lopsided, know-it-all smirk which was an obvious match for Jim's famous smile. "As I am, Mademoiselle. Bonsoir."

Chapter Sixteen

Celeste sat a while sipping tea and thinking. The whole evening had been illuminating to say the least. Phillipe, Jean-Jacques, and now this. She took the back of her hand and touched her forehead and cheek. "You don't have a fever, silly; what are you doing that for? You aren't sick." But, she felt very weak at the knees all of a sudden. "I'll sketch for a while. Maybe that will help."

She placed her tea cup on a small table and climbed the stairs to her new bedroom. She remembered her picture of Jim; the one she had redone to look like Jean-Jacques, and took it out of its hiding place under the bed. It needed no more lines to make it perfect. It was the image of the police spy now. Should she follow his lead for Celeste Lacombe and her baby's sake? What would her other self want her to do? Did this woman ever discover what happened to *her* Phillipe? Or did she leave France never knowing? Or worse?

The baby's life force fluttered in her stomach, and she giggled and smiled a warm, personal response to the child. Her fingers touched the swollen part of her abdomen. "Oh, I really don't want this. I don't want to be pregnant, you see. I told Jim that. I was taking the pill. So much for that little habit. Exactly what is *my* body saying to all this?"

She placed the picture back in its hiding place and went downstairs. She stared out of the window and looked at the moon drenched streets of Paris. Where was he now?

"Don't leave us Jean-Jacques. I've got a feeling you're

the only one who can help us now. Wonder what date it is?"

The baby moved again inside her. "Oh, I know I shouldn't have had the wine. I won't have anymore now that I know you're really here. I'll drink milk if I can get it. I'll have to be more careful about what I eat too. One of the ladies who works for me went seven months before taking her maternity leave. I think I can remember what she ate. Of course, she lived in a modern America. Look at how I'm talking to you already. Do you know I'm not your mommy? Of course, you don't because I am, aren't I ? "

Celeste touched her breasts gingerly and realized how swollen they were. She was very glad that she and Phillipe had not spent the night together.

"I can't pretend I don't know now. Everything's changed."

Just then Claire knocked and entered her house. "I thought he might be gone by now."

"Phillipe had to go home suddenly. His mother took quite ill." She paused to make sure Claire was paying attention, "Claire, I'm pregnant."

"Zut alors! For certain?"

"I felt his or her foot kick me just now when I was talking to Jean-Jacques."

"Oh? I'm delighted about the first but curious about the latter."

"He didn't come to spy." She touched her lips and smiled.

"I see," said Claire, grinning and nodding her head up and down.

"What am I going to do?"

"Sleep with Coupier and tell him the baby's his?"

Celeste shot a quick, disapproving look at her. "I wouldn't do that. Besides, it's too late. He felt the baby kick when he was holding me in his arms."

"I don't suppose there's any chance Phillipe will do the noble thing. Is that hot water for tea?"

"No and yes to the tea."

Claire poured a cup of the still warm liquid and spooned sugar into it. "Well, what do you want to do?"

"I have no idea. My, God, I'm in the middle of political chaos, and I'm pregnant."

"T'isn't something new to be pregnant, Celeste."

"It is for me."

"Not to change the subject, but Leclerc will be dropping in tonight. Tomorrow the ladies of the Revolutionary Republican Women's Club will accept the Constitution. You must come with me and wear your cockade."

Celeste let her hand rest on her stomach and sighed. "Why do you bother? They don't care what you think. They just pretend because...your women, and they have to please you. You helped win them this political coup."

Claire seemed perturbed and shocked at turns. "Why do you say that?"

"Because ultimately, men still think women aren't equal. They never will think they are the same. It will end with all of us going home and having babies and keeping the house warm, the soup hot, and the baby sleepy and satisfied."

"What's gotten into you?"

"I'm a mother now, *damn it*!" she said a bit too

forcefully. "I'm not playing games in pants running through the streets cheering that I am like a man. I don't want to fight a war. I just want to feel safe—secure—loved."

"It's that Jean-Jacques fellow. He's so old fashioned in his thinking, isn't he? He's made you swallow his stupid philosophies. Leclerc doesn't feel that way about women."

"Feel women? In what manner am I feeling women?" Leclerc had stepped into the room unnoticed. He took Claire's cup from her hands, kissed her on the cheek, then sipped some of the tea. "Have I missed something?"

"Celeste's pregnant."

"I could have told you that. I told you how she's changed so. Women get that way when they're pregnant."

"How would you know?"

He grinned. "My mother told me."

Celeste looked at him for some time. Their eyes met, and he became serious. "I don't suppose..."

"No, and it's pointless to ask."

"I could go to him, implore him to consider a proper marital course. He should marry you."

"All he wants to talk about is setting up a household in a cottage outside Paris. In the country. I don't want to go."

"Then you shouldn't. He's planning on 'keeping' you as his mistress for the rest of your life. That's what it sounds like to me."

"I don't want to leave the city. You and Claire are all the family I have right now."

"I should think. And with trouble in the air, you need us close by," said her cousin.

"Maybe we should go to Bordeaux and talk with him," said Leclerc.

"I think she should take joy in her little bundle and forget him. There are other men in this world."

Tears welled in Celeste's eyes. "You're talking about me as if I weren't here, as if I had no plan of my own."

"Well, do you?" said Leclerc.

She paused for too long which answered his question. "I'm working on that."

"The police spy? What has he told you?" asked Leclerc.

"He thinks that your passes will be spotted as a forgery immediately. He wants to help me."

"Accept favors from him? And we know well enough what he'll want in return," said Claire.

"Well, he didn't mention that."

"He wouldn't on the first try," said Leclerc. "He was here tonight, then?"

"Yes. I made him some tea. The baby kicked when he held me."

"Poor little one must want his papa and pushed the other man away. See how our society has fallen into this immoral state of affairs," said Leclerc. "Men taking advantage of young women with no plan to make a home for them."

"Oh? And does that include you?" asked Claire, her hands resting on her hips.

"I want to settle down, Claire. It's you who keep building the wall not me."

Celeste needed sleep. The wine was making her very drowsy. "I've had enough tonight. If you want me to go with you tomorrow, I will."

Claire was overjoyed. "And wear the cockade?"

"I don't know about that. I have to think about the baby now. Can't get injured over some ribbon."

"*Please.* The other women will not be bold if you and I aren't."

"All right. I'm heading to bed. You two worry about the cause of Liberty. Liberty? Has a nice ring to it. Maybe I should call him or her Liberty."

Leclerc frowned. "You'd better go to sleep; you're starting to get delirious."

She left them to plot and plan. Making lists of names. Contriving deadly plots to save their lives at the risk of other's. When she finally sat down on her small bed, she placed her hand underneath its frame and took out her sketch of Jim/Jean-Jacques. She stared at his eyes for some time.

"Are you worried sick about me? You are, aren't you? I'm here for a reason, Jim. I have to write and finish this life's book in three months if I'm ever to understand it all. I'm really not alone, Jim. You're here in an odd sort of way. See, there's this Jean-Jacques fellow, and he looks just like you. Especially when he smiles. And I let him kiss me tonight, and it's like kissing you. Phillipe's here too. I still feel a twinge of affection for him; I won't lie to you about that. And the woman I'm here with is pregnant. Isn't that just too bizarre. Put that one in your time travelers' journal. Are you telling my secretary weird stories about where I've gone? And Sam? How's he holding up with all the summer campers buzzing around the two of you?"

She started to cry again. "I miss you, and I still have three months to go. It's unfair. You said that Time Travelers, Incorporated always sends someone with the client. I'm not a client, I know, but...I didn't even pay you, did I?"

She thought about Jean-Jacques. "Did you get the book I gave you?" She cried more. "That's the one who's here with me. The police spy who wrote the book I gave you. Some surprise, huh? Better stop crying, or I'm going to mess up your picture, and it's all I have of both of you. Be patient, Jim. And pray to your 'someone in charge' that I'll come home to you."

She sighed and relaxed her body onto her bed. She held the picture to her chest. "Keep us safe until we can be together again." Celeste closed her eyes, and she and the baby slept.

Chapter Seventeen

Claire Lacombe and her friend, Pauline, as well as others of the Republican Revolutionary Women's Club, spoke at the Committee's next meeting. They accepted the Constitution publicly and pledged allegiance to any duties asked of them. Celeste attended with her cousin just as she had promised, and afterwards the ladies had refreshments at Nanette's house. Celeste behaved as expected—shy, quiet, and reserved compared to her volatile cousin. It wasn't because it was her nature; it was because Celeste was focused on other matters: Phillipe, Jean-Jacques, leaving Paris with one of them, and the baby.

Neither man had shown his face in a week's time. Celeste was worried that the responsibility implied by rescuing a pregnant woman from a desperate situation might have been too much for Jean-Jacques. Perhaps he had become bored or frightened or found another more attractive and less...maternal lover. She wouldn't have blamed him if he had. What man would want to be saddled with fatherhood when the baby wasn't even his? Celeste Lacombe had never shown one ounce of interest in him before June 21.

A week passed with only one visitor—Tallon. He seemed excited because he had more work for her, but confused by the sketches she had prepared for him.

"Celeste? A new style?" he said, shrugging his shoulders, shaking his head, and frowning. "It isn't that I don't want you to try new techniques, but I rather liked your previous work. And we talked about what you needed to do on this one." He pointed to the pages. "You've forgotten?"

"It's just...that...well, to make a long story short, I'm pregnant, and I've not felt too well lately. I spent a night in prison..."

He interrupted her. "Was it serious?" he said, shocked by the news.

"No... it was a police spy who..."

"I know what you're going to say. It's because of that damn cousin of yours. Why don't you send her packing?"

"She's the only family I have now, and Phillipe isn't around much to help me."

"Well, he'll be visiting soon to fetch his mother's poetry book. I thought you'd like to make some scribbles here and there around her poems."

"His mother writes poetry?"

Tallon stared at her as if she had just slipped into a coma. "Why yes, she's not particularly good at it, but they pay well, and so I take their business. I've been friends with his father for many years."

"And because of all that's going on, you feel compelled to hurry the job?" she asked.

"What do you mean?"

She was playing detective, and Tallon's reaction to her words told volumes.

"She's not well. That's what I've been told."

"Ridiculous, I've never known a woman to be more robust and healthy." Tallon wasn't aware that he'd just called Phillipe a liar. He wasn't smart enough to realize that the only one who would have told her this piece of information was

Phillipe.

The whole idea of Phillipe lying to her gave her an emotional jolt. Her lover had left for some other reason that night. There was nothing wrong with his mother. Celeste sat down on the stool by the window to think things through.

"Can you have them ready by the end of the week? I can make the small amount of copies they need so that he can pick them up in two weeks. I think it's meant as a birthday present for her."

"Yes, of course, for Phillipe's mother. I'll get them done right a way." She was thinking on another plane.

"And use your old style. I like it better. T'is warmer and looks feminine and sweet."

"And passive and shy," she wanted to add but did not.

"Here's your pay for these. Have you seen a doctor yet?"

"No, I don't know to whom to go."

"Here's a bit more so that you can find a good one, and a mid-wife, as well. After all, the child is a de Brouquens. Only the finest for him."

She smiled in gratitude but wanted to scream that it would be nicer if the child's father felt compelled to give her comfort now.

"Why do you think it's a boy?" she asked.

He turned as he was walking to the door. "Don't know why really, just guessing." Then he was gone.

How was she going to sketch like the other Celeste? There are many things she could fake, or play the role expected, or improvise if need be; but there was no way in hell that she could draw and paint like the other Celeste. She hadn't the same soul or heart. Hadn't the same life experiences that Celeste Lacombe would have drawn upon to create her own technique. She loved as the other woman must have loved, but that was all she could mimic.

When he left, she sighed and stared at the poems. The book would be called *The Poetry of Madame de Brouquens*. She smiled. It'd never sell a copy on Barnes and Noble.com with that title, but, she tried her best to draw some tiny rosebuds over the love poem, ivy down the side of one long ballad about nature, and two, small, rotund cherubs holding a ribbon between them across the top of the one on motherhood.

"Oh," she thought, "I suppose I should read what my would-be mother-in-law thinks about being a mother." She read two or three, but they were terrible. "Madame de Brouquens...your poetry sucks."

The door opened, and Leclerc and Claire came inside. "We thought we might go to a small restaurant and have something to eat. Leclerc is in a generous mood today. Do you wish to come with us?" said Claire.

The idea seemed to be an answer to a prayer. She put her work aside and fetched a shawl. "I'll go with you, though I shouldn't drink any wine."

"Why not?" she asked, and Celeste reminded herself that her 1793 cousin wouldn't have had the prenatal health care information that Celeste had. "I just don't think I should drink it now that I'm pregnant. But, I *am* hungry, and I would like to have something to eat with you. I'd like to see the city a bit. Haven't been able to see much on my trip."

"Trip? What trip?" said Leclerc.

"Ah...I mean...well...I've sort of been trapped inside, daydreaming, traveling in my head, and haven't seen much of the ah...Paris under the new regime, so to speak." There was no way out of her words. Of course, she couldn't make her comments make sense to him. She was hoping that she might see Jean-Jacques if she went with them.

As if reading her mind, Leclerc said, "Have you seen your new friend lately?"

Celeste found her shawl on a peg near the door. "No, he hasn't been by."

Claire gave a knowing look at Leclerc. "He's probably thought it all through, Celeste, and realized you'll never love him because you are having Phillipe's baby."

"Maybe. I miss him."

"Are you in love with him?" asked Claire.

Celeste thought for a moment before saying, "I love them both."

Claire shook her head and a few of her curls escaped their binding. "Well, don't tell him that if he comes with transportation out of Paris. Play the part. It's important to make the right choices. This man may be your lifeline now."

"What do you know?" she asked as they sauntered down the streets and headed for the marketplace.

Leclerc said, "I've tried to get some information on Phillipe and his family, but I'm drawing a blank. If you want to get the real story, I suggest we go to Bordeaux."

"A trip? Oh, I'd love to go traveling," said Claire.

Celeste touched her stomach, "I'm not that far along. I suppose we could if you could find a nice comfortable carriage in which to travel." The thought of finding the answers once and for all as well as venturing to another location in 1793 intrigued her.

"Very well, ladies, I will finance a small vacation out of Paris that is if Claire is willing to dismiss politics long enough for us to do some investigating."

"I'll talk with Pauline and Nanette. It isn't the best time to be away, but we won't be gone too long, will we?"

"Probably a week," he assured her.

Celeste was thrilled with Leclerc's favorite cafe and ordered some tea and pastry. Leclerc spent most of the time talking about traveling: that he knew someone who would give them a room for the week, that he had an idea where to find de Brouquenses' vineyards, that the political atmosphere was moving on its own course, and that Pauline was capable of continuing the course of liberty without them. He planned to rent the carriage that day. There were many aristocrats fleeing Paris for the comfort of their country estates. Leclerc wanted to make an early bid on a good carriage. He even mentioned that they could stop at Orleans, Blois, Civray, and Ruffec so that they might speak with the other women's clubs. Claire became notably enthusiastic at the thought of 'spreading the word' to her other female compadres.

Celeste dissected her pastry with true admiration for its flaky crust and listened to them. It was a chance to settle the record once and for all, and she had no intention of passing it up. It made a difference to this Celeste's life and hers as well. She could have kissed Leclerc for coming up with the idea.

She looked for Jean-Jacques as she listened and ate.

Nodding her head occasionally gave her two companions the erroneous idea that she wanted more food, so they ordered it for her. It was her way of pretending to be a part of their conversation, and she was surprised as new delicacies were placed before her. When she realized the mistake, she started to giggle uncontrollably. They both looked at her and ceased chattering.

"What is so funny, cousin?" asked Claire with irritation.

"What? Oh, nothing. I just was thinking about something else."

"Something or someone?" said Leclerc.

"You're good. You should be a detective."

"A what?" He looked at Claire. "Does she mean a spy?"

"I suppose." Claire shrugged and sighed. "I'm losing her. She daydreams so much. Like she is asleep when she is awake."

"Perhaps she is in love," said Leclerc.

Celeste smiled and said, "You Frenchmen are all alike."

Just then Nanette burst through the street crowd and into the patio of the cafe. "I am so glad I found you two!" Terror rang in her voice.

"What is it, Nanette?" Leclerc stood up and held the woman by the shoulders. She was was shaking with emotion.

"Il est mort! Il est mort!" Her body was quivering with emotion.

"Who's dead? Calm yourself, woman," said Leclerc.

She sobbed, "Jean-Paul...Marat! Il est mort! Assassiner! Oh, L'Ami du Peuple! *Il est mort!*"

Leclerc looked at Claire and Celeste while the sobbing woman collapsed in his arms.

Chapter Eighteen

On July 13, 1793, the 'friend of the people', Jean-Paul Marat, a small-framed, frail-looking doctor turned writer; who founded the journal, *L'Ami du Peuple*; and who had viciously attacked the major powers in France, was stabbed to death by a beautiful, pale skinned, wide-eyed, childishly sweet looking woman named Charlotte Corday.

Jean-Paul had lived his last few years as an outlaw of France because of his writings. He had once been forced to live in the sewers of Paris to escape imprisonment. In 1790, he avoided persecution by secretly traveling to England, staying there until 1791. He returned to Paris when the Committee took charge and began writing his newspaper again. The skin disease he'd tolerated his entire life had become more inflamed while living in the sewers. This condition required that Marat soothe his skin by taking medicinal baths once a day.

Living with her aunt in Caen, a woman from a noble family, Charlotte Corday—whose thin, pretty face and expressive eyes should have gained her many admirers—became interested in the Girondins who had been taken from power that June. She was introduced to a man by the name of Charles Barbaroux who educated her on the subject of Jean-Paul Marat's immense influence over the people of France and the Promethean power of his newspaper. Charlotte decided to go to Paris and become active in the Girondins' cause. She solicited an interview with Jean-Paul Marat and was refused until eventually, under the pretext that she had the names of dissidents in Normandy,

Charlotte Corday was permitted to speak with Marat while he was taking his therapeutic bath.

Jean-Paul wrote the names she gave him on a piece of paper, scribbling in ink atop a small table that rested near his tub. He smiled at her and assured her that the people she had just named would be guillotined. Charlotte then drew a knife she had hidden in the folds of her dress, and stabbed Jean-Paul in his heart. Death was immediate from one thrust of the dagger. So was her arrest. She was brought to prison where she was questioned by Jean-Jacques Coupier and others. Witnesses lined the hallways. More than one might have expected. And they all claimed to have seen Charlotte with the bloody dagger in her hand. Some claimed she spoke condemnation to Jean-Paul's corpse; others reported that she had said nothing at all. Just stood quietly. Wide-eyed. No emotion. Almost as if she were surprised by the whole incident.

The flame of freedom had been ignited months before his murder; yet, with the death of the French citizens' most popular and most antagonistic writer, the blaze of bitterness and anger fueled the women of Paris into a conflagration that would destroy the lives of thousands of men, women, and children all over France.

It was not the beginning of the nightmare; but, surprisingly enough, it was the end of the women of France's political position. Claire and Pauline, as well as many of the Republican Revolutionary Women's Club, began two months of mourning for a man who had caught the imagination and idealism of revolutionaries not only in France but all over the world. The women had no intention of letting his memory die with him.

They turned him into a martyr for Liberty. They turned him into a god.

The respect the men had for their female compadres waned from July to September as, like Antigone, the sans culotte—the Amazons—turned Jean-Paul Marat's funeral into a macabre spectacle; thus, focusing all their attention on the burial of this one man, and turning his bloody corpse into a symbolic parallel of the 'body of the Republic'. They seemed to be saying that neither Jean-Paul nor the Republic should die. It was their attempt to keep Marat alive, if only in the people's memory, but it made them appear to be more concerned with his demise than the birth of a new nation.

The overwhelming emotion they showed, the high drama they pursued, showed the men of France that their women were motivated by anything but logic, and they cast aside the sans culottes' political views as unworthy of serious attention.

The immortalization of Marat was not the Committee's primary concern, and the women's sentimentalism on the subject made them appear over emotional and feminine rather than the tough, equal warriors the women had portrayed themselves to be earlier.

The Committee had a plan of its own. The members turned the wound in Marat's heart—the symbolic heart of the people—and the women's wailing, into the battle cry for 'The Terror'. More than one person would pay for Marat's death.

Leclerc's plans to go to Bordeaux were canceled. Jean-Jacques was inundated with more work than he could handle. Claire took on the grandest role of her career; Leclerc had volumes to write; Pauline and Nanette created the set for the grandest funeral since Alexander the Great; Phillipe's family started pondering the possibility of taking a trip out of the country; and Celeste, who was not allowed to stay in the background anymore, was dragged into history as a snail might be pulled into a whirlpool.

Celeste knew the moment she heard Nanette's words that she was on a horrific collision course, and that three months might be more than she could endure. She knew she may not be able to direct the outcome of this other Celeste's life, but she had to try. What happened to her no longer mattered. She was living for Celeste Lacombe now. Somewhere in the deepest regions of her soul, she knew that this young girl, this soul mate sister, talented artist, and soon-to-be mother would not survive. A small human being was kicking her in the stomach when she skipped breakfast. She knew what she had to do; the choices she resisted or accepted on this preselected path mattered to three lives not one. She forced Jim's words from her mind, "If it's your time to die in this life, you'll die in that time period."

Her hands shook, and her mouth went dry as she, Leclerc, and Claire raced to the scene of the murder. Her knees buckled, and she felt faint when they brought the linen wrapped corpse of France's newly slain martyr from his apartment. Her heart pounded against her chest as if it might burst when she saw Jean-Jacques's face as he led Charlotte Corday to prison. He didn't see Celeste in the crowd. Maybe he wasn't looking for her anymore. Maybe she didn't matter.

The Corday woman had no expression on her face, nor did she say anything to the crowd who cried out for her death. Celeste watched as the woman was led away. She found the whole scene fascinating.

"You've changed the course of history, Charlotte. Why did you do it?" she thought. The notion that it might be interesting to plead the murderess's case flew through the attorney's curious mind. Celeste tapped her head with the futility of such a notion.

Claire Lacombe could no longer wait in the wings, however. She heard her cue line and walked into the center of history's stage. She marched up to Charlotte Corday, as that woman was being pulled into the streets, and spat in her face.

"Whore!" she screamed. "Murderess."

Then Claire stopped the procession carrying Jean-Paul's corpse and threw the linen sheet aside. The people in the crowd gasped not only at Claire's audacity and boldness but also because of the hideous wound that still flowed crimson rivers down the side of Marat's still, cold, pale body.

"This is what they have done to all of France!" she said, pointing to Marat with an open palm, outstretched fingers, and a graceful swish of her wrist—a move that only a trained actress could have managed.

"Stabbed us in the heart—in the performance of our most unique creation of life in words. But." She looked around so that she was sure that everyone was paying attention to her, paused for effect, and then said, "They have not killed us! *Liberty shall not die!*"

The crowd applauded.

"See the wound fellow citizens, countrymen of France! See how it still pours life into the streets of our awakening nation."

Leclerc was fascinated with Claire's speech. He turned to Celeste and said, "How do you get her off the stage?"

Celeste shrugged, smirked, and said, "We have no hook!"

Claire touched the wound on Marat's chest then looked at the blood on her hand. "This blood is our blood. Shed for our freedom, our independence, our salvation from the tyranny of the Royalists. And like a woman's flow, it shall continue to give life to this nation. It will seed the Republic with the children of righteousness, the children of our future, our youth, our destiny as a new nation where all citizens are completely free to make choices—where there is equality for all."

Jean-Jacques moved to stop Claire who was on a dramatic roll. He touched her arm and mumbled something to her, but she pulled away from him.

Claire's voice intensified. "No! No man shall stop me nor prevent any other woman in this great land, from bearing sons who shall be from the seed of this man. He, whose words brought life to that same Liberty, now has given every woman a reason to give life to his heirs. His seed is our future streaming forth from his words. The seed of his shed blood. His sons. Marat's heirs. He *shall* be reborn." As she spoke this last statement, Claire showed the blood on her hands to each man and woman standing close to her.

"Good Lord!" said Leclerc plainly put out by his lover's passion.

"Young woman, cease this show and let us get on with our job."

"I'll tell you what job we have my sisters," she said, paying no mind to Jean-Jacques's words, "it is what each woman can do—what no other citizen of France can."

Nanette screamed, "I am Marat's wife!"

And Pauline screamed, "I will give him sons. Let me touch the wound."

Celeste shook her head in disbelief and mumbled, "My heart is in the coffin there with Caesar, and I must pause till it come back to me."

Leclerc heard her and said, "What?"

"English playwright. Before your time."

Pauline placed her finger in Jean-Paul Marat's chest wound and showed the blood on her finger to Claire and then sobbed. "My God, they have butchered him."

Then Nanette did the same and began crying so much that she fell to the cobblestones and had to be pulled away from the corpse. Jean-Jacques called for assistance, and soon he had enough men to pull the women from the dead man's body. He placed the linen over the poor man's lifeless frame and told his men to take the body to an address that he whispered to them. Then he turned back to Claire. "Go home, Claire."

"Home? Yes. But, only to make arrangements for the funeral of our husband and the father of our future children."

Jean-Jacques rolled his eyes upward to heaven and motioned for the men to move the body. Then he looked at the murderess. "Take her to prison. This shouldn't take long."

Claire ripped open her blouse in an action obviously planned to depict her grief in a sort of Biblical manner, but all it did was show every man there how beautiful her breasts were. Then she fell to the ground beside her 'sisters' and wept.

"If I didn't know better, I'd swear I just saw the Easter

morning performance of *At the tomb!*"

"What are you going on about?" said Leclerc finally turning his head so that he could see her.

Celeste judged that he was not in the mood for humor.

"Nothing. Don't mind me. We'd better get her home before she begins act two."

Leclerc gathered Claire's limp figure into his arms and carried her to a less populated street.

"Put me down," she said, dropping the act so suddenly it left both her lover and her cousin speechless.

She stared at Celeste. "Why didn't you come over? I can't think of a better symbol for my rhetoric than your swollen belly."

Celeste looked at Leclerc. "Take her home," he said to Celeste. "I have a news story that needs written.

Celeste could tell he was furious and disgusted with Claire's impromptu performance.

Nanette and Pauline found them as they were turning the corner for home.

"What did you think?" Claire asked Pauline.

"Wonderful! I have some ideas for his funeral."

"I think we need to approach the Committee and ask whether we could put some sort of monument to Marat in the Place de Revolution."

"Great idea. We'll tell everyone to dress in mourning for—say two months at least—and we'll need to make some floral wreaths for his body."

"Wait a minute," interrupted Claire, "I have a tremendous notion, but we'll have to return to his apartment."

Pauline was practically grinning with a heightened sense of anticipation at Claire's plans. They were as excited as three high school girls who had just decided on the perfect theme for this year's junior prom. "You're so creative. What?"

"Let's get the bathtub, his pen, anything that indicates his final moments."

"What will we do with those?" asked Nanette.

"I'm not sure, but give me some time, and I'll come up with something."

"Will Leclerc put something in the paper about the murder?" asked Pauline.

"Oh, I'm sure of it. I hope he mentions my speech too."

"Pure inspiration, Claire. You were very dramatic. It brought tears to the eyes of every woman in that crowd."

"Celeste, do you want to come with us? We're going back for the tub."

"No thanks. I'm not feeling well all of a sudden. I want to go home."

As she walked away from the women who were busily making plans to immortalize Jean-Paul Marat, Celeste felt a sudden rush of panic.

"I want to go home all right. My home. My clothes. My lover. My bed." She looked at the round belly protruding from her blue and white striped, peasant skirt. "My body."

Chapter Nineteen

Celeste found it impossible to stay out of the 'funeral festivities'. As Claire's cousin, she was expected to be present at all club activities involving the funeral of Jean-Paul Marat. She used these times to search for Jean-Jacques who she suspected might be in the crowd, but she caught only quick glimpses of him, and he never seemed to notice her. It was very frustrating. She was becoming more frightened as the baby grew inside her. She wanted to act but couldn't without enlisting the aid of one of the three men in her life: Phillipe—the baby's father, Leclerc—who said that he would take her to Phillipe, and Jean-Jacques—who had promised that he would help her get out of France. The modern woman wanted to pack her oil paints and head for the nearest train, plane, or taxi; but without a man to help her, she was stalled in any attempt she might have to rescue Celeste Lacombe. She knew how much Jean-Jacques despised Claire and hoped that his revulsion of her cousin was the reason for his inattentiveness. Any other reason terrified her, because, in her own mind, he was Jim, and if he abandoned her it might mean that Jim Cooper could leave her too.

"It's time to go to the wake, mon petite cher," said Claire interrupting Celeste's ink marks on a page of poetry. "Are you coming, Leclerc?" she asked.

"Do I have a choice?" he answered.

"Marat must live again. The women of France shall make him immortal. I have written an ode that I will deliver before the crowd. I am shocked that you are not more sentimental on the subject."

"Yes, yes, poor man. Get your shawl, Celeste. Don't go without it."

Celeste placed the black shawl of mourning over her head and let it drape over her shoulders.

They walked to the Place de Revolution where Marat lay in state on a wide, heavy pedestal. There were steps leading to his now gloriously clothed and groomed corpse. The man looked asleep—free from any concern for the chaos his words would cause. It was July 16, 1793.

Nanette and several women Celeste did not know carried the infamous tub and placed it under the pedestal. Then Nanette touched the wound, and blood poured from his body as if he'd just died. Celeste was amazed at the sight of the fresh blood that trickled into the tub. Then one by one, each woman took the blood from the tub onto a finger and marked her blouse, just above her heart, with a stain. After doing this, the woman placed a floral wreath on the man's body.

Claire read her ode—that seemed hastily written but full of emotion and, all in all, not amateurish in the least—and then offered another dramatic display of her astonishing rhetoric. She began with, "There is oppression against the social body when a single one of its members is oppressed. In this case, we are all oppressed; the friend of the people is no more."

She wept and fell by the side of the tub. Her head lifted proudly, she continued mentioning all Jean-Paul's deeds: how he had been victimized by the Royalist; how he had to suffer in hiding; how he came home when he was needed; and how treacherous Charlotte Corday had been. She finished with, "May the blood of Marat become a seed for intrepid Republicans, and may the women of France people the soil of Liberty with as many Marats as we can." A carefully staged and executed performance enacted to perfection by the Queen of the Republic.

Leclerc observed everything. Celeste watched as the historical event skimmed across her vision, but she kept looking for Jean-Jacques. Eventually she was rewarded. He was standing near a building just behind the pedestal making sure no one bothered the corpse and listening to everything Claire said.

Leclerc mused, "The body may decompose, but it shall come back to life through the careful ministrations of the women of France." He smirked as Claire touched the wound and placed blood on her blouse and then on her peasant skirt to symbolize his life becoming the 'semen' of a new race, a new order, a new world, and a new land of free citizens.

"Nicely put," Celeste said in reference to his comment. "Could you stay here until I speak with someone? Don't leave without me," she said to Leclerc.

Leclerc looked around to see who might be there. Celeste pointed to Jean-Jacques. "Yes, of course, shy one. I'll keep one eye on her and one on you."

She hurried over to Jean-Jacques. At first, it seemed as if he hadn't noticed her, and then he smiled. "What are you doing here? Oh, yes, of course, Claire."

Her next words were much harsher than she wanted them to be. "Where have you been? I've been waiting for you to come back to the house." Celeste silently cursed herself for sounding like a shrewish wife.

"Oh, I've been very busy investigating murders, taking

Charlotte to court, making sure these crazy women don't do something horrid to the poor man's corpse. And, of course, there's the list."

"List? What list?"

"The Committee has begun a list of those aristocrats they wish to...imprison."

"You mean execute."

"I think that's where it's going. By the way, you're starting to show." He pointed to her stomach.

"Yes, I know, but have you done nothing to find a way for us to get out of Paris...out of France?"

He pretended to be watching the crowd as he spoke with her. "Now, now don't panic. I've thought about you everyday...when I had a chance that is. And I've made some connections. Things look very good. But, when I say it's time; you have to be ready to leave. Decide it in your head now, Celeste." He looked directly at her and watched her reaction to his words. "I won't have time to wait for you. This is very tricky business."

"What can I take?"

"Nothing. We'll buy what we need when we get to Boston."

"I have one picture I must take with me and some warm clothes."

"And any money you may have, of course."

"My art supplies?" she said sadly.

"Will have to stay behind. And there can be no farewells to Claire or her lover. No one must know what we are doing. Be ready. Now go, it won't impress your cousin's friends to see you conversing with a police spy."

She started to hurry away and then stopped and turned to him. "Jean-Jacques?"

He stared at her in bewilderment. Why would she need anything more than his brief comments, his expression seemed to say? "Yes?"

"You risk your life for a woman who is carrying the child of a man you hate?"

His smile was soft and reassuring, as though he thought she would ask him something difficult. "Yes."

"Why?"

His smile widened making a long, thin line that dimpled his right cheek and brightened his handsome face now tanned by the July sun. "Simple. I love you. I don't want to live without you."

Celeste smiled, and her eyes twinkled with a sparkling blue light that was an answer to the man whose life and career were on the line because of his plan to save her. She ran back to Leclerc. Her face was flushed, but no one noticed.

"I think Claire is ready for the parade. Are you going to walk with her?" asked Leclerc.

"I'll have to listen to it for days if I don't."

Claire ordered the bathtub lifted onto the shoulders of four women. Pauline took Jean-Paul's shirt—which had rested on the side of the tub and was completely saturated with dried blood—from a sack. She held it above her head. The sobbing women cheered. Then Claire walked down the steps and began the march through the streets of Paris. The other women followed her moaning, "Marat is not dead! Marat is not dead!"

Leclerc turned to Celeste. "You can't walk far in your condition, so I'll meet you back home in about an hour."

"If I can walk that long."

Leclerc smiled at her and placed his hand on her head. "You are the future of France, shy one."

The comment caught her off guard. "Leclerc, I need your help, and for some reason, I trust you more than Claire right now."

"She's an actress caught up in high melodrama."

"You promised to take me to Bordeaux. Perhaps it's the growth of the baby, I don't know, but suddenly I have a need to settle the score with Phillipe once and for all."

"I understand. Yes, I did promise, but Claire and her infatuation with Marat..."

"Lives in the fantasy world of theater. She has made his death into her play. But, you and I are rooted in reality, and my needs are not fictional. I still want to go—need to go, desperately."

He raised his eyebrows. "I understand. Claire won't tear herself away from this spectacle."

"Can *you* take me?"

"The two of us?"

"Will you?"

He stared at Claire before he answered. "Yes, of course. But, I don't think she'll like it much." He frowned. "How about the first week of August? Will that be soon enough?"

She thought of Jean-Jacques's promise and hoped that the trip would be concluded before he found a ship to America. He had told her to be ready. What if he came for her, and she wasn't there? Even a man in love would be insulted if she chose to go to Bordeaux and hunt for the true father of the baby he had promised to adopt as his own.

"As soon as you can find a way to take me. I'll be in your debt. I trust you."

He motioned that the march with the tub was beginning, and that she should go. She waved to him as she began walking with Nanette, Pauline, and Claire. Her gaze rested on the blood on Claire's skirt and was suddenly sick to her stomach. She stopped on the side of the street and vomited. One of the women stood beside her to see whether she could help, but Claire continued, oblivious to her own cousin's wretchedness.

"You shouldn't be walking with us if you're ill," said the woman.

When Celeste looked up, she noticed that a guillotine was being erected in the middle of the plaza.

"Oh," said the woman who had noticed her glance. "It's for Charlotte. The whore will die tomorrow, and we will be here at noon to witness it. You'll be there, of course. With your cockade on. I can't wait to see her bleed as he did."

"They plan to guillotine her? So soon? Without a trial?"

"She's had a trial. Everyone knows she's guilty. Why wait? It's just the beginning. Now that we have a list, watch the heads fall. The guillotine is such a wonderful invention, n'est ce pas? Though some feel that it is too swift a death for the vermin that infest our land. It will still be worth watching, don't you think?"

"Charlotte's been tried by a jury of her peers?"

mumbled Celeste incoherently.

"What?"

"Never mind. America seems so far away."

"America?"

"Please go on. Leave me. I'm going home."

The woman followed the crowd and left Celeste to ease her stomach while she watched the men erect the guillotine. *"Good God, get me out of here!"*

She realized one horrible truth about time travel: it is not the same as *reading* about the past in a history book, and it is *never* edited to cushion the traveler from the truth. It is true, and the only way a person can understand life in the past, is to live there.

Chapter Twenty

Charlotte Corday was brought to the plaza in a horse drawn cart. She was wearing the same dress she had worn when arrested. Her hair had been cut, and a white dust cap was on her head. Her hands were tied behind her. There were thousands of people in the streets ready to savor every one of her last minutes on earth, and they spat on her if they were close enough, swore at her, and called her cruel names. Her face was red from crying, and her eyes were wide with fear. You could see that she wanted to be brave for the cause; she had acted out of patriotic passion; and, now, the full revelation of what she had done was as biting as the first frost on the warm autumn ground.

She had expressive, pretty eyes that were set in a beautiful, pale face. Her cheekbones were high but softened so that a person looked at her long eyebrows and wide eyes first. Her lower lip protruded from the thin upper lip making her mouth appear weak. Her face was long and thin. There were two unattractive features, however, a decidedly tiny, pointy chin, and a long nose with a wide bridge and a narrow tip that looked as though it were in direct line with the chin. The woman's eyes were so spectacular that once a man had gazed upon her curvaceous figure and her pale blue eyes that seemed more like colored crystal, he would have forgiven her the sharpness of the chin and nose. Celeste could not help but wonder what had driven this woman to such a self-destructive act.

Charlotte's hands trembled, and her footsteps faltered as the guards took her from the cart. One of the henchmen looked angry and upset and refused to look at her. The executioner didn't seem particularly happy about killing a woman, but it was evident from the way he moved around the guillotine that he knew how to work the new instrument of death. Another man called out to the crowd the name of the crime for which Charlotte Corday was charged. It was noon, July 17, 1793, only one day after the funeral of the man she had allegedly killed.

They picked up her body, and laid her, face down, on a wooden table that would slide under the blade. Then they took leather straps and fastened them so that her legs, stomach, and chest would be flat and secure against the board, and that the dress and its petticoats would not hamper the execution. There were dogs in the crowd who barked, yapped wildly, and rushed to the platform circling underneath the wooden planks of the guillotine as if they had been called to dinner. When her body was resting in its correct position, the man motioned to the executioner, the wooden table shot into its spot under the blade, and the cold, sharp, glistening edge of the blade came down immediately and severed Charlotte's head from her shoulders. The blood from the wound gushed everywhere, pouring down the frame of the wooden guillotine. The dogs whined and whimpered joyfully and began lapping at the pools of blood that flowed from her dismembered corpse through the wooden planks. No one stopped them.

The executioner raised the head of the condemned woman for all to see, and the citizens of France cheered as if their team had just scored the winning point in the game.

Celeste watched with a mixture of fascination and horror. The guards undid the straps holding the dead body to the wooden table and hurled it into the crowd who cut and tore it to shreds with their fingers and daggers as they chanted, "The murderess is dead, but Marat will never die!"

Celeste stared at the Charlotte's severed head. Suddenly, the dead woman's eyelids opened slowly, and her expression showed pain and bewilderment as if she had heard her name called.

"Her eyes opened!" Celeste told Leclerc anxiously. "Did you see? Her eyes opened. She still senses what's happening."

"Don't be ridiculous. That's impossible."

"But I saw it!" She shook his arm and pointed for him to look before it was too late.

Leclerc stared at Charlotte's head.

"See! Her eyes were closed when they first held her head up, now they are slightly open."

Leclerc stared for a moment and said, "You're right. Something to write about in my paper, I think. The murderess suffers even after death."

"No, you don't understand, that's not what I meant! Don't you see the cruelty of this execution?"

"Oh, no, I think it's a marvelous invention and probably less cruel than beheading someone with an axe. The only thing that disturbs me is that it is *so* quick that the crowd losses some of the drama. Pity. There's more excitement when the victim's face can be seen; his or her shirt and hair pulled away from the shoulders; their head bare for all to see; the priest giving the last rites; and that wonderful moment when they must kneel before justice and bow their head before the crowd who has accused them. Something so humbling there. The executioner in his grim black cloak; his identity hidden behind his hood instead of like this. And then there's always the hope that things won't go right away. That the blade isn't sharp enough to be fatal on the first strike. They say the guillotine is kinder, but you may have a point."

Celeste dropped her hold on his arm. She felt dizzy and nauseous—as if she might just topple over into the street from the sheer reality of what she had just witnessed.

"You can't mean that! Say you don't mean that. That's not what I meant."

"Of course I do. Why are we here? To see justice done. Why should there be mercy? She killed a man, Celeste! I'm sure that the loss of entertainment with this new form of execution will be criticized in all the national papers. I need to get to my office immediately. Can you find your way home? Claire is too close to the platform, probably trying to get a souvenir of the day, so I doubt she can take you home."

Her hands were shaking; her legs felt as though they might break beneath her. "I'll...I'll find my way home some how."

Leclerc was gone in an instant, and she immediately regretted her remark because the crowd started to push her in their zeal to get to the corpse.

An arm fastened around her waist. "Come this way," said Jean-Jacques.

Celeste followed as he led the way through the crowd. He moved her swiftly to a place of safety—what appeared to be his home. He opened the door to his modest flat, and shut it behind him quickly. His face looked pale. His voice was heavy with emotion.

"That was awful. I had no idea. Good Lord, what have we become? I've got to get you out of here. We both have to get out of here." He put his hands over his face and covered his eyes.

"I thought you helped condemn her."

"I simply told what needed to be told when she went before the Revolutionary Tribunal. I knew they would find her guilty, but, I've never seen a woman executed before in my life. The way the crowd reacted. I'll never forget it. I don't want to live here anymore."

He pulled Celeste into his arms. "Stay here for a while. Until things have calmed down out there."

"Yes."

"Can I make you something to drink?"

"Yes, I think tea would be fine." She wanted a stiff whiskey, but couldn't very well say that.

"Sit. Sit. I'll make you something. Make yourself comfortable."

He went about his apartment playing the role of host.

"Have you found a way for us to leave?"

"I'm working on it? Have you seen or heard from Phillipe lately?"

"No. Why?"

"Just wondering."

"Just worrying?"

"Well, a man may have his fears, n'est ce pas? There's a ship called the *Diana* that sails in early September. I'll see what I can do to get us passage. It will be a crude trip; she's not a passenger vessel."

"I don't care."

"Neither do I."

He swept her from her seat and held her close to his body. "I'll find work in America, or we'll own a farm, not that I know anything about farming. We'll do what we have to to build a family. I want a family."

Celeste rested her head on his chest and listened to his heartbeat. It felt good to be in his strong arms, and when she closed her eyes it was just like being home—peaceful. "You have no idea how desperately I want to go to America with you."

"Do you mean that?"

She pulled her head back so that she could see his face. It was so pathetically hopeful she grinned. "Yes, Jean-Jacques." And then, she pressed her lips against his, giving him a long, passionate kiss and some much needed reassurance.

"I want you."

"I want you too."

"Can we? Do you think it's all right to...?" His hand moved up her spine and flitted gently across her neck.

She kissed him again. "Probably not." She allowed his hand to touch her breast.

"Good Lord, you are so beautiful. I will be good to you. I love you so much."

She took her hand and touched his cheek. "All in good time. I have some business to settle with Monsieur de Brouquens first."

"What?" He pulled away from her. "What do you need to 'settle' with him?"

"It's something that has passed from one year to another

and will haunt me forever. If I don't take care of it now, it will ruin our relationship."

"You'll see him again?" He was suddenly cool to her.

"If that's what I have to do to finish our business, I will."

"I see."

The tea water was hot, and he poured her some of the mixture and sprinkled some sugar into it.

"What if I told you that I don't want you near him? What would you say?"

"I would say that I wouldn't go near him. Is that what you want?"

"Do what you have to do, Celeste, but when the *Diana* sails, I will be on the ship whether you are by my side or not. Is that clear?"

"Yes."

"I have to leave France soon."

"I understand."

"And I want you to be on board with me as my wife. I want that done promptly. If you say you love me, why would you want to go near de Brouquens? I will not force you to never speak with him again until you are my wife. If you feel you must end it in some manner with this aristocratic bastard, I will not stop you."

"I will be ready to sail with you, I promise."

"And then you and I and the baby can make a new start in this modern land of democracy."

"We'll be together there, I swear."

They spent an hour or so together sipping tea and

speaking of the life they would share together. Then he walked her home.

Claire was awaiting her arrival, and she was furious.

"Where have you been? I've been searching all over Paris for you."

"I spent the afternoon with Jean-Jacques."

"Why?"

"Oh, Claire, will you just leave me alone? I weary of your attitude."

"I risked my life to bring you back something you can give your child for its heritage. I retrieved her cap. Charlotte's. I thought you might want to give it to your son or daughter for posterity. Some day it might mean a great deal."

"I don't want it," said Celeste, wearying of her cousin's zeal.

"Don't be silly."

Celeste became angry. "*I don't want it*, and I don't believe for one minute that you saved it for *me*. You are just saying that to make me part of your *hideous* club, and I don't want to be. I am tired of trekking all over the city just so that everyone can see the cockade I wear on my breast, so that they'll think that your cousin is as political as you are. I'm pregnant, Claire, in case you haven't noticed, and I will *not* be a part of your little play at being a political Amazon anymore."

Claire paused before saying, "Play? Do you think this is some sort of character I'm playing? That I am not passionate for the cause?"

"I think the only one you are passionate about is yourself. It's all a play to you, and you've given yourself the lead role and demanded center stage. Marat had it first, and you think that you should be the one in the limelight now that he's gone. A bizarre inheritance. Even Leclerc bores of you."

She wasn't sure what had made her say these cruel words to her cousin, but they poured from her like the blood of Charlotte Corday and Marat.

Claire said, "How can you be so cruel to me? I have supported you all along."

"In what manner? You are a merchant's daughter. The only reason you are so zealous for the cause is to save your own neck. If they think you are in love with Liberty, you cannot be under suspicion. Isn't that right?"

"No. Leclerc..."

Celeste, fueled by her mood, couldn't stop her words. She wondered if they came from the other woman whose body she shared.

"And he is the same as you. An editor of his own paper can save his own neck by directing others to the spot where the rich live. 'I'm not the one you want; you want him or her. See how loyal I am to the cause.' In the end it will be the same for you as it is for the aristocrats. Hypocrites! Even Pauline. You're all a bunch of hypocrites."

"My word, such rhetoric from the little shy one," said Leclerc who had been napping upstairs and had heard all that the two had said.

"Oh...I'm sorry. I didn't know that you were there," said Celeste.

"And so you would have said these things behind my back rather than to my face? No, no, shy one, I think you have spoken from your heart for once. Don't hold back. Say what you wish."

"Don't you both see what's going on? People are dying. The rebels are naming names so that they are not the ones to die. You all stand around and applaud and tear, like dogs in the streets, at the remains of your victims. Marat, Corday, they are victims of your dementia."

"Cousin."

"Yes, cousin, and how do you treat your cousin who is about to give birth to an aristocrat's bastard? Do you help me, no, you force me to be the center of your horrid Theatre´ de la Mort. I will not play a role in your drama nor will I cheer when you do stupid things like wiping his blood on your skirt and telling everyone that you will bear a dead man's child. Leave me out of this. I'm trying the best I know to survive." Celeste broke into tears.

Leclerc said, "Claire meant that business about Marat's children in a purely symbolic way."

"I don't care how she meant it," Celeste said, interrupting him. Her face was red with the fire of her rage, and her voice was hoarse with screaming. The whole neighborhood must have heard her.

"Does this mean that you won't come with me to the Committee meeting and beg the court to pay for a memorial, an obelisk, erected in the Place de Revolution for the man whose pen helped us to be free from tyranny?"

"Ah!" Celeste screamed and then rested her body against the side of a large table. "You never listen to me, do you?"

Leclerc said, "I think perhaps you and I should leave Celeste alone for a while. The pregnancy has..."

Celeste pointed her finger at him in a sharp, daggerlike manner. "*Oh, no you don't!* You won't place the blame for my speaking the truth on my feminine state. It's about time I spoke up for how I feel; it has nothing to do with motherhood."

Claire stared at her cousin. "What's wrong with you? I'll forgive this outburst because I love you, Celeste. I'll stay at Leclerc's if you want me to until you ask me back. I won't stay here with you feeling this way about the cause and our club."

Leclerc added, "Pauline wanted to go over the plans to speak again on excluding nobles from obtaining any gainful employment or serving in the army. Her thrust is on national security now while Claire's interests have shifted to the obelisk; but then you wish to be left out of all that, correct?"

She collapsed into a chair. "All of it."

Leclerc took his hat from a peg on the wall by the door. "I'll return tomorrow to speak with you on the other matter. I can tell you are frustrated beyond reason and may have good cause."

When they left, and the fury was out of her system; Celeste gave vent to her tears. "I'm sorry," she said to an empty house. "Come back. Don't leave me."

She went to the portrait of Phillipe and stared at it for a while then shook her head. "You're not here for me." Then she found the picture of Jim/Jean she had kept under the bed. The smile on Jim's face warmed her heart.

"Hey, you," she said, wiping away her tears with the back of her hand, "where are you? I don't want to be here anymore. Can you check the Internet for a ticket home? I miss you, Jim. And I still have so much more time here. I wonder if you time travelers have any idea how long three months can be when you have to stand in line for your food, piddle in a pot, cook on a primitive piece of equipment, carry someone else's baby in your belly, and watch people applaud butchery? I bet summer is wonderful in Richfield Springs. I could paint a zillion pictures there right now. We could be spending the weekends watching the birds and rabbits flit around the trees next to the cabin. We could swim in the lake. Please be there when I get back."

She fell onto the bed and cried herself to sleep. During the night, she dreamed of the conversation she had had with the woman at the prison before she'd traveled to 1793. The woman who had been accused of murdering her husband.

She woke suddenly and sat up in bed. "Oh, my God, Charlotte! I thought I'd seen those eyes before. She didn't do it, did she? She didn't kill Marat. That helpless expression on her face. All the facts against her. She's a scapegoat for someone else and died for the cause. And that woman in the 2000 jail cell is Charlotte. Reincarnated. But, how do I call the office to tell Brenda I have to take that case. Will it be too late when I return in September?"

She collapsed on her pillow. "They were *wrong*! History was wrong! That Charles Barbaroux killed Marat. He must have been there just before she came into the room. That's why they found a list of names in Marat's hand. The woman was so astonished; she said nothing and let them take her away take the rap. She was far too refined and cultured to stab a man to death like that. Even Claire couldn't do it, and she's more the type than Charlotte Corday. Her eyes. No way. She's too frail to plunge a knife into a man's heart so fiercely and thoroughly that he would have died instantly with just one thrust. The wound. Claire walked up and touched the wound. I saw it with my own eyes. There was only one slash mark. Charlotte's tiny hand trained to pour chocolate from a teapot would not have had the physical strength to kill a man with one thrust of a dagger. Not to mention the emotional strength to go from her aunt's warm and cozy home in Caen to murdering a man in his own apartment while he lay naked in his bathtub. Give me a break! Marat was dead before she ever walked into the room. Barbaroux probably hid somewhere close to Marat's tub and, pretending to be Marat, called to Marat's man telling him to let her in. Marat's back was turned to the door so that the servant wouldn't have noticed anyone else in that room. The back of the tub would have temporarily supported Jean-Paul's dead body. No doubt, Barbaroux used a towel to muffle Marat's cry for help, and then tied it around the dead man's head to make it look like a bathing cap. Charlotte would have noticed the wound when she went around to the other side of the tub to see Marat's face and make her petition to him. The servant would have been suspicious of her if she had looked harmful in the least. Unless he was in on the plot. Charlotte saw Marat was murdered, picked up the knife to examine it; but, by that time, Charles would have summoned the authorities. He *used* her loyalty. Bastard. And look how quick to judge they were. Anymore time and someone like Jean-Jacques would have figured it out. But, it's too late now; she's dead. Charlotte must have known she was set up. What could she say? Maybe she was in love with Charles. She goes down in history as a murderess. It's all happening again in New York City on a smaller scale, of course. My God! I have a chance to save her when I return home.

"I have to take her case, don't I? I am the only one who can. Jim's 'someone' thinks I'm capable of getting her off. All I have to do is look for clues that would support a theory that another person was in that bathroom before her. There is a 'someone' who pulls the strings in the time travel mechanism, isn't there? Someone knitting people's lives together. Saving them from a less fulfilling destiny. And I have to save Celeste Lacombe and her baby, as well as myself, or I'll never be able to help that woman, and she'll get the death penalty. I guess by coming back to 1793 and viewing what I must have witnessed in my other life as Celeste Lacombe was the time tunnels way of showing me what I needed to do in my 2000 life. Someone's future, as well as my own, is at stake. Lord, it's a heavy task you're asking me to undertake, but you must think I can handle it. All I have to do is make it home."

Chapter Twenty-One

Claire and Leclerc left Celeste alone for one full day, returning in the evening to see whether her mood had lightened. They found her in good humor and finishing her work for Tallon who had promised to come for it the next day. Claire tiptoed around her cousin keeping her comments on a domestic level. Leclerc acted as if nothing had happened and went to buy food for them. and that enabled the two women to make amends.

"I apologize, Celeste," Claire said with tears rimming her eyes. "I'm all that you said I am—probably more. I am completely selfish and have been since our childhood. Forgive me, cousin, for my passion and stupidity. Perhaps I am just frightened. As frightened as you."

Celeste hugged the woman. "It's a fearful time, Claire. I accept your apology. And by the way, that cap you worked so hard to get for me?"

Claire's eye brightened. "Charlotte's cap?"

"I'd like it now if you have it. I...think it might give me some inspiration, and you're right about its historical importance." Celeste was thinking of one antique dealer in Milford, New York, who would positively salivate when he saw it.

"Do you meant it?" she said, wiping her eyes with the sleeve of her blouse.

"I want the bonnet. Thank you. It was a horrible sight to see, Claire, even you must admit that."

"I think I am just beginning to understand it. I thought it

was all a political performance, and I confess that I did get into the movement for all the right ideals; however, I've never been a good one for reality and well you know it. Always wanting to play childish stories—games—trying so hard to be what I was not. I couldn't stand by and watch the dying women beg in the streets, Celeste. I had to get involved. And then, I met Leclerc, and you know what happened after that. The obelisk will be my next task as secretary for the club—a very peaceful chore, you must admit. Then the whole group of women have decided to concentrate all our activities on strengthening the national security. It's an important matter and long overdo. One small group can't do all that's necessary."

"I know, but you try."

"Yes, we try. I realized after you yelled at me, what this all must mean to you. How can you survive without Phillipe? And he dare not come to Paris. He should leave France immediately. With you."

"I know. Leclerc is taking me to Bordeaux soon, but you don't have to come with us if you have more important things to do."

"Nothing is more important to me right now than this small family I have with you and Leclerc. Pauline and I were just saying how we would refuse help from a pregnant woman, or a mother of small children. It isn't their place to be fighting for freedom."

"Why not?"

"Because they have a job. They are raising the future of France, and that is a difficult task. Simply finding food for their children, or work to get money to sustain that family, is tough enough. I don't want you to come to anymore meetings. It's not good for you."

Celeste looked into Claire's eyes. "You'll come with us, then? To Bordeaux?"

"I'll be right by your side the whole time and kick Phillipe in the shins if he doesn't swear a lifetime of loving you." She giggled.

Celeste started to laugh. It occurred to her that she hadn't laughed for weeks. It lifted her spirits just to giggle like a schoolgirl. "Oh that should scare him."

They both laughed so hard; Claire fell to the ground weeping. "Look at us silly girls. Just like the old days when we used to toss those rag dolls of ours at each other until we laughed ourselves silly and mother had to pull us apart. Remember?"

Celeste Montclaire froze. Her mood shifted. Suddenly, she could not stop the tears. "Yes," she lied, "I remember those days."

Claire hugged her cousin. "You're all I have now. Besides Leclerc. I make him unhappy and happy by turns."

"Isn't that the way it's meant to be with men and women?"

Claire shrugged like a nine-year-old girl who had just decided that her cousin could eat the distasteful purple jellybeans so that she could have all the rest. "I suppose. I still feel that he wants something more from me. Something that I can't give him."

"Does he talk about it?"

"We don't talk much about love we just do it." Claire's head rocked back onto the top of her shoulders; then she stretched her neck and rolled her eyes to the ceiling. "We mostly share revolutionary ideas and write speeches." She righted herself and looked at her cousin. "We aren't a very romantic couple."

"Are you going to get married?"

"I don't think that's a good idea for an actress. To get married might upset my career plans."

"You don't love him?"

"I'm not sure."

"Does he love you?"

"I think so. He's," she paused, examined her cuticles, then looked at Celeste, raised her eyebrows, wiggled her head mischievously, shrugged her shoulders, and said, "he makes love wonderfully. I've never had such a man. And you know I know what I'm talking about."

Celeste lied again, "Yes, I know, you naughty girl."

Claire moved to a small chair and rested her body in it, let her feet dangle low to the floor so that her back was far away from the chair, then placed her hand behind her head and rested.

"Why are we women so...?"

"What do you mean?"

"You're in love with a shadow man and a mystery man. One loves you without asking anything from you, and the other takes all you have but doesn't seem to love you."

"They both give what they can, Claire. What more can I ask of them? Claire?"

"Yes?"

"If for any reason I should leave suddenly, please don't be offended. I know I shouldn't talk like this, but if you had to run for your life, *I'd* understand, and if Phillipe and I..." she was cautious to place blame for a sudden disappearance on Phillipe rather than Jean-Jacques who had warned her not to say anything to Leclerc or Claire. She felt guilty all of a sudden for making plans on her own and not taking into consideration what the other Celeste might be feeling or how much she might miss her cousin. She knew so little of the women's relationship. Did Celeste love her cousin or loathe her? Depend on her or wish she'd butt out? And she would never know because the other Celeste rarely made her presence known—the shy one, indeed. But, the baby inside her body was all too lively, and she, or he, was making its existence obvious.

"I'm going to be a mother, and I'm not sure I'm fit for the job."

Claire came to her and touched Celeste's forehead lovingly. "Silly. You're the perfect one to be a mother. You always said you wanted a real family all your own."

Claire's words were encouraging. Jean-Jacques wanted a family. Wanted Celeste to be his wife. Celeste Lacombe must have wanted that too, deep down in her heart. She had to be on the right path.

"Anyway," said Claire, interrupting Celeste's thoughts, "I will cry if you go away, but I won't interfere. I always knew that some day you and I would end up on different roads. It's inevitable. We're not little girls anymore."

As an afterthought she said, "I have something for you." Claire raced up to her bed, made some noises, and then returned with something behind her back. "A gift for the baby." She produced a beat-up, old rag doll. "For *you* and the baby."

Celeste stared in bewilderment at the 1790 doll. "You still have it?"

"You must remember Geraldine." Claire shook the doll's yarn curls and pinched its tiny nose. "Have you forgotten how you cried so when I said that I threw her in the river? I was so bad to you."

"Ah...of course...I remember Geraldine; I thought she was gone forever."

"I kept her all these years because I was too guilty and afraid of how you'd feel about me if you knew that I had treated you so unjustly."

Celeste took the doll in her arms and hugged it as the other woman would have done. "Dear Geraldine. How I've missed you."

"So you're not angry?"

"I am furious and would beat you about the ears with her except the battle would tear her even more. Thank you for not hurting her and for returning her to me."

Another antique, she thought, but one Jim Cooper wasn't going to get.

The day was to prove pivotal in another way. Tallon came to retrieve the rest of the sketches for the poetry book. His face was lined with sorrow as he handed a letter to Celeste. "I have not read it, Mademoiselle, but from the one sent to me, I fear it is bad news.

Celeste opened the letter slowly, afraid to read Phillipe's words, yet anxious to discover any truth that might help her understand the past life of the man who had run away from her. The letter read:

Mon Coeur,

The news I have to tell you is as a dagger in my heart. I wish the pen would break, and the ink in this well dry up so that I would not have the ability to tell you what needs be told. My family has been arrested. My father's lands seized. My mother may never read her own book, and I may never see our son. Worse, of course, is the fact that I may never see your fair face again, Celeste. Know this, I have never loved any woman save you. If, by some act of God, my family escapes, I will return to you.

You warned me to leave France, and I am now to be the victim of my own stupidity. I will never be given another opportunity to write to you as I have been allowed to see Tallon only, which enabled me to slip this note to you by his hands. I am sure it will be the last time they'll permit this.

Farewell, mon coeur, my only love. Get out of France but keep in touch with Tallon. Save our child who may very well be the last in the family line of de Brouquens. Go and don't look back. When you are finally safe, remember me.

Je t'adore,
Phillipe de Brouquens

Celeste had finally received her 'Dear Jane' letter. Just like that—goodbye. She looked at Tallon.

"I'm sorry, Mademoiselle, but it doesn't look good for him. I finished his mother's book. I did not read his letter to

222

you, but, since you may be the only one close to the family who might survive; know that I have the manuscript, and that it is yours if you wish it. I know it's dreadful poetry, but the woman may never live to see the final copy."

Celeste thought of Jim. "I want it."

"Bien," he said handing it to her. She gazed at the artwork she and her past life persona had created for the text.

"How did you know to go to Bordeaux?"

"Pure chance. I thought to visit a relative and stop by Monsieur de Brouquens's estate to show him the final draft and the art work you had done for it. I was shocked to see the house in disarray. Despite what you have heard to the contrary, they have moved a wooden cart with a guillotine into the city. I have heard that it has passed through several towns already, but has found a permanent spot in Bordeaux. Since Phillipe's father is a known Royalist, his family was taken first. Nothing's been done yet, but I fear it is just a matter of time."

"I must go to him."

"I wouldn't if I were you, Mademoiselle." His face showed true terror at the thought. "Not a wise move on your part. Do you need money?"

She was thinking so fast that she didn't immediately respond to his offer.

"What a silly question, of course, you do. Here." He handed her a small purse. "Get out of France. You have his future inside you."

She thought of Jean-Jacques's plan to leave France. The *Diana* wouldn't sail for several weeks. There was time to help Phillipe and still leave with Jean-Jacques. She had to find

Leclerc. It was a risky endeavor, but she knew she couldn't sleep at night if she didn't try to help him. Claire owed her one, Leclerc owed Claire, and she owed Jean-Jacques a happy wife and a new life. She could do this. Her mind was made up. Her heart belonged to Jean-Jacques Coupier, but, for Celeste Lacombe's sake, she had to rescue Phillipe de Brouquens. The existence of the tiny baby in the woman's womb made it mandatory.

Chapter Twenty-Two

Leclerc agreed to the adventure; it appealed to his romantic nature. Even Claire expressed excitement at being the heroine in Celeste's play. They told no one where they were going and packed lightly. She did not mention their plans to visit Bordeaux to Tallon for security reasons. Claire made up an excuse for not continuing with her speeches, asking Pauline to take her place. Leclerc published a large edition and locked the door to his office.

"This is really rather embarrassing actually," said Claire. "Here I am a known rebel, and I'm packing off to save the life of a loathed aristocrat." She was smiling at the prospect, however, for she was helping her cousin and that was what mattered now.

Leclerc and Claire went to a cafe to meet with friends the evening that Jean-Jacques whisked into the apartment. He tossed his cloak to the chair as if he had just come home from the office and placed his hat on a peg by the door.

The instant he arrived, Celeste felt ill at ease. How could she keep him from the truth? How would he react to the news?

"Wonderful news!" he exclaimed.

"Yes?" she said, "I have news too. You go first." She sauntered up close to him and smiled. Her fingers undid the buttons on his suit coat. Then she stood on tiptoes to give him a meaningful kiss.

"What's this?" he growled. His manner was suddenly seductive, a hint of her Jim, now that they were alone and away from public scrutiny. "Is there a bit of a sparkle in your eyes today, shy one? You look wonderful."

"Yes, I'm very excited. The baby has been good lately, and I'm feeling better."

"Excellent. Then the news I have for you will bring you great joy."

"Let me get you some wine. Sit by the table while I get it. Here, let me get you a pillow for that chair, it's far too stiff."

"Pillows? Wine? If I didn't know better, I'd say that you were a woman in love."

She stopped what she was doing to emphasize the full import of her words. "I am. With you." She placed the tankard on the table in front of him.

He stood and took her in his arms. "Do you mean that?"

"With all my heart," she said and then kissed him.

"I am bursting to tell you my news."

She motioned for him to sit down again and continued drinking the tea she had poured for herself earlier.

"I have found another ship. It leaves in two days, and I've purchased two tickets for us to ride her to America. It wasn't easy to talk the captain into taking us on board as she isn't a passenger ship, as I've mentioned before, and he's been having trouble getting to port here in France. He might not return because of all the political distress here, and has told me that he plans on warning his Boston friends to do likewise. This may be our only chance if trade is interrupted. I've come into some money recently..." he suddenly paused and stared at her. "What's wrong?"

Her voice faltered. "I can't go right now. Not right

now."

His features darkened. "I told you to be ready."

"Yes, but you also told me that we wouldn't have any chance to leave until September."

"What could keep you from starting a new life with the man you just declared your love to?"

"Phillipe."

"Phillipe?" He let the impact of the other man's name settle into his thoughts before he said another word. "Why would you have a care for him now? He's left you on your own with a baby to fret about."

"He's in trouble. Taken to prison."

He turned his eyes from her. "That is, indeed, unfortunate, Celeste. But, I have made our plans, and you said you would leave with me at a moment's notice."

"I know I did, but Leclerc, Claire, and I have made plans to...to..." she wasn't sure how much she could tell him. He was already in a temper by the look in his eyes and the tone in his voice. "I have to see him one last time."

"If he's even there when you arrive."

"What do you know?"

"Nothing that I can tell you, only that he's doomed."

"All the more reason to...see him."

"Celeste, you aren't planning anything stupid are you?" She looked at the cup in her hands.

"You're not planning on rescuing him, are you? If that is your strategy, I can tell you that it is the stupidest idea I've ever heard."

His remark angered her. "I never realized what a

controller you are, Jean-Jacques."

"Controller?"

"You're saying this because my plans have interfered with yours. You told me that you weren't going to leave France until September, and this is my last chance to tie up my business once and for all with Phillipe."

"That's been done for you. You can only do yourself harm by going to him. Besides, I'm leaving whether you're with me or not."

She could feel her heart pounding in her chest. Her throat seemed to squeeze shut, her lips went dry, and she said, "You mean that you would sail without me?"

"If you tell me you love me, and that you want to start a new life with me as my wife, and then turn to me and say, 'Oh, no, wait, just let me go to my former lover who used me as he did his horse so that I can try to save his miserable neck. Then we'll go to America, and I'll make you happy the rest of your life,' what am I to think?"

"That I am a ...good, kind, compassionate woman."

"To hell with Phillipe de Brouquens, I say leave while we still can."

"When the going gets tough; the tough get going?"

"I've never heard it put quite that way, but, yes, something like that."

"I have to follow my plans. We've spent Leclerc's money renting a carriage, and we leave tomorrow at dawn. Can't you wait for me?"

"There are reasons, that I can't go into that makes it mandatory to leave promptly. Besides," he took his cloak from the chair, swallowed the wine in one gulp, and turned to the peg by the door for his hat, "if you're worried about Phillipe, then you can't really be in love with me. You still love that bastard."

She tried to stop him. "No...you don't understand."

His words were bitter. "I understand that you would rather risk your life for a man who used you, than sail away with one who never would."

She had hurt him, and she'd never meant that to happen. "Please wait. I *do* love you. I don't love Phillipe; I just have to settle things with him."

"They were settled when he unexpectedly went home the last time he visited. Bordeaux is in hell right now. It is folly to go, and it was foolishness on my part to give my heart to a woman who is in love with another man." He started to leave.

Celeste screamed after him, "Jim, I mean, Jean-Jacques, no! I want to go with you to America. *I do.*"

"Then don't go to Bordeaux and be here tomorrow morning. We have to travel to the port, and I want to get out of here as fast as possible. It isn't just *your* future alone that concerns me now."

"Just give me a few days."

"Ships don't wait..." he looked into her eyes, "...and neither do I."

Chapter Twenty-Three

Jean-Jacques left Celeste alone, confused, and in a panic. There was so much emotion going on inside her heart; it seemed to block out any other sensation. She was in a trance when Leclerc and Claire came home.

"What's wrong?" Claire asked.

Celeste wasn't sure how much to tell them. She hesitated, weighing her words before she opened her soul to them. He had told her to keep quiet, but these two people were ready to embark on an adventure that could harm their reputations with the patriots forever subsequently placing their necks on the guillotine; so she threw aside all Jean-Jacques's words and spoke the truth.

"Jean-Jacques wants to take me to America. He loves me, and I love him."

"Wonderful. Oh, I am so happy for you," said Claire.

"That's not the problem. Jean-Jacques told me that we would leave on a ship called the *Diana* that sails in September. So, I arranged for us to leave for Bordeaux immediately. America is so far away, and I want to start a new life by dissolving any ties I have with Phillipe."

"That may have been done for you already," said Leclerc.

"You were going to leave us without saying farewell?" asked Claire.

"Jean-Jacques forbid me to say anything to you about our plans as he was frightened you might try to prevent us from leaving."

"I think it's a superb idea; I told you to leave France. I'd go myself if I weren't needed here, and then there's my family and all. I hear that Boston is a pretty spot."

"He said that you wouldn't be able to get me proper papers, but because of his allegiance to French authority, he could."

Leclerc shrugged his shoulders. "That makes sense."

"Still you would have gone without telling us, and we would have been so worried."

"I wouldn't have left without at least leaving a note, Claire."

"So, what's wrong?"

"He has tickets to leave on another ship, one that is available right now; and I told him that I couldn't go, that we had plans we could not alter."

Leclerc smiled. "Oh, I bet that made him happy."

"He thinks I don't love him now; that I still love Phillipe."

Leclerc said, "From a man's perspective, he has a point."

Celeste said, "I can't leave now."

"He'll wait," said Leclerc.

"He said he wouldn't."

Claire said, "Cousin, by the look in that man's eyes, wild horses couldn't tear him from your side."

"Do you think he'll wait? He said he wouldn't. 'Ships don't wait, and neither do I' he said."

"He's a handful; I'll grant you. So stubborn and into his own ways. Got a chip in his shoulder about something, that's for

231

sure," said Claire.

"What am I to do?"

"Leave with us in the morning. Claire's been working on a disguise; I've been purchasing clothes that will make me look like a poor brother; and you already have the look of a soldier's widow if we dress you in dark colors. Now that Claire has had the tailor widen your dresses, we should be able to find something for you to wear."

"But Jean-Jacques?"

"You have a destiny, shy one. You can't turn back now as you yourself said. You have to finish the final chapter of this book before you can start a new one. He should have been more understanding of your feelings. Brute! If needs be, I'll see that you're on that ship, or, if we don't make the one he's leaving on, I'll find you another, and then you can search for him in Boston to your heart's content. If he goes without you, which I doubt he will."

"He said that it was dangerous to stay; that he had secret reasons for wanting to go as soon as possible; that he had just come into a great fortune. He was very angry with me."

Claire touched Celeste's shoulder, shrugged, and smiled wryly. "He's that type. You're in for a time with that one. How I envy you," she whispered into her cousin's ear.

"Then we'll head for Bordeaux tomorrow at dawn?" Celeste asked.

Leclerc shook his head. "I've even made arrangements to stop along the way. We shall have a fine time on this summer vacation of ours. However," he winked, "we'll all have to sleep in the same bed as that's all the money I have."

"Oh, I have some too," Celeste said, suddenly remembering the money Tallon had given her. "I don't want us to be frugal on the trip."

Claire clapped her hands. "How exciting this all is! It's like something out of a grand drama. All three of us trying to save Phillipe. Riding the highway. A woman with child striving to rescue the father of her baby and then heading off to start a new life with a man who loves her waiting in the wings. He does plan on marrying you, I hope."

"As soon as possible."

"Then we'll make short work of our business in Bordeaux and be home in time to smuggle the 'princess' onto the ship so that she can meet her prince in a new, savage land."

Celeste looked surprised. "Savage?"

"They say they have naked Indians running around Albany, New York. People have sent home reports. Do you think you'll move there? *Naked* savages! Maybe I should go too."

"Oh, heavens, I don't know. I just want to cry, sleep, not sleep; I have a headache."

"And you're both giving me one too," said Leclerc and then smiled. "Silly women, why do I get caught up in your ridiculous schemes?"

"Because you get to sleep with the two of us in one bed and go on an adventure that you can write about as soon as you return home. You'll probably have enough material to write a book or something," said Claire.

"That may very well be, but if we don't sleep now, we'll have a rough day of it tomorrow. I'll blow out the candles; you two go to bed."

Claire and Celeste undressed in Celeste's bedroom and then curled up beside each other. Leclerc slept alone in the other room.

Claire whispered, "Do you have Geraldine?"

"Yes, in my bag, why?" Celeste whispered to her cousin like a small girl at a sleep over.

"Take it with you for luck, all right?"

"Yes, of course." Celeste thought of what she needed to take with her: the bonnet of the dead Charlotte Corday, the book of poetry Tallon had given her, the rolled up and tied picture of Jim/Jean-Jacques, the painting of Phillipe she had taken from the easel, rolled up, and tied with a ribbon, the rag doll, the blue and white stripped skirt, her torn cockade, and some money. It occurred to her that this might be the last time she would see her little house again. She comforted herself with the knowledge that she would at least be able to take her satchel all the way to Bordeaux, Boston, and back home to Richfield Springs. She must not lose her precious souvenirs.

She prayed. "Help me, whoever is pulling the strings on this one. And don't let that arrogant Jean-Jacques leave without Celeste. I can't do this without you. I have five people trusting that I know what I'm doing: Celeste, Leclerc, Claire, Jean-Jacques, and the baby. Should I mention Jim Cooper too? Keep us all safe and get me home. Please!"

Chapter Twenty-Four

France in the dead of July's summer heat can be harsh enough, but riding in a carriage, pregnant, wearing uncomfortable clothes, with two other passengers squeezed tightly into the cab with you, bumping your posterior on what actually is no more than a wooden seat with leather over it, and getting dust in your mouth every time the horses start to go faster, was beyond anything Celeste had experienced in the realm of discomfort.

The horse dung dropped along the roadside as they traveled, and the cow pastures—resplendent with excrement—gave an interesting aroma to the adventure; and this, added to her stomach being tossed at any given moment, made Celeste ill during ninety-eight percent of the trip. There were no gas station service machines along the way where you could buy bottled water or Pepto-Bismo, no rest areas where you could relieve yourself, and the food they did eventually find to eat was stale or a candidate for botulism. The water they drank when they could get it was lukewarm but tasted pleasing to Celeste's parched palate.

The nights weren't much better. Leclerc, Claire, and Celeste tossed and turned, jockeying for a better spot in their one grand bed, clothed only in their undergarments. The flies were everywhere in the inns and with no identifiable relief for the pests. Watching flies buzz around the food and the cook as she prepared their dinner was enough to make Celeste lose her increasingly voracious appetite. Celeste ate fruit whenever she could get it.

The carriage occasionally broke down, and the three had to leave it and sit by the roadside until the wheel, horse, or dislocation problem was fixed. Sitting on a rock for four hours in the excruciating heat while other tourists passed by was mind numbing. Celeste thought of cool breezes running through her hair as the ship to America took her to a new home and wondered if peace of mind was worth this trauma. The worst part of it all was that Leclerc and Claire took the whole business in stride, claiming that travel was unusually *delightful* this July.

Eventually they drove into Bordeaux. Leclerc made arrangements for them to stay at an inn rather than divulge his presence to any of his or Claire's associates who might live near the town. There was a very active woman's club in Bordeaux, but Claire remained low key because of their planned intrigue.

Once they were settled, Claire and Celeste headed for the makeshift prison. The moment Celeste saw the traveling guillotine on the cart with the barricade around it, her mind went to Charlotte's death, and she knew she'd made the right choice in helping Phillipe.

Claire asked one of the guards whether Phillipe de Brouquens was imprisoned there, and was informed that he and his entire family had been imprisoned three days ago and were being held there until a council could be elected to oversee all the cases on the docket. Celeste asked whether he had legal counsel, and the man laughed in her face. She wanted to know whether she could talk to him and immediately knew that her remark had been a mistake. The guard was suspicious of her instantly.

"Now what do we do?" asked Claire after they had walked

across the street and were far enough away from the guard that he would not hear their words.

"How will we reach him? Leclerc?"

"He's only a writer and has no clout here," said her cousin.

They sat on a bench near the inn and stared at the cobblestones while busy citizens hurried about the streets, gossiped about politics, or waited in line for food.

"I can see why Phillipe likes it here. It's very pretty," said Celeste. "I wonder where his vineyard is?"

"This prison can't be all that difficult to break into," said Claire with a sudden burst of enthusiasm for the problem. "We'll wait until nightfall. Let's hire a carriage and take a tour of the countryside."

"Now? My rump is still numb from our last traveling expedition."

Leclerc sauntered by with a loaf of bread which he handed to them to eat. "I was one of the lucky ones. It's black, but it's the best I can do. No luck with the prison guards?"

"The good news," said Claire as she munched on the disgusting, dry bread, "is that he's still alive and hasn't been tried. The bad news is that they have no court set up yet for hearing any cases, and we can't see him."

"Apparently the guillotine just arrived and has been left in the Place Dauphine. There is great concern about what will come next. A small group of fanatics who came with it met no opposition. I've heard some say that a few cannon shots fired into their ranks might have stopped them as they passed along the Rue de Faubourg-Saint-Julien; but the people of this city showed no resistance. Oh, Claire, this looks very bad. I had no idea it would be like this. Ideals discussed in Paris with friends, and the reality of murdering for those ideals—not just merchants or politicians, but all the innocent members of their families as well—is suddenly very disturbing to me. It just never crossed my mind that entire families...I mean...even small children have been arrested for crimes of which they couldn't possibly have any knowledge."

"Why would children be arrested?" asked Claire.

"Sometimes just the husband and son have been charged, but in other cases entire families who have, for any numerous reasons, displeased someone in charge, will be killed."

"After a trial?" said Claire.

"What trial? The men who will be 'elected' to this court will simply follow the dictates of their own bitterness towards people they have hated for years. A way to pay them back for some imagined hurt from years past."

"But the plan was to attack..."

"Forget the plan, Claire, this is not imprisonment for infractions against the poor, but death because you have blue blood in your veins. Anyone connected to these families, by any sort of relationship, will die. I've heard it was a blood bath in La Réole. There was a revolt against the Convention here, but in the desire to be freemen like the people of America, a new surge of patriotism has attached itself to this city. Young men from the leading families drilled for warfare on the slopes of the Chateau-Trompette, they say. Apparently, these men made a great deal of noise at the theaters at night about their bravery, never daring to shout 'Long live the King'. They speak of being independent of

Paris and the Convention in hopes to achieve their own political party. It will not be long before Tallien and Ysabeau arrive to severe heads. The Revolutionary army hasn't entered the city yet; but when it does, people will die quickly. There are so many rich families and important persons in this town that the number of homicides will be overwhelming. I must assume that the de Brouquens family is an influential one. That means trouble for Phillipe and our plan."

"How can we get Phillipe out?"

"We can't."

Celeste fell silent. She had never seen Leclerc this worried, and the expression on his face frightened her.

"If we're going to do anything, it had better be quick," he continued.

"I can't even get in to see him."

Leclerc shot a nervous glance at some women who had strolled close to them and appeared to be listening intently to what they were discussing. Leclerc said, "Let's speak in a less public place. We are being watched—perhaps overheard."

They went to their room at the inn, shut the door, and brainstormed every conceivable way to free Phillipe.

"How can we free a man who is locked in a makeshift cell in a building whose interior design is lost to us? If we only knew which window, or which door, or what hallway. I don't like disguising myself and then hedging down a floor saying, 'yoo hoo, which one of you is Phillipe de Brouquens?' " said Claire.

"You can do it if we disguise you as a cook or something. They have to feed them while they're in there. You could say that you are the de Brouquens's cook."

"She's probably already been there, and they'd know what she looks like."

"True."

"I've never really seen him that much," said Claire, "and we can't send Celeste."

They sat for some time thinking quietly until finally Claire said, "I'll say that I have papers that need to be signed?"

"The book!" cried Celeste. "The book of poetry Tallon published for Phillipe's mother. We could say that Monsieur de Brouquens owes money on the publication of his mother's book of poetry, and that you've been sent to get it. A good citizen of the Republic should be paid his wages. Say that Tallon is a patriot. They'll never know. Here," she said going to her bag and showing them the portrait of Phillipe, "this might help refresh your memory of what he looks like. Then you can tell us where Phillipe is located, and we can wait until the evening and sneak in and rescue him."

"Brilliant. Claire?"

"I'll wear my peasant's skirt. I won't have to say too much to him once I find him because he hates me enough to remember *my* face and realize that if I am here—so are you. Playing along about the money owed will alert him to be ready for action."

"Excellent," said Leclerc. "Go now while the guards and guests of the prison eat their midday meal."

Claire hurried to make her disguise. Four hours had passed while they sat inactively hatching schemes so that when it was time to act, it was refreshing to move swiftly through the streets. Celeste never doubted for a moment that Claire could pull off the charade; she would be doing what she did best.

Leclerc and Celeste sat impatiently on a bench near a tall tree across the plaza from the 'jail' and waited for their 'secret agent's' return. Celeste refused small pastries Leclerc purchased to wile away the time. She couldn't think of eating at a time like this. Her stomach was contorted, and she still had not fully recovered from her travel sickness.

They saw Claire's face as the door opened to allow her to leave the prison. Claire's expression showed her companions that she was still enjoying her role as she bobbed and weaved her head, shoulders, and neck to make herself look submissively ignorant of any wrong she might have done.

Then she hurried towards them. The look on her face was not encouraging.

Celeste asked, "What is it? Hold nothing back from me, cousin."

Claire couldn't speak at first. Finally she said, "I can't tell you."

"Is it that awful?"

"The worst thing. We shouldn't have come."

"Are they going to execute him?" Celeste said, her lips trembling as she spoke the words.

"Assuredly, as well as all the members of his family. The trial is forthcoming. Monsieur de Brouquens is well known for his Royalist affiliations. Phillipe assured me that anyone connected by blood to his family would probably be put to death. He told me that you should return to Paris at once."

"Oh, God, his father and mother too?"

Claire looked deeply into her cousin's eyes. "Yes, the old

241

ones, even the household servants, as well as...Phillipe's wife and three young daughters."

Chapter Twenty-Five

Leclerc and Claire held onto Celeste as her body slumped to the bench. A wave of complete nausea hit her. Celeste felt as if she were in a vacuum; her head seemed to be spinning into a tunnel of darkness. Sounds became distorted. People—abstract in appearance. Her skin seemed hot from the inside out, as her stomach twisted like vines around a tree trunk. Her focal point diminished, and she felt as if she were losing touch with reality. So that was why he never returned to her. He'd been married. Maybe his wife had found out about his mistress in France and put a stop to it. Maybe her Phillipe had met the same fate this one soon would.

Phillipe had lied to her. Used her trusting nature against her. He hadn't been worthy of her love, and she'd waited for him. She'd gone on living with no heart and no thought of what her future could become with a new love. She'd even forsaken her art for this man. She'd changed her life's goals because of Phillipe's disappearance. And then there was Jim. All he wanted was his love returned. She had wasted time and talent on a man who didn't deserve her adoration. He had taken advantage of her innocence, robbed her of her virginity, and lacked the courage to confront her about his real life, forcing her to commit adultery. She began to sob and talk very loudly and very fast. She would never have come close to him if she had known that he belonged to another. It wasn't her style.

"I can't believe this. He lied to me."

"Hush now, let's go back to the inn," said Claire. "We'll

talk in our room."

"He lied to me!" she screamed. "I'm having his child, and he doesn't even have the courtesy to tell me he's *married*! How could I be so stupid? The clues were there all along. He can't marry me—why? He said he had to leave because of his dying mother who Tallon said wasn't ill. Wants to set me up in a cottage. Can you *believe* this man? A cottage in the country far away from prying eyes! And now we know why."

Leclerc tried to get Celeste to move and eventually, stifled her words with his hand. He stared straight into her eyes. "All that is true, but he did take care of you and was planning on continuing to do that for the rest of your life," admitted Leclerc. "I should have realized this was going on."

Celeste took his hand from her mouth. "What about his wife? Did she know? Poor woman. There she is having his little girls for him, and he's out screwing another woman in hopes of gaining a son. I committed adultery. My immortal soul..."

"Let's get out of here. People are watching us," warned Claire, noticing the people gathering to view the spectacle.

"His wife is about to be guillotined because she is married to that liar!"

"We'll have to drag her back to the inn," said Leclerc shrugging.

Celeste sobbed hysterically. "My whole life was ruined because I loved this man."

"Not entirely ruined, Celeste," said Leclerc. "You can't help that you loved him. Lots of aristocrats take mistresses. Happens all the time. It's better than begging for coins in the street or suicide. And you have life in you, as well. Frustrating circumstances now perhaps, but a blessing for your future, I think."

"Is this supposed to make me feel better, Leclerc? I thought you didn't like him, and now you're sticking up for him."

"I'm just saying that he probably did...does love you. His marriage being arranged by his father; he was expected to follow the rules his world established long ago. He had to keep the blue blood in the family, and his wife must have had a good family name and a fat dowry. But that doesn't mean that he didn't love you, Celeste. He knew you would never agree to loving him if he told you that he was married."

"I'm having his baby!" she cried. It was the sort of deafening noise an animal makes when it has been caught in a trap.

"Keep shouting that up and down the street, Celeste, and you may soon be in the cell next to him."

That thought stopped her words. They managed to get her to drink some cool water and sit peacefully on the bed for a whole minute.

"Now what do we do?" asked Claire.

Leclerc was infused with energy. "Get out of town as fast as possible."

"Phillipe looked so frightened, Celeste. He told me to tell you to return to Paris immediately. Oh, he is in agony about you. He does care so much for you. I am almost certain I saw his wife and children in another section of the prison. You must see that your child is the de Brouquens's future. His family is lost, but

245

you can get his only heir safely back to Paris where you can hide until freedom is declared. You need to think about that. You loved him Celeste. Don't cheat that love by destroying the only future both of you have—the baby."

"And what about Jean-Jacques?" Celeste put her head in her hands.

Her two friends said nothing.

Celeste's face was wet and red from crying when she looked up at both of them. "I left him to go hunting for a fool. I'm a fool. He's been sailing now for days, and here I sit knowing I love him and that he is lost to me forever."

"I told you that I would arrange passage for you on the *Diana*."

"And then I can spend years looking for the man hoping that he will accept my apology after I've shunned him. Where can I find him? I have no idea where a bachelor might decide to live in that vast country. He's convinced I don't really love him. That I'm still in love with Phillipe because I risked my happiness to save that liar. And what about you two? You both helped me, risked your own money and reputations to follow me on this adventure."

"That's all right," said Claire shyly, "we didn't mind helping. Just because it didn't turn out the way we all hoped it would, doesn't mean that we would have changed our plans to help you. We helped you uncover the truth. You felt that it was important to help Phillipe."

"But Leclerc's money?"

Leclerc could not stand still. He moved back and forth like a frightened rabbit. "Look, Celeste, what's done is done and cannot be undone. Forget him. Concentrate on your own happiness and the life of your unborn child."

Celeste stopped weeping long enough to think about what he was saying. Then her forehead wrinkled again, her lower lip quivered, and she began to cry all over again. She collapsed on the bed.

"You weep for this man, girl?" came a voice from the door.

"Who are you?" asked Claire to the intruder.

It was a middle-aged woman whose hair was starting to turn gray and whose features were every bit as beautiful as they must have been when she was sixteen. She was dressed in fine satin of the most beautiful color of burgundy, and it was accentuated with the most exquisite handmade lace. She had a sad smile.

"A mourner such as yourself. My name is Emilia. I saw you and your friends in the plaza—witnessed your tears. You went to see Phillipe de Brouquens?"

"What right have you to interfere? Leave our room at once," said Leclerc.

"I thought I could help."

"How can you help her? You don't even know us."

"Oh, that's not true. I know all about her. Her name is Celeste Lacombe, and I'll wager you're her cousin, Claire. I also know a great deal about the de Brouquens family."

"Emilia?" said Claire.

"Yes," answered the woman. "May I come in?"

Celeste motioned for the woman to come into their suite and shut the door.

"I have been in love with Monsieur de Brouquens for thirty years. And now after all these years, it's come to this."

"You mean Phillipe's father?"

"I have loved him and lived outside his family for all of my adult life, and I know that the man loved me as much, if not more, than he loved his wife. I'm sure she must have known about it—maybe not. I feel no shame about the union. How can you be ashamed of loving a man and wanting to be with him forever? He would never have been able to marry me under the strict dictates of his social role. Their society is crumbling, and maybe it should. I know that Phillipe had no choice but to marry Estelle. In fact, I was indirectly invited to the wedding. She's a lovely woman, and they have three beautiful children, but I know he loves you very much. Unfortunately, he can't help you now. You have to get out of France immediately. You've lost one chance, but maybe you can rectify it. I overheard what this man said. You need to be on that ship because if they catch wind of the fact that you're mother to an heir of the de Brouquens's family title, they will kill you and the baby. There is no rhyme or reason to anything now."

"She's in that much danger?" said Leclerc.

"Yes. I am leaving the country soon. Going to live in Spain for a while. I don't want to leave him until it's over. I'll be in the crowd the day he dies. I have to be. He'll look for me. You have a chance at a new life, Celeste, don't refuse your heart now. You aren't really in love with Phillipe now, are you? What does your heart tell you?"

"I love another." She heard herself say the words and smiled. It was good to talk to the old woman. Emilia seemed to understand everything she had gone through in the last few months. Speaking with her reminded her of the many nights of long discussions she'd had with her own mother.

"I know all about the man, and he does love you. He had to run just as we all do."

The woman ambled sadly to the door. "These are hard times for a mother...for women...for families."

"How do you know about Jean-Jacques?" Celeste asked.

"He's my son. The son I had to Monsieur de Brouquens; the illegitimate brother of Phillipe de Brouquens. It was his father's wish to baptize him last week and acknowledge him fully before his probable demise. A secret ceremony held at our cottage just prior to their arrest. He gave Jean-Jacques a title, a huge inheritance, a legal birth certificate—signed by his own lawyer—which makes it a matter of public record who his father and mother are. Then he gave him a personal request—to go to America as soon as he could. If and when Jean-Jacques comes back here, the de Brouquens estate will be his. But, now you understand why it was of the utmost urgency he leave the country right away."

"Why didn't he tell me that he was in danger?"

"And tell you that he was your former lover's brother? What might you think? That he only wanted you to prove something to the de Brouquens family—steal the woman Phillipe couldn't live without? I'm sure he was testing you, as well. It's his nature to be suspicious, after all."

"So he simply told me that he was trying to rescue me without disclosing the danger he was in."

The woman smiled a tired, sad smile. She looked closely

249

at Celeste. "Listen well, my dear. Jean-Jacques told me all about you when we parted last week. Since you are here, I'd have to assume you didn't go with him." She glanced at Leclerc. "Do as this man suggests. My son loves you. He's had a hard life and should enjoy some happiness. So do you. He said that he was going to Boston, and that he would marry you if you agreed. I'll bet you'll find him there. But, whatever you do, girl, do it quickly. My son's life was in danger from the moment his father publicly acknowledged him. That's why he gave him enough money to flee France. Now you need to do the same."

Emilia Coupier looked at Claire and Leclerc. "Get her out of Bordeaux tonight." She gave Celeste one final look, smiled, and departed.

"This making any sense to you?" Celeste stammered.

Leclerc shut the door so that no one would hear him. "I'm taking control now. You're too filled with emotion to think straight. Perfectly natural. Pack, Claire. Pack for all of us. I'll find a carriage, if I can, and we'll take supper here at the inn before we leave."

"We can't travel at night," said Claire.

"We have no choice," he said.

"I'll never find him," said Celeste weakly. "How stupid I am. I'm sorry. How could I get both of you into such a horrid situation?"

"We can mourn about all that in Paris," said Leclerc. "Right now I'm more interested in getting one pregnant woman, one lover, and one editor home before all hell breaks loose."

"I can't thank you two enough for helping me."

Claire smiled. "It's all right. Maybe it's just what I

250

needed to see, Celeste."

"What do you mean?"

"The old man and his wife have given up. Phillipe is frightened. His wife is terrified. But, the faces of those darling girls facing their fate at the mercy of the guillotine will haunt me for the rest of my life."

Leclerc took his hat. "I only hope I can find someone willing to ride their horses into the night."

The two women packed and spoke only of their domestic preparations until Leclerc stormed into the room two hours later.

"I found some bread and cheese to eat along the way. It will have to do as supper; I don't think we should wait a minute longer."

"Then you've found transportation."

"A merchant is willing to drive us in his wagon as far as Civray. From there we'll take a rented carriage that he assures me will be easier to obtain than the ones in Bordeaux. I'm not sure I trust him, but it's the best I can do. Are you two ready?"

They shook their heads.

"Fine. We'll go at once."

"You mean we'll be riding in a *cart*?"

Leclerc rolled his eyes. "I think that's what I just said, Claire. Move."

The old man was nervous and motioned for them to move swiftly. They pulled their cloaks over their heads and tried to be unobtrusive. The horses moved at a steady but determined rate, and soon they were far away from the city. Celeste could be heard sniffling occasionally, but no one made notice of her grief.

The old man kept his focus on the road ahead, never looking at any of them, nor did he try to start a conversation, either.

They rolled into Civray just as the sun was beginning to touch the Western skyline. The old man seemed glad to be rid of his guests and motioned, with a crooked finger, toward an inn where they could spend the night, then motioned with the same finger to a stable where carriages could be rented for long rides. Leclerc paid the man, and he hustled away without giving them a backwards glance.

"Friendly old goat, isn't he?" Leclerc said sarcastically. "Let's get some food and a place to rest. My back is breaking from the ride."

The tavern was crude but did have a room for rent. The bread and cheese had been filling enough, but they all agreed that they needed a full meal if they were to travel long hours tomorrow. After eating a surprisingly decent meal of red meat, wine, potatoes, and freshly baked bread, the three travelers settled in for the night. Sleep seized them within seconds of dropping onto the bed, but it didn't last long.

They awoke to a loud banging on the door.

"We want Claire. Open up!"

They looked at each other in bewilderment.

"Just a second," said Leclerc, throwing on his clothes and rushing to the door. "What do you want?" he asked the guards whose guns were loaded and pointing into the room.

"Is that Claire Lacombe and her cousin Celeste?" the tall one with the too long mustache asked.

"Why? Who wants to know?"

"They are under arrest."

The old man who had driven the cart pointed the same crooked finger at Claire and Celeste. "These are the ones who were by the prison yesterday—and the man."

"Come with us. You're all under arrest for suspicion of trying to help a condemned Royalist, being family to Phillipe de Brouquens, and falsely identifying yourself when asked by guardsman for your identity."

Leclerc sprang into action. He pulled the gun away from one guard's hands and pushed the others out of his path.

"I'll be back," he said to the women as he ran passed the men and out of the inn.

One man stayed with the women, pointing his gun at them, while the others chased Leclerc. "Please keep him safe," whispered Claire. "Oh, Celeste, who would think that I would be the one to bring the trouble to you?"

"It's all right, Claire. Somehow we'll get out of this."

But at this point Celeste wasn't sure of anything. She wanted to survive this time traveling vacation, but it looked as if she had made the fatal mistake of following her head instead of her heart. What was it they said about curious cats? Jean-Jacques was on a ship bound for Boston probably watching the sunrise while she might very well be facing her last.

253

Chapter Twenty-Six

Leclerc escaped. Claire and Celeste traveled by carriage to Bordeaux. The women's hands were tied behind their backs; their baggage placed under their feet; and two men on horseback rode behind the cab. Despite Claire's attempts to charm the two guards who sat inside the carriage with them, they refused to tell the two women much except that they were prisoners under suspicion of being Royalist sympathizers. Claire and Celeste would go before a court where they could plead their cases. Neither of the men was amused with Claire, but they showed some sympathy to the 'mother'.

It was late when the carriage arrived in Bordeaux, so the two prisoners were hurried to a cell without much comment from any authority figure. Celeste tried to search for Phillipe's cell when they walked through the hallway leading to their new home, but they were in the women's section of the prison, and he was nowhere. She wondered which one of the aristocratic ladies was Madame de Brouquens one and two. All the women looked frightened, disheveled, and hungry. They pulled their shawls around their shoulders protectively, or gathered their children close to themselves for comfort. Their facial expressions showed disillusioned hope as they eyed the new neighbors.

Could these women help them? Probably not. Were they friends who would smile at them and ease their grief? No, they were strangers in the same miserable state as they were.

The 'prison' smelled of spoiled food, dried blood, and urine. The hole they were placed in was decorated with a rustic cot covered with straw, a basin and chipped pitcher, a worn stool, and dirt. A window, just above their heads, brought some light and gave a view of the street.

Celeste and Claire's hands were untied once they were inside their chambers, but they were not told anything about their fate. Their bags were tossed in after them and lay in a heap at their feet.

"Who would have guessed that I would be the one to put us in such jeopardy? A Royalist! What an insult!" Claire said. "Let's hope Leclerc makes it back to Paris on that horse he stole."

Celeste smiled. "He did look rather heroic, didn't he? Like a knight from bygone days the way he pushed through the guards and screamed back at us that he would return to save us."

"I've picked a good one, eh?" Claire said with a melancholy smile.

"Do you think they'll find us guilty?"

"Of what? Pretending to be Tallon's assistant? What can they do about that? Punish me by keeping me here for a while? And they'll let you go because you're pregnant."

Celeste rested on the stool and touched her stomach to ease the baby's kicking. "Has it ever occurred to you that almost everything you've ever told me is wrong?"

Claire stared at her, letting her cousin's comment sink in, and then burst into a fit of laughter. "That's not true!" she said between gasps for breath.

"Besides getting me out of prison, you've been wrong about almost everything. The disguise got you into trouble. The fact that you are the biggest rebel in all of Paris hasn't stopped them from charging you with being a Royalist sympathizer. Nothing would surprise me now. I can only hope Leclerc comes back with reinforcements to get us out of here, or we may very well be dead. Has that thought crossed your mind?"

"Heavens no, cousin. Somehow we two will make it out of here. Haven't we always survived? Ah, look," she motioned to the hall, "bread. We've not had much to eat for hours, and I'll bet the baby is hungry."

The guard told them to move back into the cell while he brought them their rations. They did as he said, and when he locked the door he asked, "Is that Phillipe de Brouquens's child in your belly?"

Claire gave Celeste a worried look. "Why would you ask such a question?" asked Celeste.

"Just answer the question. Are you married to him?"

"No."

"Is that Phillipe's baby? People heard you talking in the streets and saying how you were his lover. You're pregnant, so I want to know whose baby it is?"

Celeste didn't think fast enough to lie. She had no other answer for him. "It is Phillipe's baby."

She placed her hand on her swollen abdomen, and the child kicked against her stomach no doubt wanting food. The baby had been relatively quiet all day, but he must have had some sense that bread was nearby.

"A court has been appointed, and the family's trial is set for nine in the morning three days from today. If they are found guilty, they will be executed at noon of the same day. That is the custom."

The surly looking man watched her face to see whether she would give away her emotions. She tried to remain calm. "What has that got to do with me?"

A nasty expression of arrogance and true glee of the power he plied over her came into his eyes. "If they find the family guilty, then *all* members of the de Brouquens family will be executed. If that child is the legitimate heir to their family, it will have to die, as well."

Celeste was stunned into silence for a second and then screamed, "But you can't do that! You wouldn't kill a pregnant woman. No one is that heartless!"

"No one wants to kill women at all, but if they are wealthy aristocrats, as the de Brouquens are, and loyal to the king; they must pay. All of them. It's a matter of blood now. Blue and red." He smirked at his small joke.

Claire shouted, "But not a pregnant woman."

"I'm not sure what they'll say about your plea. Maybe they'll just let you stay in prison where you'll rot away anyhow until the baby is born. Obviously, you are an aristocrat's whore who profited by the misery of others. You were given comfort, money, a house when others died in the streets. You let him have your body, and now it holds his future."

"No," Claire cried, "it isn't like that at all. Don't you know who I am? Claire Lacombe! You must have heard of me. Secretary—*president* to the most outspoken women's club in all of France."

He was impressed. His eyebrows rose, and he smiled and looked closely at the woman. "I've heard of you. You are the one who spoke at Marat's funeral."

"Yes. And this is my cousin. She wears the cockade. She's one of us. She followed her heart with this man. She's a French citizen. She can't help it if she is weak when it comes to handsome men. Happens all the time to my sex. You can't blame her for loving him. She didn't even know he was married and had children until yesterday. He lied to her. Told her he would take care of her but couldn't marry her because his father wouldn't let him. What was she to do, die for lack of food? He helped her. That says something for the man, yes?"

"It simply says that he paid for her, but I will tell the judge what you've said. He might know you."

"She just wanted to see him one last time to say goodbye. We weren't going to rescue him. What rubbish. How would we?"

For once Celeste was hoping Claire would *keep* talking.

The man looked both women up and down. "I can understand why the man would fall for you," he said to Celeste. "And there are ways to make sure that things go well for you in court, if you understand my meaning."

Claire did. "Yes, of course, if you will promise to help *both* of us."

"Do you mean it?" he asked.

Claire paused before she said, "Only if you come back with a pardon for *both of us*."

"Two pardons for two women? I want both then."

Celeste stared at Claire.

"Yes," Celeste said finally. "Two women for two pardons."

"And one of you *before* the trial."

That comment received Claire's anger. "Why? If they pardon us, we're going to make good on our deal. We're prisoners. You hold the key to the door. What choice do we have? No. After the trial, Monsieur, and we know we are free."

"No. I'll have to free you immediately if they pardon you, and I won't get what I'm risking my reputation for. One before and one afterwards. You first," he said pointing to Claire. "Tomorrow night. I'll come for you."

He looked at Celeste. "There are ways a woman in your condition can please a man. I'll bring Phillipe to your cell so that you can say your..." he smirked, "farewell to him. Don't think because you are with child that I shall not want something from you. As a matter of fact, I fancy you all the more for your obvious femininity."

Claire hesitated and then said, "Yes. All right. Tomorrow night."

He blew them both a kiss and walked away from their cell but did not leave. Celeste and Claire listened as he spoke with a mother in the cell across from theirs.

"Do you agree to my terms?" he asked.

A young girl's voice whimpered, "It isn't up to you, mother, it's up to me to decide."

"No, Jeanette," said the mother.

"If it means saving you and my sister. We can't help Papa, but maybe if I do this we'll make it out of here."

"Good girl," said the man. "I will be kind to her. She's doing the right thing, believe me. Your trial is up tomorrow. I can't help your husband, but I can take mercy on helpless women...provided I am well compensated."

The cell door opened, and Celeste caught a glimpse of a girl who couldn't have been more than fifteen exiting the compartment. She heard the girl's mother sobbing as the guard whispered flattering comments to the child as they walked down the hall.

"Good Lord, the man's a fiend!" said Claire.

"You can't go with him, Claire! Please don't go through with this. How degrading! Leclerc will come."

"We don't have *time* for that. I *have* to. Do you have any idea how long it will take Leclerc to get to France, find help, and then get back here? You could be guillotined by then even if *I* survive. Promise you won't tell Leclerc what I had to do to help us. He'd be so hurt. Better still, think about yourself now. You'll have to do what the guard wants when it's your turn. They mean to kill you with your lover, Celeste, make no mistake of that. They hate his family that much. Whatever Phillipe's father did to reap this much hatred on his family, it certainly twisted the nose of someone mighty important. It's a small price to pay for the life of your child, Celeste. Besides, you may never see Jean-Jacques again anyway. Where is he now when you need him? America? You have to save yourself in this life, cousin. No one is going to care more about your neck than you."

In this life. Celeste thought about her cousin's words and realized how true they were. Like it or not, she would go with this man if it meant making it to the equinox alive. She had to save the baby, Celeste, and the Charlotte Corday in her own lifetime. She thought of Jim. He'd be hurt to think of her in this man's arms. Well, it's *your* time tunnel not mine, she thought.

Chapter Twenty-Seven

The food was worse in prison than one might expect, but it had one saving grace—it was brought to them. No lines at the bakery. No fights in the streets. They were given black bread, cold water, and some fruit. The guard promised soup for lunch, and it was obvious that they were getting special privileges because they were going to have sex with him. The mother-to-be was famished, and Claire gave her cousin her allotment of fruit because of the baby.

"You have to keep up your strength," she said.

Celeste hesitated and then ate. Her stomach relaxed, and her headache went away.

That afternoon, Celeste was taken to a private cell. A dark figure stood in the shadows. "Hello, my love," said the somber voice.

"Phillipe?" she said.

Phillipe looked disheveled; his face was covered with dirt. He hadn't shaved for days, and his hair was greasy looking and unkempt. His eyes had lost their customary twinkle; his countenance resembled a man who had already died.

"I am so sorry." He ran to her and cradled her in his arms. "I told you to stay away. Now you know the truth. I've been married for many years. My wife is a sweet woman but could never be the one I was destined to love my whole life."

Celeste pulled away from him. "Fine words now. Liar. You could have told me the truth and let me decide what I wanted to do about it." Then she slapped him.

His head dropped, and his chin rested on his chest. He couldn't look at her. "I understand how you feel."

"No, you don't!" Celeste started to cry. The anger that had festered within her for so many years burst forth. "I adored you to the point of pushing away a man who loves me far more than you ever could. I could be with him now." She remembered the other Celeste's predicament. "And what were you going to do about our child?"

"I would have taken care of him. Of both of you."

"Acknowledge that he's yours?"

He shook his head and stared at his filthy hands. "No, I could never do that. Please understand that I *had* to marry according to my social standing."

"Even if I could understand all that, Phillipe, I could never forgive you for lying to me and abandoning me in...Paris without..." she hesitated. This Phillipe had written to her. "Oh, what's the point," she said finally tossing her hands into the air. "It's all a mess now, isn't it?" She went into his arms. "There's no point in arguing about it now, is there?" she said softly.

"I'm afraid we're all doomed, love. And the ladies in my life...including my daughters...will die with the family name."

She pulled away again. "I don't have your name."

"You've got to think of some way to survive, Celeste. When I was taken, the only thought I had was that, at least, you would be free. What were you thinking when you came to Bordeaux?"

"Of rescuing you. Leclerc and Claire came too, and you know what a sacrifice it was for them. Plus, Leclerc used some

262

of his own money, and Claire had to disguise herself so that no one would recognize her."

Phillipe smiled. "They are good to you."

"Leclerc fought passed the guards and fled to Paris to get help."

He paused before saying, "But the trial is soon, my love."

"I know. Claire has plans that frighten me. The guard."

"Tell her not to bother. The guards prey on the women here. They make promises, and the women, young girls mostly who are innocent to the ways of men, fall for their game. They tell them that they can free them by speaking on their behalf. These men have no power. They can't save anyone. And who are you to quarrel with them about them breaking their word to you after they've had their way, and you are led to the guillotine. They'll smile as the blade cuts into your spine. But, when it is your life, you will do anything."

"You mean; he won't keep his word."

Phillipe held her by the shoulders so that she could look into his eyes and see his meaning. "He'll use both of you."

"Oh, God, help us out of this hole."

"I don't mind telling you that I am frightened for myself and my family. But, I won't let them know that. I shall die as nobly as I can. And you will do that too. Pride is the last, and only thing, they cannot take from us."

She stared at him, then backed away slowly. "I don't intend to die with you, Phillipe." Her voice was cool, and her demeanor isolated from his crisis. "Somehow, and I haven't figured out how yet, I'll get out of this. There's more to our story than you know."

"Do you mean God?" He smirked and whispered, "He has forsaken us, Celeste."

Celeste was suddenly empowered. She thought of Jim's words. "No, I don't think He's forsaken me. There's someone waiting for me in America. All I have to do is find him."

Phillipe's words were bitter. "Another man?" He let out a disgusted snort and shrugged his shoulders. "So soon, my love?"

"Don't get righteous on me. You cheated on your wife, time period or no time period that makes you an adulterer anyway you look at it. I didn't know the truth; you did."

"But you said that you loved me."

Celeste looked up so that Phillipe wouldn't see her true thoughts reflected in her eyes. "I can't explain it all now, just know that I will have a life; I will survive, and your baby will live."

Phillipe stood straight, pulled his shoulders back, and raised his chest. "Then a de Brouquens will survive this?"

"Yes."

"And you will bring him back to France when this is all over?"

She answered quickly, "No. I will go to America, if Leclerc can work his magic and live there in peace. I will always remember the time we shared together, and I am sorry for this because it isn't right, and it isn't fair. Especially for your young daughters."

He held her close. "Then we'll not have loved in vain?"

"Destined to love until the karma is changed," she said,

thinking of 1990.

"I don't understand?"

"Trust me," she said kissing him gently on the lips. "Final farewell, Phillipe. God be with you in this life and the next."

Without looking back, she asked the guard to open the door of the cell and take her back to hers. It was over. Not even a second glance to see how he'd reacted to her words. Never again, in any lifetime, would she love Phillipe. She knew the truth...and...it had set her soul free to love again. Jim Cooper! She couldn't wait to see him again. This time, she would not let him get away from her. She would cherish him as she should have cherished Jean-Jacques Coupier.

"Was it bad?" asked Claire when Celeste walked through the door.

"Yes and no. It's over, Claire. Finally." Celeste sighed heavily. "Now all I have to do is find my way back to Jim...ah...I mean Jean-Jacques. I was so stupid to let him out of my sight."

Claire smiled and shook her head. "No, cousin, you did what you had to do—uncover the truth and try and help someone else—and that isn't such a bad thing."

"Perhaps."

"Well, the guard was here while you were gone."

Celeste's eyelids opened wide with fear. "Oh, Claire, Phillipe told me that you shouldn't listen to him. He's using you. He has no power and only wants free sex."

"Oh, I guessed that one. But, we can stall for time which is what we need right now."

"You mean you're just teasing him?"

265

Claire waved her hands dramatically underlining her words. "There are many things a woman can do for a man without opening her legs, Celeste."

Celeste shook her head. "I don't think I want to hear this."

They were brought steaming hot broth in wooden bowls, fresh baked *white* bread still warm from the baker's oven, and just picked apples and grapes for lunch. Claire smiled politely at the man who grinned back at her.

"This is actually pretty good," said the hungry Celeste. "And white bread. Two loaves. Flirt a lot, Claire."

"All for a smile and a show of flesh," she said, tying the strings of her blouse so that she would be covered again. "I told him that I was experienced in pleasing a man. He can't wait."

When the guard came to take away their bowls and give them some hot tea, he said, "I think they'll be ruling on you first," he said to Claire, "because they really don't have very much on you, and your reputation as a rebel has become known to the magistrate. Unfortunately, as you are being released, the case for your cousin will be brought to the jury. It doesn't look good for you," he said to Celeste. "There is a man on the jury who claims Monsieur de Brouquens has wronged his family for years, and I know he will push for the family's destruction. He'll want the life of the child. And he has already made comments that you were legally Phillipe's wife before Phillipe married his other woman. Is that true?"

Celeste guessed. "That is a lie."

"Apparently, the judge's sister lives in Paris and has tried, on many occasions, to get a job working for Tallon. She has often spoken about how Phillipe used his influence to get you that job."

Celeste and Claire fell silent.

"As long as we have a deal," he looked at one woman and then the other, "I might be able to help your cousin for a...price, of course."

Claire smiled, "Of course."

"How soon will they try Phillipe's case? You said in three days."

"Possibly sooner. Who knows? They've just established a court." He looked at Claire. "You are so beautiful."

"Get my cousin out of this mess, and you'll be *well* paid," Claire said.

"If I can." And he was gone.

There was a moment of silence between the two women.

"Leave, Claire. It's not your fault that I'm in this mess. Go back to Paris and live. Find Leclerc."

Claire's eyebrows knitted together, and she scowled. On some women it would be an ugly expression, but, for some reason, on Claire, it was rather charming. "Do you think that I would leave you? We're all we have. I told you that before. I have no intention of leaving you behind. I'm taking you out of here no matter what I have to do."

Celeste drank some of the lukewarm tea the guard had given her. Claire's words were comforting, but they did nothing to ease her growing fear. Maybe her time was up in both centuries.

Chapter Twenty-Eight

The judge found nothing substantial against Claire Lacombe. She was found innocent with only a slight slap on the wrist. Claire refused to leave her cousin though she was technically released two days after their imprisonment. The guard was very pleased with that aspect of their deal, and Claire followed through with the promise to give him what he wanted for their release. Though she hadn't really needed him to help her out of this jam, she knew her sacrifice could help her cousin. She would intervene on Celeste's behalf and go with him so that Celeste would not have to. The situation revolted Celeste, especially when she remembered Phillipe's words, but she admired Claire's loyalty. The man wasn't ugly, but the thought of him touching Claire made Celeste ill. Their sisterly conversation back in Paris had created a bond that circumstances could not deter. Claire's thoughts had turned to rescuing her cousin and the baby.

Phillipe's trial came one week after their discussion. The de Brouquens's family was found guilty at nine o'clock Thursday morning. The whole family was in the courtroom to hear the verdict, but the women were taken from the room when they continued examining information about Phillipe's mistress and his other unborn child. Celeste was not present.

The entire family was taken to cells in the lower level of the 'prison', according to what the guard had overheard, to be prepared for their execution at twelve o'clock that day. Celeste shivered with fear at the thought that the man she had once loved, his wife, and small children would be murdered that very day in a public display of hatred and blood lust. She remembered Charlotte's death and closed her eyes every time she had a mental vision of that grotesque spectacle. The babies would die the same way as the father.

The guard returned at eleven with more news. The judge had declared Celeste Lacombe guilty because she was pregnant with an aristocrat's child, and the early morning verdict that all members of the same family were to be destroyed. That reason, and the fact that she had taken a job from another woman, and benefited in other ways from her association with Phillipe, had condemned her. One man, unknown to the guard, had spoken on Celeste's behalf and requested a stay of execution to discover the committee's feelings about butchering a pregnant woman, and for the humane notion that Phillipe's wife need not be humiliated at her own execution by viewing her husband's whore in the cart with her and her daughters.

So this is how it ends for Celeste Lacombe, my past life, thought Celeste. In trouble with Phillipe again, she dies in 1793. Can I change it now, or do I have to wait until 2000? Will I ever get the chance to change anything?

She and Claire were moved to a new cell with a better view...of the guillotine. The guard was positioned outside their cell with no apparent inclination to move.

Celeste asked, "Why do you stay?"

"It's my job to watch you. I have to report how you react to his execution."

"I thought you were going to help us? Claire and you..."

"I can only do so much. I helped her; I just can't do

anything for you." He turned to her and smiled. "Enjoy the view."

The cart bearing the doomed family came through the crowd of people who were cheering them to their deaths. The little girls looked frightened, but Phillipe and his father looked proud and gallant. Phillipe seemed so handsome, courageous, and arrogant, she couldn't help feel a pang of pride at the fact that he had loved her. Despite all he had done to her, she knew that he had loved her. So, this was how she would find out what happened to Phillipe. Why had she been so damned curious? Watching him meet his fate would be the answer to all her questions. Now she knew—he had died in her lifetime, as well.

The woman who must have been his wife was pulled roughly from the cart. She was taken to a stake, or pole, in the ground that was under Celeste's window. Celeste could not see the woman's face, but she and his wife could both view the family's execution. Celeste dropped her head and closed her eyes. She was glad that this gentle lady never knew. Look at how her life ends. Loving and caring for a man who loved another and then watching all whom she loved die before her. They had placed her in front of the guillotine so that she could watch the whole execution of each one of her loved ones; and the audience could witness the horror on her face. It was part of the entertainment. And Celeste could see by the reactions of the crowd that they were enjoying the intense melodrama set before them. Celeste felt the baby kick. Yes, she thought, I am his wife now too. It is your Daddy who dies today.

The old man was the first to be strapped to the palate, and his head was swiftly dropped into a basket under the blade. It was removed, and his body was dropped onto a spot by the guillotine. Celeste wondered which bonnet in the crowd belonged to Emilia Coupier, and how she must feel holding back her tears so that those around her would not suspect her of Royalist sentiments.

As soon as they caught wind of what had just occurred to their grandfather, the little girls began to cry and scream. Their mother cried out to them to be good girls. They called to her in vain. She could not hold them nor comfort them. Their small, delicate hands were tied behind their backs; they could not reach up the side of mother's pretty dress to grasp her gloved hand for support. She would not be able to whisper encouraging words to them or kiss them on the cheek as a sign of her undying love. And she could not teach them to pray for their immortal soul's salvation. She could only call to them, and her words were almost completely whisked away by the cheering crowd.

Phillipe tried to show no emotion, but his father had just been butchered before his eyes, and his face was now red with anger. His mother begged to go next. "My husband. My husband," Phillipe's mother called from the cart to the crowd, and they laughed.

Out of respect for her age, she went next. She was a large woman of fashion, and the audience enjoyed the guards futile attempts to fasten her heavy body onto the wooden board. It was humiliating to watch. The crowd applauded as if it were the third act of a comedy when the sharp shaft cut the old woman's neck in two. There were comments from the crowd that there had been considerable doubt whether the old woman's fat neck would be too *stiff* to break. Madame de Brouquens, the elder, must have had many enemies by the sounds of it.

Then the oldest daughter was led to the guillotine. She was fair skinned and pretty with her father's lovely eyes and her mother's delicate frame. She could not have been older than ten. The young girl should have been gleefully planning her next birthday party, not facing public ridicule and death. The guard made some movement about her neck to move a bit of lace and take away her bonnet. She looked at her father and then at her mother. With her hands tied behind her, she was led to the wooden palate. They tied her face down to the board, and Celeste thought she heard the woman beneath her cell call the girl's name. And then it was over. That fast. That final.

"This is hideous!" cried Celeste to Claire who came to watch with her. "How can you have wanted such brutality, cousin?" Both women held onto each other, and soon the tears began to fall for the fate of the girl who would never feel her first kiss. The blade had taken her life swiftly and with no remorse from the crowd who cheered for more bloodshed.

Celeste moved from the window and said to the guard, "I can't watch anymore. You can't expect me to watch this."

"Why? They are hideous rich beasts, and it is good that they die. They starved us all while they squandered money on fancy clothes, food, and fine living. They showed no remorse to the thousands of French citizens who died at their feet while they sailed along the road with their arrogant noses in the air. Afraid they might dirty their hems on the filth of the poor. Did they feel guilty when our children died from malnutrition and lack of medical care? Then why should I care when one small rich bitch dies. They deserve what they get," said the guard.

"But the little girls! They have done nothing wrong."

"The verdict against them stated that all the family members must die, and die they shall. Why do you care? I thought you wore the cockade." He was becoming suspicious of the two women.

"I had no idea," said Claire as they led the eight-year-old girl to meet her fate. She wasn't as brave as her older sister. She screamed, wiggled to free herself, and shook with fear. Phillipe almost collapsed with emotion as he watched his brave girl's head fall into the same basket that held her grandmother's. Phillipe's wife sobbed uncontrollably and begged to be spared anymore grief by being the next one to die. The crowd applauded her words.

The three-year-old, who had to be lifted above the steps to make it to the guillotine, didn't quite fit on the table, and she kicked the guards and cried violently to be let go. "My Papa will beat you for this," she screamed and thrust her little fist in the guard's face. It was clear the executioner did not want to harm the baby. There was some tension in the air as the crowd, thrilled to see the hesitation on the man's face, waited excitedly to see whether he would flinch from his duty, if he would beg for the child's freedom.

"Why don't you do your duty? Hurry it up," roared the crowd.

The executioner did not move a muscle.

One of the guards finally managed to tie her hands behind her small back and strap her into place. She called to her mother and father. It was the tearful cry of a baby who is frightened beyond her limits. The executioner realized that he could no longer prolong her agony, and to make sure her death was swift, pushed the table before the girl anticipated it, and the baby died without realizing it was her time. A small sign of compassion.

Phillipe was led up the steps of the guillotine. He did not appear frightened. His head was held high, and he mumbled his prayers. He called to his wife one last time, but Celeste could not hear what he said.

Celeste could hear his wife below say, "Phillipe, mon coeur. I love you."

Phillipe acknowledged his wife and then his gaze lifted upwards as if he were looking for a guardian angel to take him to his family in heaven. He saw Celeste in the window. As they were bending his body to be tied to the table, he smiled up at her. She waved to him. Then the palate moved under the blade that sliced his head from his shoulders.

It was too much for Celeste. She cried, "This can't be happening. Please say that this is some sort of macabre dream. Claire!"

"I'm here. I'm here," was all the revolutionary could say to her cousin.

When the guards took the weak and shivering woman from the stake and motioned that she could move to the scaffold, Celeste began to sob hysterically. She fell to the floor to the cell and cried until her heart would burst. "Oh God!"

Claire wasn't sure how to react, but assuming her role was to be sisterly, she knelt by Celeste and cradled her against her chest.

"There, there, cousin, it's over now. Once and for all."

"She cried for him," said the guard bitterly.

"Why? Wouldn't you have expected that?"

"Not from a woman who wears the cockade. I must take this information back to my superior. I must tell them that she cried at his death. Just like a wife." He looked at both of them. Celeste wasn't able to focus on his words or his face. She would never forget what she had just seen.

"He's dead. The father of my baby has been butchered, and all you can think about is politics!" she wailed at him angrily.

"I'm a soldier guarding those who have committed atrocities against the people. The case against the arrogant and heartless de Brouquens's family sealed their fate not I. He used you. Why do you care what happens to him? Unless you are like them."

"A three-year-old baby girl was just murdered out there today. You didn't watch that, did you? Why? Do you have a child?"

"No, I'm not even married."

"Then how would you know what it feels like to see your own child die like that. An innocent child. To hell with all of you. This isn't a revolution; it's pure and simple greed and murder. That baby did nothing to harm anyone."

"I've already told you about the verdict. Why do you go on so about it? Claire, you understand now, don't you? You of all people. This is what *you* meant by 'putting the terror on the agenda', isn't it?"

"I thought I did, but that's all changed now. I want to go home. You said that I could. And I want my cousin out of here with me, tonight. You promised to help, and I did what you asked."

He looked like a man in a tough spot. "All right! Quiet down now. I can arrange it, I think. I can tell them that she shed no tear for the bastard, and you can both leave tomorrow morning. If I don't, she dies at noon."

"That wasn't what you said originally."

"I was supposed to lie so that I might see her true reactions to the death of her lover. I have. She's guilty. Unless...you...come with me now and do what I want."

Claire looked at her cousin. "I've already done that."

"Once more to take her place in the bargain."

"You're lying," Claire said.

"No, I swear, I can fix it."

"You'll help both of us?" asked Claire.

"Yes. Both. I swear."

"He's lying, Claire, don't go with him. He's proven what a liar he is, how can you trust he won't turn on me? How can he be lying one minute, and then expect us to believe his words the next?"

"I can understand your concern, but I can assure you that your fate is in my hands right now. That's plain enough. When I come back with your cousin, I shall have permission to set you free."

"Don't do it, Claire," said Celeste.

Claire looked at her cousin and smiled gently. A loss of pride to save her beloved cousin's life. It wasn't much to ask of a fighter like Claire Lacombe. And it was something she could control. "What choice do we have now, Celeste? I don't mind.

Really. I'll be back soon, I swear."

The man took hold of her shoulders as soon as he took her out of the cell and kissed her hard on the lips. "Come, sweet one. I've been thinking about this all day."

He directed her to the hallway, but before Claire left she said to Celeste, "I'll be all right. And so will you. You just keep praying it will all work out. I'll be back in an hour."

Celeste took one last look at the butchery that had occurred in the street that day and felt a cold blade of panic run up her spine. "This had better work, Claire," she said to no one. Then she stayed awake all afternoon, unable to sleep even a minute, waiting for her cousin's return.

She never saw Claire Lacombe again.

Chapter Twenty-Nine

A myriad of horrible thoughts about what might have happened to Claire went through Celeste's mind the least of which was that her cousin had abandoned her to her fate. She couldn't believe Claire would do such a thing.

She was left alone to ponder the incidents of that day. She had witnessed the brutal murder of the man she had loved and lost in two lifetimes. She had viewed an old man, and his beloved spouse die knowing that the man's lover, Emilia, was watching every moment of their destruction. Three innocent babies had met an untimely death. And Jean-Jacques had fled France at the very moment his father had met his demise on the guillotine. Was there any rhyme or reason to any of this? And now Claire was gone, and all the comfort of her cousin's support and wisdom had vanished. Her stomach growled for food, and the baby kicked constantly. She couldn't blame her little son—for somewhere along the path to Bordeaux she had decided it was the son for which Phillipe had hoped.

There was no news until dinnertime when a guard brought her food. It was not the same guard as the one who had dallied with Claire. This one was stern and unsympathetic.

"Excusez moi, Monsieur," she interrupted him as he slid her dinner under the door to her.

He acknowledged her with a snort and a hesitation in his step.

"Where is my cousin? She was to be brought back to me this afternoon, and she's not returned. Please tell me whether she is all right."

"She's good from what Henri has told me. But, she was taken by coach to Paris. She has been moved to her own city where there are those who wish to keep an eye on her. Of course, Henri didn't tell her that until...afterwards," he said smiling.

"She asked whether she could stay with me. I don't understand." Her voice tried to follow him, gain his attention so that he would answer her and not walk away.

"She's been moved, that's all I know," he said and turned away. "No one is allowed in here now."

Her voice softened as if she knew the answer to her own question. "Why?" It was fainter than a whimper.

"Don't you know why you were moved?"

Celeste shuddered. Maybe be she did after all. "He didn't say anything to us. He gave me the impression that they wanted to watch my reactions to the family's execution."

"This is a holding cell for those meant to be executed. That is why your cousin has been taken to Paris. She's a troublemaker and might have tried to spare you from your fate. Anyway, I was told that you are allowed no visitors."

"The guard," she said cautiously, "told us that I had not been marked for death, and that a man spoke on my behalf. That they wished to examine my case more closely."

"They condemned you this morning along with the de Brouquens's family, but Phillipe asked for a personal favor so that his wife and children might be spared the humiliation of dying on the same day as his mistress. That they might be able to think good thoughts about him when they left for heaven. I'm rather surprised that the court agreed, but they did."

"He worried about *their* feelings?"

"Yes, quite noble, don't you think?"

Her eyelids closed halfway. "Humiliation? Was that the word he used."

"Yes. His wife didn't know about it, you see. But, like it or not, the barber will be here later this evening to cut your long hair, and at nine o'clock tomorrow you will be taken from this cell to the place of execution. You will die with the servants of the de Brouquens's family."

The bitterness sealed her throat. "*The servants!*" she coughed. "But I thought that they didn't execute pregnant women."

"They could decide to do that, but until then, your case has not been overruled because of your condition since it is precisely that condition which has doomed you. All heirs must die."

She thought of Jean-Jacques. He would survive. The de Brouquens's name *would* survive since the old man had acknowledged his illegitimate son's birthright at the end and given him an inheritance to use for escaping the family's fate. That was why Jean-Jacques's mother had urged him out of the country, and why Celeste had been told to follow him. When the reign of terror was finished, Jean-Jacques and the baby would inherit anything left of the estate. That must have been why he was willing to marry her despite her maternal condition. Did he love her, or did he just want her because he could marry the woman his half-brother loved? Interesting thought. The baby would be son and nephew simultaneously.

Would she and the other Celeste die together? Apparently

so. It must be her time to die in 2000, and she would meet her fate here. But, she didn't want to die. This was all so stupid. Her other personality was a poor artist barely able to make a living, in love with a selfish, misguided aristocrat. She was carrying his child yet to be born who would never sound its first cry. So this is how it ends for Celeste Lacombe. Alone. Abandoned. Poor, pregnant, and having missed a perfect opportunity to be with a good man who probably loved and sympathized with her plight by shunning him in that one moment when he needed her to be his completely. Stupid choice. And, of all things, cousin and friend to the one woman in all of France responsible for the countless executions of the very family whose heir Celeste had loved.

She had shown allegiance by wearing the cockade. She'd mourned Marat. She'd lived with two outspoken rebels whose words would now kill her. Could there be any other human on this earth whose existence could be more paradoxical? She remembered Charlotte. "I won't be there to help her," she thought. To plead her case and finally solve this unjust murder. No one will know the truth. And then there was Jim. Waiting for his lover to come home on the equinox. That thought made her cry.

The guard said, "Now, don't do that. It's of no use. I can't get your cousin for you, she's gone. She will have to be careful from now on. There have been rumors spread about her, and some important people are looking into the idea that she may be an outspoken traitor bent on harming the revolution."

"Claire? Never."

"Well, everyone is suspicious of everyone these days.

Would you like some more food?" His voice had undergone a change. "I could probably find some more for you."

"No thank you. I've lost my appetite."

"Try to sleep. Do you want a priest? There's one outside who is volunteering his services to anyone who wishes to repent."

She shook her head. "Oui. Why not?"

Celeste drank some water, ate some of the soup that was still very hot, and tasted the bread. Her hands started to shake, and she wrung them in an attempt to still her trembling fingers. She stared at her hands, and then covered her eyes with them. She tried to stop the motion but couldn't. She felt cold and hot at turns. Then she vomited her food. Her throat began to squeeze shut, and she swallowed more water to ease the tightness. Her hand went to her stomach protectively. "No, we can't die," she said to her son. "We have to survive. But how?"

The guards had an interesting way of ignoring her the rest of the afternoon and into the early evening. Their emotional separation from her implied that they found executing a pregnant woman distasteful. Isolation, loneliness, and fear kept her awake. What was the point in sleeping when eternal rest was impending?

She slumbered for about an hour or so and was awakened to another hot meal. When she was finished, a man came to cut her hair. He took his time. The beautiful golden brown locks fell into a sack he had with him. He even shaved her neck. "Do you feel the blade now, Mademoiselle?"

Celeste refused to show any fear to this man.

"Here is a gown you shall wear," he said. "You may

wear your own clothes if you wish, but this is the customary shift women wear to have their heads cut from their throat."

Celeste trembled as she held the linen dress in her hands. He had given her a cap just like the one Charlotte had worn. She looked at the bag that held all her souvenirs: the portrait, the bonnet, the sketch, the skirt, the torn cockade, the doll. She would not wear the dress. Her white and blue striped skirt would do. They might as well realize what fools they are—killing one of their own.

Eventually, the guard found the priest and ushered him into the cell.

"You wish to confess your sins and take Holy Communion, my child?"

"Ah...yes...I suppose I do at that."

"Kneel before me."

"That might be a bit difficult with my belly."

"I see, yes, of course. Please, Sir," the priest said the the guard, "would you be good enough to leave us while the lady confesses her sins. One's confession should be private."

The guard agreed.

"A prayer before you confess?"

"Yes, Father."

"Holy love. One who shall be redeemed in a matter of minutes once I slip the key into the lock. Be ever-aware that thy Father in heaven, who knows a good friend in a large bastille in Paris, has a very fast horse outside this pathetic excuse for a prison, and a dagger or two up his enormous sleeves. Please gather up your earthly belongings, kiss my ring, and whimper pathetically as if you are ashamed of your disgraceful sins."

Celeste looked into the half-hidden face of Jean-Jacques Coupier.

"*You didn't leave me!*"

"How could I? Now do as I say, or we're both dead."

Celeste did a performance even her own cousin couldn't top. "Bless me Father for I have sinned."

"That's an understatement."

She wailed loudly. He handed her a bag of hay that he had used to make himself look bulbous. "Take that cotton shift, fill it with hay, and then put the cap on it so that it looks like a human form."

Celeste did as he said.

"Put her in bed and turn her to the wall so that it looks as though you are sleeping. That should keep them away until morning. Put this on."

He took off his clergy robe and gave it to her. He had been wearing the exact uniform the guards wore underneath the priest's robe. "It wasn't hard to get these from my police friends either."

"But how did you know I was in trouble?"

"I knew that if you came *here*, there was a good chance you'd get in the middle of it all. My mother told me when I arrived last night."

"Then you know about your father."

"Yes, now there will be plenty of time to talk on board the ship provided we make it there in one piece. Dress quickly."

"But the ship left, didn't it?"

"That one did, yes. There are others, and I have a few friends in low places."

"I thought you left. That I had made you angry with me."

"The trouble with women is that no matter how simple they can be—if you love them—you have to keep them from their own misadventures."

She smiled at his comment. "You love me?"

"What a question? Do you think that I would risk my neck for just anyone?"

"I know about Phillipe being your brother. I thought..."

"Would you do me a big favor?"

"Anything."

"Shut up and follow me."

Celeste grabbed her souvenir bag, put it under the robe but on the lower part of her back, and tied the priest's belt around her hips so that it looked as if she were as chubby in back as she was in her front.

He slipped the skeleton key into the cell door, and it opened. "Come this way, Father," he said, using a rough sounding voice. "I'll show you out of the prison." Then he answered himself in his other voice. "Poor girl. She is at peace after confession. Well, she is with God now."

Celeste grinned and leaned up and kissed him on the cheek. It occurred to her that this was the second time she had kissed him in front of a barred cell door.

"Keep your head down under the hood of the robe and walk normally. Your pregnancy will be mistaken for my fat hay belly. Don't appear anxious. If anyone says anything to you, give them the Holy cross sign, and that should shut them up."

"A blessing?"

"Yes, and if all goes well we'll be on the road soon. I have only one horse, and you'll have to ride behind my saddle. I hope you don't mind. The baby and all. I'll take it slowly on the road. We don't have very far to go."

"We won't be going back to Paris?"

"We'll never see it again."

She thought of Claire and Leclerc. She would never see *them* again either. How strange it all seemed and yet wonderfully adventurous also.

"When we get outside, walk away from the prison and maneuver your way across the street. You'll see a lit barn. My horse is saddled and ready. Wait for me there. It will look suspicious if I walk with you to the barn just after you've exited the prison."

She whispered, "Don't take too long."

They walked slowly passed two guards who were playing some sort of game with coins. Jean-Jacques waved a good night greeting to the guards, and Celeste gave them the blessing.

She followed his instructions to the letter. After she left the prison, she walked directly to the barn as he had told her to do. He went elsewhere, but she had no idea where. She dared not look after him, or peek out of the barn door to see where he might be. It was so difficult waiting there. Not knowing whether he had been caught. Worrying that the footsteps going passed the barn door might be a guard who had followed her. If she were caught now, there would be no salvation for either of them. She tried to breathe evenly, but the pain in her chest, the tension in her muscles, and the rapid pounding of her heart against her breast kept her in a state of near panic. Her lips were unbearably dry, and she licked them often which only made them more chapped. The hay around her made her want to sneeze, and she had to stifle it. The horses looked at her with mild distrust. Jean-Jacques's horse seemed ready for action. The aroma of horse dung made her want to vomit. Even the baby was still as if he could sense his mother's stress. It seemed like hours, but, actually, it had only been about twenty minutes before Jean-Jacques was in her arms.

"I love you," she said. "Oh, hold me. I love you so much." Her blue eyes were sparkling with happiness.

He stared at her as if she were the most precious diamond in the world. "You're so beautiful. I couldn't leave you...just couldn't. I suppose my love needed testing. It's not my imagination though; I adore you!" He pulled back the hood of the priest's robe to look at her. "Ah, your hair!"

She combed it with her fingers and blushed. "I know. Does it look awful?"

"No. It makes you look more beautiful."

Her eyes teared. "Thank God you came!" She hugged him tightly.

"We need to go." He climbed onto his horse and reached down for her hand. "No regrets, Celeste?"

"The beginning of my whole life is right here with me now. How could I even imagine a life with anyone else?"

"Good!"

She reached her hand up to meet his, put her foot in the stirrup, and let him pull her up so that she sat behind him.

Celeste took her bag from her backside and placed it on her stomach—between her belly and Jean-Jacques's back—to cushion the baby during their escape.

She held onto his waist, placed her cheek against his back, and closed her eyes.

"There was no life until you came into mine. I was disillusioned, but that's all over now. I have no memory of a time without you, Jim...ah...Jean-Jacques. I thought I knew love, but how could I have understood it when you are the only one who could teach my heart to live. It was dead for so long. But, now it's alive...with you. I feel its life inside my chest for the first time; it sings a new song because of you. How many ways can I tell you how much I love you?"

"Do you mean that, Celeste Lacombe?"

She kissed the back of his head. "Get going before they spot us."

The horse moved slowly from the stable and crept into the darkness.

Chapter Thirty

Jean-Jacques guided his horse towards the slopes of the Chateau Trompette. Celeste marveled that he could find the road in the darkness, but he managed to keep them moving at a slow, smooth gallop. They stopped when they came to the end of the Quai des Chartrons. Jean-Jacques dropped from his horse and then helped Celeste from the back of the tired animal.

"Take my animal," he said to someone near the water and the man paid him some coins.

Celeste couldn't guess the time only that it must be mid-morning because of the dim light sneaking between the clouds. She had no clue how far they had traveled. A man met them there and asked for their passports which Jean-Jacques gave to him for verification. The man seemed uneasy, and Jean-Jacques hurried matters along with, "We have little time. I'm sure they must be aware that she is missing. Make haste."

They climbed into a dinghy and were steered towards their ship called the *Helena*. The water smelled of mud and reptiles, but there was a fresh smell of wildflowers nearby. There was something about the stench of the heat of August; the sweat of the horse; the perspiration and dirt on their clothes after riding; the mixture of sweet yet pungent air about the black water that, all combined, brought to her mind a similar scenario near a cabin by a lake in New York state. And that thought was pleasant enough to make her smile.

Jean-Jacques took Celeste's hand to ease her fear, and that movement reassured her that soon they would be free from

France and danger. Free to choose their own way in life...together.

Celeste noted that the tiny boat held the supplies that would have to sustain them on their trip. The man, obviously their new captain, saw her look at the jars and spoke as he maneuvered the boat.

"I've obtained a few jars of potted goose, some sacks of potatoes, French beans, a case of bottled jam, fifty bottles of Bordeaux wine, and a barrel of biscuits which, sadly, have been on board for about a year. Such short notice. It's the best I can do."

Jean-Jacques's voice was comforting. "It will do. Thank you."

Celeste knew that it was not enough to keep them alive the full length of the trip.

"We might be able to get some fresh meat and supplies while we sail," said the captain, trying to help.

The captain wasn't any taller than Celeste, and he was quite heavy around the middle. He wore a seaman's coat and hat and old black trousers with high boots. It was hard to see his ragged face and his unkempt hair in the dim light. He was probably in his early forties, but hard work and many storms must have etched those jagged lines into his face. She could not tell the color of his eyes. His hair was brown, and she didn't see any gray. She wagered that she would see more of him on the long trip.

They hadn't traveled very far when they were stopped by the authorities. A warship that was stationed on sentinel duty in the middle of the river, at the very entrance to the port, blocked any chance of escape. Jean-Jacques squeezed her hand—a signal to keep quiet. Celeste had no intention of moving an eyelash. The captain took all his papers and their passports in preparation for the expected interrogation. The moment was tense. Celeste and Jean-Jacques could be seen by those on board. Her short hair was a give away that she was a prisoner of the Republic so she pulled the priest's hood over her head and pretended to be a holy man.

"At least I look like a soldier," Jean-Jacques said to her. "It will be all right; you'll see. Be calm."

"Don't speak French," the captain warned them.

"What are you going to do?"

"Hope I can relay, in my poor French, that we are harmless and have no aristocratic refugees on board. Stay quiet. Even a priest is suspect these days."

The captain went on board the warship.

They heard the other captain say, "I can't understand a word. Ask the priest to speak for you. Surely he can speak French."

Celeste looked at Jean-Jacques. "Don't go," he said.

Just then a French boat full of men in uniforms arrived in the midst of the exchange. "Why are you blocking the way?" shouted one of the men in the boat.

Their captain gathered his papers and came back to the dinghy. He mumbled, "Perfect timing." The warship was compelled to open the path to the river and let all boats continue without further delay. "God is with us," said the captain with a smile.

The *Helena*, which had gone down on the preceding tide to

the Bec d'Ambez, was sitting silently on the banks waiting for her master to put her out to sea. It was a small, American built vessel of only 150 tons with a tall, solitary mast. She had no cargo but twenty-five cases of what appeared to be wine, but Celeste couldn't be sure. The crew consisted of three sailors, a cabin boy who acted as steward, the captain, a young man who acted as the captain's mate and who, like the captain, also came from Nantucket, and an old, experienced sailor who the captain consulted constantly.

The captain's cabin was very small. Jean-Jacques and Celeste would sleep on the tiny bed while the captain would be forced to sleep on a chest covered with a blanket and a pillow. This would be their home for at least a month.

Glad to be hidden from searching eyes, Celeste removed the priest's robes and used it and her bag as a pillow. She was still wearing the dress she had worn when she, Leclerc, and Claire left Paris. It was torn, filthy, and smelled of perspiration. She and Jean-Jacques cuddled together on the bed, throwing the captain's blanket around their bodies for comfort. They slept until sunlight awakened them.

The next ebb tide took them down to Pauillic where they were stopped again by two guard ships. Officers came on board to question the captain, peruse what was on board, and check their papers. Celeste pulled the priest's costume on again while Jean-Jacques eased the officers' concern.

"I have to rejoin my regiment," he said. "Please don't detain us further. This man was kind enough to give me passage, or else I would never make it back in time."

"Why were you separated from your regiment?" one

officer asked.

Jean-Jacques masked his irritation. "You know that I cannot tell you that. I'm not free to speak of military matters, but I can assure you that if you hinder me from my duty, I will tell the General, himself, the names of those who dared interfere with my mission."

It was enough to stop the search. Jean-Jacques's uniform had convinced them. That and a few bottles of wine. The rolling of the ship made Celeste ill, and she found herself on deck much of the time with her head over the side of the boat. She wasn't sure if it was the rolling of the boat, the nervous excitement of having almost met death head-on, or the baby's kicking that caused her to feel so sick; but Jean-Jacques showed his sensitive side as he stood beside her and spoke words of encouragement to her as she wretched into the water that swirled around *Helena's* side.

"You'll get used to the movement," cried the captain. "You just need to get your sea legs, that's all."

The fact that she had had no solid food for ten hours was the real problem. Jean-Jacques asked the captain for some biscuits, but they were quite stale, and Celeste couldn't stomach them.

"Should I soften it with some boiled water?" asked Jean-Jacques.

"If you do that, the weevils will crawl out," said the captain as matter-of-factly as if he had just informed them that the water was cold.

Celeste wretched as soon as he said that.

"I can get her some tea, and I can toast the biscuits and

soften that with sweet wine."

Celeste wondered if she would survive this part of her time traveling experience. She did not wish to offend the captain who was trying to be as kind as possible to his pregnant passenger.

"Thank you very much," she said as though she meant it, "that's most kind of you."

She ate the toast—trying to forget how infested it was—and drank the tea until her stomach felt better. Jean-Jacques watched her eat; his face filled with concern and helplessness. The food settled her stomach enough to eat some more of the toast with a bit of jam spread on it.

She smiled at him. "I'll be all right. We're safe now; that's all that matters."

The crease in his forehead relaxed a bit. "I wish we could get you something solid to eat."

"I had a good meal in prison before you came. I'll be all right."

"We haven't had much time to speak with each other, have we?"

"Everything happened so fast."

"So, you know about my mother?"

"Yes, she and I spoke. She told me to find you in Boston. Did you go to see her when you came for me?"

"I saw her for about an hour. She told you about Phillipe being my half-brother?"

"Yes."

"You're probably thinking that I want to marry you because of him. That I wanted to win you away from him so that I could claim something of his as my own. Some sort of jealous revenge, but it isn't so."

"Why don't you tell me all about it; I think we have some time."

He laughed, and the sides of his mouth raised to accommodate it. It was nice to see he could do that. Always stern and professional looking, Jean-Jacques had never shown his good-natured side. It made him look even more like Jim.

"I went to Paris to be as far away from my father and his 'legitimate' family as I could get. I was passing time in the streets one day when Phillipe came to your house. I heard his carriage man call him by name, and I knew right away who he was. In all honesty, I was initially interested in him alone. How much we looked alike and so on. My mother, who was constantly harping on me to find a nice girl and settle down, and to forget about my birthright, had told me how much my brother and I looked alike. Then I saw you. I knew that he would never marry you because he was already married. I thought that it was such a shame because you were all that a man could ask for in a woman. I started watching you when he was gone. You became an obsession, I guess, because; in a way, you and Phillipe resembled my father and mother's story. The whole thing, the parallel, just fascinated me. You'll forgive me for saying so, but how could you not know that he was married?"

"Ahm...ah...I guess love is blind."

"And I think, in his own way, he loved you too. Of course that all doesn't matter now; you've chosen a different path. I hope you aren't sorry about spending the rest of your life with me. I'm no aristocrat, but I will take care of you and give you all that I have."

"I *was* in love with him, but I was also very intrigued with you when I first spied you stalking...ah...I mean watching me."

He looked at his hands and smiled. "I didn't make a very good first impression, did I? Hauling you off to prison like that. But, it was really about Claire." He smiled. "It was so amusing the way she came for you that day. What a great actress. Such a warrior!"

Celeste laughed. "I know. Ah, poor Claire. What will become of her?"

He tilted his head sideways. "Do you miss them? Leclerc and Claire?"

She looked down at the floor boards so that he wouldn't see her eyes fill briefly with tears. "Of course, we were close. But, I don't miss the guillotine or all the unrest in Paris. You saved my life."

"I had to. There would be no life for me without you. I realized that after our argument."

"You had a right to be upset. I mean, from your point of view, I can understand it."

"If we ever make it to the colonies, I promise to make it up to you. I have some money, as I've told you, and we'll buy a house...in town if you like."

"And the baby?"

"I will love him as if he were my own. After all, I am his uncle. I need to make him a good life. Not one where he is living in the shadows of a family crest. Not living with the shame of being illegitimate. That is my gift to him. A name to be proud of."

She paused before saying, "Will you call yourself de Brouquens in America? You can you know. Your father recognized you as his own. He gave you your birthright."

"No. Despite what you might think, I do not wish to hear that name again. I will always be called by my mother's name, for I respect her above all. She has lost her lover and her son. She is completely alone now. And yet all she could think of when I spoke with her was my happiness and my future with you. And despite all that has happened to her...all that he's done to her...she still loves him. Always will."

"I'm glad your father acknowledged you as his son if only for her sake. It must have relieved her some. By the way, not to change the subject, why do you think it's a boy?"

He laughed. "Well, I don't know. I just assumed. Will you tell him that I am his father...or *her* father?"

She hesitated. "If you wish me to. Yes. There's no point in telling him about a father who died on the guillotine and can never claim him. A man who didn't have the courage to make him legitimate. I think you're correct about it being a boy. Ironic, isn't it?"

He seemed uneasy all of a sudden. "I meant what I said about loving you. It's not easy to say these things when you are a man not given to warm sentiment by nature."

"I understand. It must have been a difficult life. To know and see a father who could never give you a real family."

"Will you help me have that family, Celeste?"

"Forever in America?"

"If you don't want to go back to France, that's fine by me.

297

I'll miss seeing my mother, but a man takes a wife and must go on his own. She'll understand."

"She lost someone that dreadful morning too."

"If you had any idea of how much she loved him. How he hurt her. Used her."

"She could have gone if she wished."

Jean-Jacques stared into her eyes. "Not if you love someone. You can't leave them if you love them, no matter how they treat you. That's what I've learned about women."

"Oh? You've had many?"

"I've never had a true love, just temporary trysts."

"And you can forgive me mine?"

"Of course. He isn't in your heart anymore, is he?"

"No. There's no room in there even for his memory. I only want you. It's a totally different feeling. A mature one. And more than just physical attraction, mind you. Much deeper. The real thing."

He moved close to her and held her in his arms. "And when we can finally love, will you...find...me...?"

"Exciting? You are the handsomest man I've ever met. I want you so much. It's just that..."

"I know, not now, the baby. I can wait. Just hold me and kiss me and tell me that you'll never desert me."

A blend of fear, sorrow, and amusement passed through her heart. "No, I won't leave you. Ever. You'll be surprised how faithfully I commit when I've a mind to." She thought she might tell Jim the same thing when she returned home.

"I've had no complaints from my lovers," he said with a smile.

She returned the smile. "I bet." She ran her hand inside his shirt and felt his hot skin on her hand. "Kiss me."

He moved his hand up to her chin, looked into her eyes, and gently, then forcefully kissed her on the lips.

"You can do that a few more hundred times," she said.

He laughed at her remark. "You know, some day I'd like to write about my experiences in Paris these last few years."

Celeste's eyes twinkled, and she giggled at his remark. "You should. And I have something for you to put on the inside cover." She ran to fetch her bag and took out the picture. "Here. I did this for you."

He looked at the portrait. "This is amazing. How could you have made such a perfect sketch when you only saw me a few times and never for very long? Utterly amazing. You are good."

"Keep it; it's yours. My first gift to you."

"And I have one for you. It belonged to my mother." He reached inside his military jacket and found a tiny box. "Her father gave it to her when she turned sixteen, and she gave it to me to give to the woman I would marry. Will you wear it for me?"

"My God, this is an heirloom," thought Celeste. She slipped it on the third finger of her left hand. It fit snugly. "Is it a sapphire?"

"Yes. Emerald cut with real diamonds on the sides. It cost my grandfather quite a bit, but she was his only child and his darling. Now I give it my darling. From my mother to you."

"I am so happy, and it's all because of you," she exclaimed.

"Well, I should hope."

"No. I mean *really* happy. In my heart. My head is light, and my whole body feels as if I could float out into the sky. This is amazing."

"I'm that good?"

"Kiss me a thousand times more, and I might just dissolve entirely. The ring is beautiful. Thank you."

"Like your eyes. Sparkling blue just like your eyes. More than he'd ever give you," he said more bitterly than he should have.

"Let's make a pact never to talk about him ever again. He's gone. From the earth, from our lives, and from my heart."

The baby kicked, and, for the first time, and because of his nearness to her stomach, Jean-Jacques felt it.

"I guess someone else wants to acknowledge this happy day as well."

Celeste sighed in his arms. "I want to go home." She blushed when she realized what she had said. He'd think she meant Paris. "I mean I want a home. That's what I meant. With you."

"I was thinking, since we're on our way now, might we let the captain marry us?"

She held his hand in hers and squeezed it tightly. "If that's what you want."

They walked to the deck together. The day was gray and dismal. It had been raining, and the boards of the ship were wet and slippery. The skies showed signs of not clearing until September. The dawn should have been breaking through the clouds, but it was suffocated behind darkness. It wasn't the prettiest picture for a wedding, but they didn't care.

"What are you two doing up here?" asked the captain nervously.

Jean-Jacques hesitated.

"The course? You're wondering where we're headed. I know, it seems unusual to be steering north, but I have a dreadful fear of Algerian pirates. Our country's at war, you know, and American ships have been seized with little provocation. We're only two leagues out of Tour de Courdouan, but I'm steering her north until I can detect the waters north of Ireland."

Jean-Jacques tried to interrupt.

"I know, I know, but I won't feel completely safe until then. I don't believe that the French navy can protect us against marauders. They won't provoke the British though, and that's where I lay my bet."

"But the weather?" said Jean-Jacques.

"Won't change me from my course. It's the safest bet for us in the end. Didn't want to mention it before, but, back there, at Pauillac, when we were stopped; I heard someone talking about how a frigate, called the Atlante, met an American boat full of French passengers at the port of La Rochelle, seized it, took the passengers to Brent, and guillotined them for trying to escape."

Celeste could feel the fear rise in her throat, and she held onto Jean-Jacques's arm tightly.

The captain smiled. "Don't want that to happen to you two, and if the Algerians catch us, we'll be cast into slavery; so, if it's all the same to you, we'll do this my way."

"I see your point though I would feel better if we weren't taking such a long route with such little provisions and Celeste being pregnant."

"I understand, and I will stop and find food when I have a chance, of course. But, that isn't all you wanted to ask me, is it?"

"No." Jean-Jacques looked at Celeste before saying, "I was hoping, rather asking, if you might marry us as you are the captain of this ship."

The man smiled, and his face radiated real joy.

"Well, that's an easy one. Fancy ceremonies ain't my style, but if you wait a minute, I'll get my book and straight 'ways marry you off."

"That would be nice," Jean-Jacques said.

"Get everyone on board," he shouted to the steward.

The sky was gloomy and threatened to rain, but the two lovers stood beside each other and saw only the brightness each other's eyes.

"Do you take this woman to be your wife?" asked the captain.

Jean-Jacques said, "I do."

"And do you take this man to be your husband?"

"I do," Celeste said.

"Then by the power invested in me as captain of this vessel, it be done. I now pronounce you husband and wife. You may kiss the bride."

Jean-Jacques held Celeste in his arms as if she were the most precious possession he owned, stared into her eyes for some time, and smiled his sideways grin.

"I love you," she said, and he kissed her.

Jean-Jacques said, "The day might portend gloom, but I

promise you that from this day forward and forever more I shall not leave your side, Celeste Coupier. Ever."

She looked at his face and thought of Jim, and, in her mind, she was marrying him; but her words had to match the present moment. "I will, from this day forward, abide by my husband's wishes in all things; and I will love him, protect him, and see to his happiness forever. I now have someone who loves me, wants me, and who will take care of me for longer than one lifetime. I will be a faithful, loyal wife, his best friend, who will nurse him when he's sick, take care of his slightest whim, and never let him down. Ever."

"Hold me," Jean -Jacques said. "I've waited a long time to hear those words."

She smiled and thought of how long her Jim had waited too. "I know," she said and smiled. "I know."

Later that night, when Jean-Jacques was sound asleep, Celeste found her bag, took the portrait of Phillipe from its hiding place, and tiptoed to the deck of the *Helena*. Without looking at the rolled canvas, she tossed it into the sea. It was too dark to see the waves engulf the man's face.

"Forever, goodbye," was her final, emotionless remark to Phillipe de Brouquens.

Chapter Thirty-One

The two newlyweds slept side by side on the mattress in the *Helena's* living quarters. It was the only form of intimacy they could share. It was enough for both of them to feel the other's heartbeat, the variation in temperature on the other's skin, and sense the mutual longing to be one. A kiss. A quick embrace. Lips close enough to whisper soft words of love.

It was difficult for Celeste not to think of how wonderful it was to sleep in Jim's arms after making love to him because Jean-Jacques was so much like him...and yet so much his own person. When she had time to think about it, it was uniquely exciting to have two men be one lover. She liked Jean-Jacques's stern, commanding, courageous, domineering personality; but, Jim was more sensitive and appreciated her for her intelligence and independence. She yearned to make love to Jim. He was so sensual, charming, honest, and seductive. He knew how to make her relax and enjoy herself. He took his time because he loved her and wanted her to be happy. He knew how to make a woman melt in his arms; but, she felt totally secure with the brave and totally dependable Jean-Jacques who had become the hero in her time traveling adventure. He had been placed in a situation Jim would never have to experience. Maybe that was why she was back in time. To see how heroic, capable, and loving Jim Cooper truly was.

Nevertheless, she had a full month or so to be close to this other Jim. and she planned on letting him lead their way to safety.

It wasn't an easy escape. Once, when they were at high sea, a French frigate—a man of war—demanded, by firing a cannon at them, to stop their course and follow them even though their captain ran up the French flag and told them that there was only cargo on board.

"Stay out of sight," the captain warned Jean-Jacques and Celeste, "they can't board us because of the high water, and when it gets dark and the fog sets in; we'll steal slowly away from them. By dawn, we'll have a good distance between us and can unfurl the sails. We'll be off course, but the alternative is death."

His plan worked. When the *Helena* raced away from the enemy, their course was turned northwest, and in no way resembled a direction that would take them to a Boston port. The French frigate was far out of sight and that fact was very comforting. The fog, which had covered their tracks, made it impossible for them to take a bearing for fifteen days. The captain told them that they could come out of their hiding place when they were near New Foundland. A west wind drove them back constantly, and food became scarce. Conveniently, they met an English ship when they were almost completely out of provisions, pulled beside her, and exchanged supplies. Their meal that day seemed like a feast to them though it wasn't much.

There was little to do on board, and the whole trip eventually became boring for Celeste. Jean-Jacques began the first chapter of his book utilizing a small amount of paper, some borrowed ink, and a quill pen the captain gave him; so he, at least, had something with which to entertain his mind. Celeste strolled on deck and occasionally watched the cook in the galley.

He didn't seem to mind her intervention, and told her she could help him if she wished. Soon, she was up to her elbows in flour and laughing at his wild seaman stories. She had a new friend and a part-time career.

Unfortunately, the fog returned, and the captain admitted that he'd lost his bearings completely. He swore he felt land breezes; that they had to be close. It was a tough time for the two lovers. The captain just couldn't be wrong. The very words brought panic.

They were saved by a pilot boat whose captain called to them that their ship was too close to the rocks, and they needed to alter their course immediately or founder. His boat came near theirs, and he threw a rope to the *Helena* and climbed on board to speak with the captain. He was from Boston. They needed only to follow him to the port in America. To home. A new life free from the fear of death that would linger in the dismal pall that enveloped all of France for several years to come. The trees and fields of this new country, the roof tops of the newly built houses, and the crowded marketplace could be seen from the deck when their ship finally docked.

Celeste and Jean-Jacques guessed that they had been at sea for forty days, and by Celeste's calculations, the equinox had to be close. She had mixed feelings about leaving 1793. She wanted to be home with Jim, but she had to admit her three months had been the most stimulating days of her life. She had amassed so much knowledge of the time period, of Charlotte Corday, of Claire Lacombe, and her lover Leclerc, about the real French Revolution, had ultimately learned the truth about Phillipe, as well as falling in love with a certain police spy who had written the book she had given Jim. Amazing. A man who would make love not to her, but a woman she once was. A pregnant woman who probably did not survive the revolution until the time tunnel opened and unexpectedly transported Celeste Montclaire to 1793 to save her. A woman who would probably bear Jean-Jacques—a man she probably never married before the Gemini effect took over her mind and soul—many sons and daughters in America. Celeste had changed the woman's destiny and in so doing, hers as well. And Jean-Jacques's. And perhaps a book's plot too.

Jean-Jacques and Celeste gathered their only belongings and began climbing down the plank when the captain yelled, "Now, you can't just leave so, without first saying farewell with a huge dinner at the inn. We must celebrate our good fortune for it was God who watched over us, and we should honor Him with a feast. On me. The inn over there," he said pointing, "and they have rooms too. You'll be needing one until you can find a house and farm."

Jean-Jacques agreed to meet the captain and his crew there, and then followed the street until he found the inn. They were able to obtain a room at a good rate, dropped their belongings at the desk, and hurried on a shopping trip. Celeste needed clothing, and Jean-Jacques swore that he would burn the uniform at the first opportunity. He was in good spirits, laughing, chatting happily, and pointing to everything he noticed. He seemed reborn. He was a wonderful companion and almost the exact opposite of the man who had placed her in prison during her first week in Paris. His light mood was infectious, and soon Celeste was smiling, forgetting everything that she had experienced in the last two and one-half months. Their legs were weak from so many days at sea, but Celeste was so delighted at the shops she found; she soon forgot any pain.

"Buy the whole town if you wish. I plan to spoil you." He kissed her. "Especially that hat," he pointed to a pretty blue lady's dream with lace, artificial silk flowers, and heaps of feathers on its wide brim. "Not as nice as the ones in Paris, but the price for this one is more reasonable, wouldn't you say?"

She understood the underlying meaning of his remark. She could keep her head as well as the hat. She was tempted to speak English to the lady who owned the shop but had to pretend she didn't understand anything the woman was saying to her. The clothes, hat, undergarments, and shoes were purchased with some coins they hoped were enough. The woman smiled and gave them change.

"We will have to learn English, I'm afraid, as fast as possible if we are to find a home."

"I think I'm already catching onto the language. It really isn't that difficult," she lied. She had to get them a farm before the equinox. "Maybe the captain will help us. I've been speaking a little English with the cook. He's been teaching me."

"Oh?" he said, grabbing her around the waist, "and what did you give him in return, eh?"

"Nothing but my time, Jean-Jacques." She kissed him on his cheek.

"Which is a gift in itself, n'est ce pas?"

"It is indeed," she said, knowing that she had only a day or two left with him. She would miss him. Jim would take his place, but there was something wickedly delightful about Jean-

Jacques. Listening to his disturbing, yet fashionable for the time period, theories on the inferiority of the female sex had been more amusing than irritating. He had saved her life and would always be a hero in her eyes. Plus, he had written the book she would be able to read when she returned to 2000. She wondered how she would explain all of her emotions to Jim when she got home. But then, he was a time traveler. He should understand.

The tavern was a peaceful and warm spot for their feast. The hearth crackled with the fat of venison and chickens cooking on a spit. Black kettles of all sizes hissed as their contents boiled and simmered. The aroma was sugar, cinnamon, coffee, and cooked meat. Bread had been made earlier, but you could still detect the aroma of it. Real homemade bread not disgusting black bread. One pot had rice pudding flavored with vanilla in it. One had apples bubbling into applesauce. Potatoes boiled in another. Occasionally the cook would pour a sauce or gravy over the meat. Six pies sat on a shelf to cool. Coffee beans rested at the bottom of one of the smaller kettles; the water in the pot slow boiled their coffee. The aroma was heavenly. Celeste watched the cook until Jean-Jacques called her to dinner. She didn't want to leave the warm fire, but the captain was preparing a rum toast to his men and his passengers. They had been given the finest room—the dining hall—for their party. She thought of the 1819 House in Cooperstown and her last meal with Jim Cooper.

"To the Father Almighty who brought us home at last and who gave Jean-Jacques and his bride a new life."

The galley cook said, "Aye," and then turned towards Celeste, winked at her, and whispered, "he's hungry so the toast will be short, but wait until he's had too much rum, and you'll get memorized Bible verses as well as the history of seamanship going back to the Roman Empire."

The food was brought in on platters and huge bowls. No one paid much attention to etiquette as they ate quickly while the servings were still steaming hot. It was the first full meal Celeste had had in months. The baby seemed soothed by it and no longer kicked or moved inside her abdomen.

"Just the beginning," she said silently to the baby.

While they were finishing their dessert, two men entered the room. They were French and the captain seemed to know them—might have even invited them. The guests could speak French and English, and you could see how relieved Jean-Jacques was to find someone with whom he could converse. They were new friends from the old country who knew this strange new world, and who could help him find a home and work.

They smiled at Celeste, but pulled Jean-Jacques to a smaller table to talk. She joined them though she wasn't invited.

"Of course, you must tell us the news from home," said Monsieur Rechele who introduced himself as a country squire.

"We escaped with our families three months ago sensing the inevitable danger," said Monsieur Dupont.

"Prophetic on your part. The king's death?" said Jean-Jacques.

"Certainly," said Dupont. "Are you planning to stay in Boston?"

"We have no plans at all except to buy some land, start a farm, I guess. I have no skills but writing and police work. Neither of those will help us."

"You know something of printing?"

"I do," interrupted Celeste. She felt the need to explain as all eyes stared at her. "I worked for a printer in Paris. I am an artist. We printed books."

"Well, the printer here in Boston, a colonist, needs an artist and an assistant. Do you know anything about farming?"

Jean-Jaques laughed. "Not really."

"The man is desperate for help. You could get a job there until you have a chance to get your bearings. Then, if you like, I have some land that I will be glad to let you have at a reasonable price if you have your heart set on a farm. I brought much money with me. My family was one of the richest in France. I would be happy to let you stay in my townhouse for as long as you wish, free of charge. You can move in tomorrow."

Celeste said, "Are you sure that won't inconvenience your family?"

"The house is empty except when we come to town. My wife adores the country, and it's a good place for raising children. Sometimes she does some shopping in town, and we stay the night; but, in truth, we knew there would be more countrymen coming and wanted to help as much as possible. The house is ready for the next occupant. From what you have just told me, the Devil, himself, has our country by the throat, and it is our duty to help those who need it. But, this is a fair land, and I think you'll like it. Has a way of making you forget you ever had another home. My wife loves it here, and though I miss the life I used to have; I have no plans of ever returning. That life ended when I set sail for America. I like the colonies very much. I am learning their language and teaching it to my children. It is a primitive land compared to France, but my wife and children are alive, and we have heard that our neighbors back in France are being butchered. To hear Alais sing in the morning as she and our cook make bread," his eyes filled with tears, "makes my decision to stay an easy one. You will like America. It takes time to adjust to their ways, but you have a baby on the way and a new life as well as new friends here in Boston. Welcome."

Jean-Jacques was overcome with emotion. He tried to hide his tears, but this was so much more than he had expected. And so much better than the lonely life they had had in Paris. No questions asked. No explanations expected.

"Celeste and I will go to this printer tomorrow morning and ask him for a job."

"Monday morning you mean," said Monsieur Rechele. "Tomorrow is the Sabbath and everyone goes to church."

"Catholic church here in America?" said Jean-Jacques, who had apparently never been very religious.

"Here in America we go to whatever church we can find and practice our own religion in our homes. One must be *seen* in Boston. Church is a very social event here. All shops are closed on the Sabbath. Dress in your best, and we will come by for you at eight and have breakfast here. The children are excited about eating at the inn, and our wives have been chattering away about not having to cook."

"We'll be waiting," said Celeste, smiling broadly at the men. So this is how Celeste Lacombe would live her life. It was wonderful to see it happen before she left. To know that the poor woman would be happy.

They talked on into the evening about France and the new life in Boston. Soon, Celeste became overcome with fatigue and asked whether she might be excused. She and Jean-Jacques drank another cup of mulled cider, then bid good night to their new friends and to the seamen and their captain. Their former traveling companions were so full of rum and good food; they hardly noticed. They informed the innkeeper that they would be leaving for new quarters tomorrow afternoon. Suddenly, the stress and fright fell from their shoulders like melting snow from a warm rooftop. They had a future and could now put the dismal past behind them for good.

"Don't worry, mistress," shouted the innkeeper to his wife, "we always get a new shipment of rum on the twenty-fourth of the month. " 'Spect we'll see it Monday."

The words were spoken behind her; she could have missed them entirely, but they crackled in her ears like roasted chestnuts in a burner. The twenty-fourth was Monday. Her head felt dizzy, and she almost fell backwards on the stairway. She wouldn't be going to church tomorrow with their new friends, or moving into the new townhouse, or seeking employment at the print shop. She would be in Jim's arms by eight Sunday morning. And the surprise of this news suddenly stung in her heart. She held onto Jean-Jacques's arm. Her eyes filled with hot tears, and her throat closed tightly shut. No! She wouldn't see *him* tomorrow. Never again.

"What's the matter, Celeste? Is it the baby, my love?"

She tightened her grip on his forearm as if she might not leave him if she held onto him for dear life.

Her tears spilled down her cheeks. "I'm overcome that's all. Oh, Jean-Jacques, I do love you so. Do you understand that? You've given us such a wonderful future. So much better than our life in France."

"It's you. I was inspired by my love for you. Heaven help us both if I hadn't fallen in love with you; you would have died at the guillotine, and I would have had to flee France without you or be killed. Providence has been generous to us both. Not so for many others. Think on that."

They undressed to their undergarments and snuggled next to each other in the quilt-ladden, overstuffed bed.

"I'm very happy Jean-Jacques. More than you know."

"Me too," he said and then fell asleep in her arms.

The other Celeste would have the baby, move into a new job, buy a new house, and be the one to make love to this incredible man thereby consummating their marriage vows. She hoped she had done the right thing for the woman and her baby. How silly, she thought. Of course she had. Now she had to save the life of another poor woman falsely accused of murdering her husband. The 2000 version of Charlotte Corday. She hoped she would not be too late and wondered what Jim had told her colleagues about her sudden disappearance. She'd find out soon enough. She smiled. She knew Jim Cooper would be waiting for her in the cabin, in the room, with champagne probably, and pizza if she were very lucky.

Celeste moved from her husband's side while he snored and took her old worn sack of souvenirs: a doll, a bonnet, her blue and white striped skirt, her half-torn tricolored cockade, and a small book of poems that had been smashed at the bottom of her bag; but, the picture of Jim/Jean-Jacques would not come home with her. She sighed at the thought of leaving it behind. She had so wanted to show it to Jim. But, it had been her only wedding present to her new husband, and it had to stay. She crawled into bed beside Jean-Jacques holding the bag close to her chest. "No offense, baby, but you can stay here with your mom if it's all the same to you."

She leaned close to Jean-Jacques's face, smiled, then kissed his cheek. She looked at him for a few moments and then whispered softly into his ear, "I love you, but I've got to be going. She'll seem different tomorrow, a new mood and an altered—maybe—sweeter disposition, but brush it off, don't dwell on it. She's *your* lady love. The woman you've been spying on for months. The one you've obsessed over; the one you're in love with. But, if it's okay with you..." she stammered, and her eyes teared.

The words stopped her breath, and she couldn't go on until she controlled herself and wiped her tears away. "Don't forget *me*. Remember that little...something that I added to *her* personality. That temperamental manner of mine—only mine not hers—like when you hauled me over your shoulder to take me to prison, and I screamed to all the women in the streets. Wonder where it went. Because I'll never forget *you*. You're not like Jim in some ways. Though I love him; I'll remember the difference and ponder about it some times and smile while I'm reading your book. You have to publish that book now, don't forget. And when you see me again in New York City 2000, in the Time Travelers' office, remember. There, now it's all fixed for the future. We're destined to be together for now and always. 1793 and 2000. And Jim and I will have a family just as you will have with her. We saved her life and her child's. We rewrote history, Jean-Jacques. Do you hear me? You've given

315

me another chance at love. Sorry it took me so long to figure it all out, but sometimes I can be really slow on the uptake. And sometimes the heart can lead you down the wrong path. I'm going home now, Jean-Jacques." Her eyelids were wet with tears. "Home."

She kissed him on the lips. *"Please don't forget me."*

Chapter Thirty-Two

"It *is* you!" exclaimed Jim Cooper as he rushed to the cabin's bed where a confused and nauseous Celeste was just realizing that she was where she had been last June before the transfer.

"Home? And not pregnant! That's a plus," she said examining her stomach.

Jim stopped in his tracks. "I'm really going to need some help understanding that last statement."

She grinned and held out her arms to him. "That time travel tunnel has a real kick to it, doesn't it?"

He sat down on the bed beside her. "Good Lord, Celeste, where *were* you?"

"1793 France. Although I did manage to make my way to Boston by September. I was right in the middle of the revolution the whole time. I was the cousin of Claire Lacombe, a noted female rebel, and I lived with her and her lover, Leclerc, in my paid-for-by-an-aristocrat lover's townhouse. I saw the funeral of Jean-Paul Marat and watched Charlotte Corday's execution." She suddenly stopped her excited prattle to say, "Why did I go?"

"I should have told you that the cabin was a primo time traveling portal, and that you should never go near it on the eve of the solstice, which—by my recollection—is when this all happened." He looked at her hair and smoothed it with the back of his hand. "Your hair...is so...short! My God, you could have been guillotined."

"I would have been if it hadn't been for your past life persona. So do you like my pre-execution haircut?"

"As a matter of fact, it suits you. Hey, what do you mean? You and he...wait a minute."

"Before you jump to conclusions, I might add that I was also *my* past life persona, Celeste Lacombe—only a pregnant version. I was a good girl the whole time even with Phillipe."

"Phillipe was there too?"

She cuddled close to him. "Yes, I had time to sort out my feelings about him. Just what the doctor ordered. I found out what a creep Phillipe was and what a wonderful guy you were...ah...are. Just hold me for a minute." She held him, and then her nose wriggled.

"Is that food I smell?" she asked.

"What's in this bag?" he asked.

"Did you make cinnamon rolls for me?"

"Wainwright and Grant Tyrell just returned from the Roman Empire, 200 A.D., and Sam and I made food for all of you. I *can* cook, you know."

She kissed him hard on the lips. "I know. Can I have some rolls or are Wainwright and Grant still in the great room?"

"No, they went down to Trudy's house in Cooperstown to deal with Grant's...whatever. I really wasn't paying much attention to either of them. Grant has some issues Wainwright said. Plus, they knew I wanted to be with you when you came home. What's in the bag?" he repeated.

She smiled wickedly. "Did you get my gift and my message?"

"Too late to save you, unfortunately. And the book is great. I couldn't read much of it because of the French, but Sam did a pretty good job of translating it for me. Copyright 1797, Paris, France. I'm impressed."

"Good, because you wrote it."

"Me?"

"Your past life personality did. His name was Jean-Jacques Coupier, and he was a police spy."

"I read something about revolutionary women and a Celeste who lived in Paris but was imprisoned."

"Thanks to Jean-Jacques's cleverness, I escaped."

Jim smiled and held her closely. "I saved you? Like some knight in shining armor?"

"Absolutely. I was totally enthralled. I'll have to read the book again."

"But you said he was in America by 1797. How could the book have been published in France then?"

"Go check."

They went into the great room where the book rested on the table exactly as if it had never been touched. Celeste shivered, and Jim gave her his own robe to keep her warm. The inside cover of the book proclaimed that the book was written in *America, in 1797* and came from a Boston printing company. And even more critical, it was now in the English language.

"It wasn't like that a week ago. This is incredible!"

Celeste stared at the book, smiled, and said, "I know. I changed history, or, rather, we changed history. And look at this."

On the next page was a sketch of the author.

"That wasn't there before," said Celeste. "I remember distinctly looking for a portrait of the author and saw none. Now there is one, and I know who drew it. Me. I started the picture of you the day you gave me the art supplies, and I was drawing it for you when I transferred. I had it in my hands while I slept. It went with me. When I met your counterpart, I changed the picture to look like him, and was going to give it to you to show you what he looked like; but, I guess he liked my wedding gift enough to use it in his book."

"Wedding gift?"

"See my ring," she said, waving the beautiful antique before Jim's eyes.

"We need to talk."

"Not until I speak with my secretary. What did you tell her anyway?"

"I told her the truth."

Celeste twirled around to see his expression; to see whether this was some sort of joke. "You told them that I time traveled?"

He shrugged his shoulders. He wasn't joking. "What was I supposed to say? You have a detective in your firm. If I tried to conceal the truth, they'd know I was lying. Then they'd be up her draining the lake looking for your dead body; of course, after I told them the truth, they still didn't believe me."

"Why on earth did you tell them about time traveling?"

"Well, Sam and I realized that we have been advertising this on the Web for some time now, why should we hide it? It's not a secret, and if we keep getting hits on that site, and people read what Stephen has to say in his story there, we'll get more customers. Stands to reason it isn't private anymore."

She laughed and buried her face in her hands. "I can just see my secretary's face when you told her. I better call."

"Ah...it's two in the morning."

"Oh yeah! I'll leave a message on her voice mail. Where did you put my cell phone? This is important. It might save a woman's life."

He handed her her purse, and she retrieved her phone. She dialed the number. "Meanwhile, Snoopy, you can see what's in the bag. It's for you—except the doll. And yes, it's all real."

She left a complete message and got back to Jim. "It's Charlotte Corday's death hat. From the guillotine."

"Maybe you should start from the very beginning."

"It's a long story."

"I've been nervously waiting to hear it for three months."

"Wouldn't you rather..."

"Yes, of course, I would, but I think I want to hear about your relationship with Jean-Jacques Coupier first."

"Afraid he might be too much like you?"

"Exactly."

She munched on rolls and sipped the hot coffee. Later, she peeled oranges, bananas, and chomped on fresh, juicy apples. The joy of being home had inspired her appetite. The story came out slowly and with mouthfuls of food. "I'm famished."

"Take your time. The story's changed from what he wrote."

"Good. Did the girl he wrote about die in that book?" she asked.

321

"I think so."

When she finished two hours later, he asked, "So, what do you think about time traveling now that you know it's true?"

"It was incredible, totally fascinating. Awful and wonderful all at the same time. I've never been so intellectually stimulated and stressed out at the same time; but, oh, how much I've learned!"

She put her arms around his neck. "Mostly about myself. You're right, Jim, there is someone else pulling the strings. They wanted me to know that my love for Phillipe was unfounded, and that my love for you was real."

"Say that again." He gave a sideways grin. "I'd like to hear that again."

"I love you, Jim. I'm never leaving you. Forever friend."

"A blessing, indeed. Welcome home."

"I wouldn't doubt we've been meeting and missing for centuries. But, this time we stay together. I fixed it in 1793 by marrying him. Celeste Lacombe got a new life with the illegitimate half-brother of the man who impregnated her. And Jean-Jacques wasn't put out by it in the least. They belonged together. And so do we."

"Does that mean you'll say yes if I ask you to marry me?"

"Does that mean I get to be a member of Time Travelers, Incorporated?"

"I think legal advisor is a good title for you—sure. You can still keep your firm. I'm a liberated man, you know."

She thought of Jean-Jacques and laughed. "Thank God!"

Then she looked at him closely. Deeply into his eyes and further into his soul.

"Make love to me," she whispered.

"With pleasure."

She kissed him and then said, "Hold that thought. There's one thing more I have to check."

She walked into the great room and turned the old, withered book to its last page. Just before the words 'the end' there was one line.

"She was a vision, I suppose, or a dream; but I never forgot her presence in my life."

Then Celeste found her traveling bag and took from it the book of poems written by Phillipe's mother and artistically designed by Celeste Lacombe. Her fingers traced the flowers, cherubs, and vines.

"Something of you still rests with me, Celeste Lacombe," she whispered. She smiled to herself and placed the book aside, then dug to the bottom of the bag to find an old, beaten-up rag doll named Geraldine. Celeste stared at it for some time until she just had to cradle it close to her chest.

"Baby!" she said softly.

The tears fell gently down her cheeks.

The End

Epilogue

Claire Lacombe continued her political life for only a matter of sixty days after leaving Celeste in Bordeaux, continuing as a driving force in Paris until September 6, 1793, when she was attacked publicly by Chabot of the Jacobins and denounced as not being a true 'female citizen'. This attack on her was spurred by her insistence that they release the mayor of Toulouse, and because she was offering refuge to Leclerc, who they considered a noble, at her townhouse. She was called a Loyalist sympathizer for trying to protect certain nobles. They also insisted that she was an irritant for 'intruding everywhere'. She was considered dangerous because she was a very eloquent speaker. Her rhetoric proclaimed allegiance to the Constitution, but then she would attack the constituted authorities who were trying to uphold it. They told her she could no longer speak at the meetings, and she was so outraged that she screamed from the gallery that if they tried to remove her, or silence her, she would show them, "what a free woman can do." She was arrested several times and usually freed the next day which only added to her sense of patriotism, outrage, and drama. The cruelest insult to her sense of rebellion came on September 23, 1793, when she was called "harmless" and a "counterrevolutionary bacchante" because of her lust for the good things in life...primarily men. This made Claire so furious that she denounced Robespierre. She earned a bit of fame around this time and was allowed to continue as head of the women's club which had been dissolving rapidly since Marat's funeral and was almost extinct by the end of October 1793. She was arrested just as she was planning to rejoin her theater troupe in Dunkirk. This time she was trapped. She stopped denouncing Robespierre and the government, but she was not released from imprisonment. Her friends begged for her freedom, but their pleas did not help her. An old friend, Victoire Capitaine, reported, after a visit to her cell, that Claire was in poor health, looked fatigued, and was giving herself to anyone who promised freedom, or who had something she needed for survival. She had lost her pride, and the brightness that had made her sparkle before her audience. After fifteen and one-half months in prison, Claire was freed. She left Paris for Nantes where she was supposed to perform again. She earned a salary of 183 livres a month and stayed with the troupe until the spring. She corresponded with her former Parisian comrades but suspended any political activities. Her friends wanted her to return to Paris and tried to find her employment in the big theaters there. She lost interest in politics completely, choosing to dedicate herself to her art, her friends, and her many lovers. She finally returned to Paris with an unknown actor as her chief companion. At this point, we know that she was in debt to her landlady to the tune of 386 livres, and it is assumed that she could not find employment. That is all we know. She simply disappeared from the pages of history. Until the end, Claire Lacombe signed her name—Lacombe, free woman!

On October 28, 1793, Leclerc married the activist and best friend of Claire Lacombe, Pauline Léon, who resumed the management of her family's chocolate business. All during the month of September, Leclerc denounced the members of the

Convention using his ladies in the gallery as his mouthpiece. Pauline, like her friend, Claire, attacked the men in charge of the government; but, by November, changed direction entirely choosing to dedicate herself primarily to taking care of her household; thus showing her patriotism by becoming a good wife to Leclerc—a proper example to all women in France of how best to help the fatherland. It might have been Claire's imprisonment, or the change in the direction of the political tide that made Leclerc marry Pauline, keep a low profile in the next few months, and enlist in the army. We know that he kept out of politics, kept quiet, and got out of the 'fire'. Pauline went to visit her husband in Lafére, where he was stationed with his battalion, to hold him in her arms once more before he left for the front. They were arrested there and imprisoned by order of the Committee of General Security. They were released a few months later, and both of them ceased writing anything at that point. Pauline continued to sign her name on all documents— Anne Pauline Léon, the wife of Leclerc.

Jean—Jacques Coupier and his wife Celeste Lacombe Coupier lived the rest of their lives in Boston. They both attained employment with the Boston printer and lived in the city. They never bought a farm and were quite happy to become part of the social whirl in such a large and popular American town. They went on holiday to the country to visit their new French friends during the hot summer months. They moved from the townhouse to a fine, red brick, Colonial house on one of the side streets that led to the printing office. The people who owned the shop, having no children of their own, left the printing business to Jean-Jacques and Celeste who began one of the first newspapers in Boston. They had three children—two sons and a little girl. They never returned to France; however, in 1803, they sent money to his mother who made the long voyage to America to join her son and his wife in the new land. None of them had the slightest desire to return to France, and members of the Coupier family still exist in Boston to this date.

Jim Cooper and Celeste Montclaire were married on December 16, 2000, in the First Presbyterian Church of Cooperstown, New York. All their friends rejoiced with them, and the reception was held at the 1819 House restaurant. Celeste's entire staff, and all the members of Time Travelers, Inc., including Dr. and Mrs. Templeton from New Orleans, Louisiana, were there to celebrate their great happiness. A young woman who had been suspected of murdering her husband was also there—saved by her experienced and impassioned attorney.

The two newlyweds honeymooned in the cabin in Richfield Springs, and on the morning of December 22—making sure that Jim Cooper kept his mind on Trudy and not Isaac Cooper so that there would only be a general transfer—they time traveled to Toddsville, New York, 1900, where a surprised Isaac Cooper drove them, in his 'newfangled' horseless carriage, to the home of Cuyler E. and Gertrude Carr of Milford, New York. Though the weather was freezing, they enjoyed a three-month stay in the Victorian time period free from danger and violence. Jim went to the store with Cuyler every day; and Cuyler, who was so excited to see his old friend, introduced Jim to all the familiar sights, as well as helping him buy items to add to his 2000 antique collection. Celeste found a new friend in Trudy Carr, but spent most of her time holding, rocking, feeding, and playing with the Carr's baby son, Cuyler E. Carr Jr.

Appendix

The information on Claire Lacombe, Leclerc, and Pauline Léon, and details of the women's club, as well as Marat's funeral—with actual selections of Claire's rhetoric—came from: Dominique Godineau's book The Women of Paris and their French Revolution, The University of California Press, Copyright 1998.

I would also like to mention the Memoirs of Madame de La Tour du Pin which began as an autobiographical work of nonfiction on January 1, 1820. Later, her story was translated from the 1913 French edition to an English version by Felice Harcourt in 1969 and published in America in 1971 by The McCall Publishing Company of New York.

Madame de La Tour de Pin was an aristocrat who escaped, by incredible good fortune—one might even say a miracle of God—the fate that awaited her family in Bordeaux. She sailed to America with her small family and ill husband *days* after giving birth to her daughter. Trying to take care of her son, her sick husband, and breast feeding her infant on the small amount of food they had on board the ship, did not dissolve her joy at being out of the danger that existed for them in France.

The first news she and her family received after finding refuge in Boston was that her father-in-law, Monsieur de La Tour du Pin, had been guillotined just weeks after their escape. They stayed in Boston for a while, where they were eventually introduced to other French immigrants, and purchased a farm in Albany, New York. This strong willed, genteel, refined, cultured woman learned to wield an axe to cut firewood, run a farm, smile and wave without batting an eye to the naked Indians she met along the road to town, and make and sell her own sweet pads of butter in the mold she brought with her from France that bore the de La Tour de Pin family crest.

Her life in the New World was not an easy one. She was ill to the point of near death several times and lost a child while living on that farm.

When the time seemed right, her husband insisted that they return to France in order to reclaim their former real estate. She begged him not to return, but he would not listen to her. There was nothing left for them in France; and to the day she died, Madame de la Tour de Pin yearned to return to America, her small farm in Albany, the wonderfully rugged life she lived there, and the grave site of her small child. Her adventures had taught her more than anything her educated tutors in France could—that she could count on her own strength and wits to survive...anything.

That is the true spirit of freedom.

—Hollie Van Horne